SHADOW PLAY

ALSO BY IRIS JOHANSEN

SHADOW PLAY

IRIS JOHANSEN

ST. MARTIN'S PRESS ❧ NEW YORK

SHADOW PLAY. Copyright © 2015 by Johansen Publishing LLLP. All rights reserved. Printed in the United States of America. For information, address St. Martin's Press, 175 Fifth Avenue, New York, N.Y. 10010.

www.stmartins.com

Designed by Omar Chapa

The Library of Congress Cataloging-in-Publication Data is available upon request.

ISBN 978-1-250-02010-9 (hardcover)
ISBN 978-1-250-02009-3 (e-book)

Our books may be purchased in bulk for promotional, educational, or business use. Please contact your local bookseller or the Macmillan Corporate and Premium Sales Department at (800) 221-7945, extension 5442, or by e-mail at MacmillanSpecialMarkets@macmillan.com.

First Edition: September 2015

10 9 8 7 6 5 4 3 2 1

CHAPTER

1

Walsh watched the detectives and forensic team milling around the open grave, their flashlight beams lighting the darkness. Stay in the back of the crowd, he told himself. The rest of these locals were only curiosity seekers, and the cops were used to dealing with them. If he blended in and didn't call attention to himself, no one would notice or remember him.

Damn kid. The girl had been buried for years and might never have been recovered if those Boy Scouts hadn't chosen this area to set up camp. It must have been the recent rains that had washed away the top layers of dirt and revealed those old bones.

Or maybe not.

He remembered how strange that little girl had been, how he'd hated her before that final blow. And he'd heard there were weird stories about this wood where he'd buried her . . .

He felt a chill as he remembered those stories.

Forget it. They were just stories. He had come here to make sure that the report was true that the girl had been unearthed after all these years. He had carefully monitored the town and vineyards since the night she had been buried. Now that he was certain, he'd fade away for a while. He was good at fading away. He'd done it eight years ago, and no one had connected him to anything that had happened in this valley.

And no one must connect him to that child the forensic team was so carefully taking out of her grave.

She had to remain unknown and lost, as she had been all these years. It was too dangerous to him for her to be anything but the heap of bones she'd become after he'd thrown her into that grave. He would have to keep monitoring the situation to be sure that threat didn't become a reality.

It would be okay. Years had passed, life moved fast, no one would care about this child who had been lost so long . . .

LAKE COTTAGE
ATLANTA, GEORGIA

"You have a FedEx package," Joe Quinn said as Eve came into the cottage. "It's on your worktable. It came from somewhere in California."

She nodded. "Yeah, Sonderville. Sheriff Nalchek called me last night and asked me to bump his reconstruction to the top of my list." She made a face. "I almost told him to forget it. I'm swamped right now, and I don't need any more pressure."

"You're always swamped." Joe smiled teasingly. "You thrive on it. And it's natural that you're in demand. Everyone wants the world-famous forensic sculptor, Eve Duncan, to solve their problems."

"Bullshit." She went to the kitchen counter and picked up

the coffee carafe. "There's usually no urgency about putting a face on a skull that's been buried for years anyway. It has to be done, but there's no reason that I can't do it in an orderly fashion. Every one of those children is important."

"So why did you give in to Sheriff Nalchek?"

"I don't know." She poured her coffee and came back to Joe. "He wore me down. He sounded young and eager and full of the horror that only comes the first time that you realize that there are vicious people out there who can do monstrous things to innocent children. I got the impression that he was an idealist who wanted to change the world." She sat down beside Joe and nestled close, her head against his shoulder. He was warm and strong, and she loved the feel of him. She loved *him*. Lord, it was good to be home. That trip to the airport today had been achingly difficult. She had watched her adopted daughter, Jane, fly away back to London, and she had no idea when she would see her again. "He kept telling me that this little girl was different, that he was sure that he'd be able to find out who she was and who had killed her if I'd just give him a face to work with. Who knows? Maybe he's right. In cold cases like this, the chances are always better if the officer in charge is enthusiastic and dedicated."

"Like you." Joe's lips brushed her forehead. "Maybe he thinks he's found a soul mate."

"Oh, I'm dedicated. Enthusiastic?" She wearily shook her head. "Not now. I'm too tired. There have been too many children in my life who have been killed and thrown away. I'm not as enthusiastic as that young officer is. I'm only determined . . . and sad."

"Sad?" Joe straightened and looked down at her. "Yes, I'm definitely feeling the sad part. But it's not only about that skull in the box over there, is it?" His hand gently cupped her cheek. "Jane? I could have taken her to the airport. I thought you wanted to do it."

"I did want to do it. It may be the last time we see her for a while. She's off to new adventures and finding a life of her own." She tried to steady her voice. "Just what we wanted for her. Look what happened when she came back from London to try to help me. She got shot and almost died. Now she's well and going on with her life." In her line of work, sometimes the evil came close to home. Most recently Jane had been one of the targets. Those weeks with her daughter, while she had been recuperating, had been strained and yet poignantly sweet. Jane had come to them when she was ten years old, and she had been more best friend than daughter to Eve. But that hadn't changed the love that had bound them all these years. Now that Jane was out on her own and becoming a successful artist, it was terribly hard to adjust to the fact that most of the time she was thousands of miles away. "It's exactly what she should be doing. What's here for her? Hell, I'm a workaholic and always involved with a reconstruction. You're a police de-tective who they tap to work cases that don't give you normal hours either. It was just . . . difficult . . . to see her get on that plane."

"And you didn't let her see one bit of that pain," Joe said quietly. "You smiled and sent her on her way."

"That's what every parent does. It always comes down to letting them go."

"And more difficult for you than for others. First, you had to let go of Bonnie when she was killed. Now Jane is moving out of our lives."

"Not out, just away." She made a face. "And evidently I

couldn't let go of Bonnie because I insisted on keeping her with me, alive or dead. I was so stubborn that whoever is in charge of the hereafter let me have my little girl's spirit to visit me now and then." Though she had initially resisted that blessing. She had thought she was hallucinating, thought that grief had made her mind fly to any solace possible. She had only wanted to be with her Bonnie and was spiraling down to meet her when she had been stopped by the realization that the visits from Bonnie were no hallucination. She drew a deep breath and gave Joe a quick kiss. "Which makes me luckier than a lot of people. I refuse to feel sorry for myself. I have you. I sometimes have Bonnie. I'll have Jane when she moves in and out of our lives." She nodded at the FedEx box across the room. "And I have a chance to help the parents of that little girl find resolution." She got to her feet and took a sip before she put the cup down on the coffee table. "So slap me if you see me go broody on you." She headed for the kitchen. "How about lasagna for supper? There's something about the smell of baking garlic bread that lifts the spirits and makes everything seem all right."

"Besides outrageously tempting the taste buds. Sounds good. Need help?"

"Nah, you know my culinary expertise is nonexistent. I'll do frozen."

"Eve."

She glanced over her shoulder.

He was frowning, and his gaze was narrowed. "It's just Jane leaving? You've been pretty quiet the last couple weeks. Nothing else is wrong?"

And Joe noticed everything. She was tempted to deny it and put him off, but she couldn't do it. They had been together for years, and their relationship was based not only on love but honesty. "Nothing that can't be fixed." She shrugged. "I guess I'm just going through some kind of emotional adjustment. I wanted everything to stay the same. I wanted to keep Jane close to me. Mine. Though I always knew she didn't really belong to me. She was too independent and was ten going on thirty when we adopted her. And Bonnie was mine, but then she was taken." She smiled. "And that spirit, Bonnie, who comes to visit me now and then is very much her own self now. Beloved, but only flashes of being mine." Her smile faded. "But I'll take it. I just want to keep her with me, too. I don't want anything to change."

"Why should that change?"

"It shouldn't change. That's what I told Bonnie. Nothing has to change."

His brows rose. "Ah, your Bonnie. She said something to disturb you? When?"

"A couple weeks ago. She scared me. She said she didn't know how long she'd be able to keep coming to me. She said everything was going to change."

"How? Why?"

"She didn't know. She just wanted to warn me."

"Very frustrating." He chuckled. "If your daughter has to pay you visits, I'd just as soon she not upset you like this."

"That's what I told her."

He got to his feet and took her in his arms. "And so you should. Send her to me, and I'll reinforce it." He kissed her. "Though I doubt if that's going to happen. She only appeared to me a couple times just to make sure I knew that you weren't hallucinating." He looked directly into her eyes. "I know you need Bonnie. She's the anchor that keeps you here with me.

You were spiraling downward and almost died before you had your ghost visits from Bonnie. She brought you back, and I thank God for her." He paused. "But if for some reason she stopped coming, I want you to know that we'll make it all right. I have so much love for you, Eve. I'm full of it, you're my center. You always have been and always will be. If your Bonnie drifts away from you, I'll just pour more of that love toward you. I'll find a way to stop you from hurting. I promise you."

He meant every word. The knight was about to mount his stallion and launch himself into battle, she realized. God, she was lucky.

She gazed up into his face, the strong square contour, the well-shaped lips, the tea-colored eyes that held both warmth and intelligence. So familiar, yet so new, every time she looked at him. "Hey, I'm just having a few twinges, nothing major. It just seemed when Jane got on that plane that the changes were starting. A sort of harbinger of things to come." She pushed him away and turned back to the freezer. "But change can be good, too, can't it? After all, Bonnie wasn't definite about anything. Forget it." She took out the lasagna. "Jane told me she'd call me as soon as she got off the plane in London. I think I'll start working on the new reconstruction after dinner, so that I'll be awake when she calls . . ."

But Eve's cell phone rang before she even finished loading the dishwasher after dinner.

"Sheriff Nalchek," she told Joe with a sigh. "You finish here. I may be more than a few minutes."

"Dedication and enthusiasm," Joe repeated with a grin. "At least he waited until after dinner."

"Not necessarily. California is three hours earlier." She punched the access button. "Eve Duncan."

"John Nalchek." His deep voice was brusque. "Sorry to bother you, Ms. Duncan. I just wanted to make sure that you'd received the skull for reconstruction today."

"Yes, FedEx is usually pretty reliable."

"What do you think of her?"

"I haven't opened the box yet, Sheriff Nalchek."

"Oh." A disappointed silence. "But you'll do it tonight?"

"Possibly." No promises, or he might be calling her in the middle of the night. "Or tomorrow."

Another silence. "Okay. I don't want to rush you."

The hell he didn't. "There's no rushing a reconstruction, Sheriff. There are several stages, measuring and processes that have to be done before the actual sculpting. It will take as long as it takes."

"What stages?"

She tried to be patient. "The first stage is repairing, then I go to the measurement stage, which is vitally important. I cut eraser sticks as markers to the proper measurements and glue them onto their specific points on the face. There are twenty points in a skull for which there are known tissue depths. Facial-tissue depth has been found to be fairly consistent in people the same age, sex, race, and weight."

"What happens next?"

"I take strips of plasticine and apply them between the markers, then build up all the tissue-depth points."

"It sounds kind of iffy, like connect the dots."

"If you wish to simplify it. I guarantee it's not simple, Nalchek. And that's only the beginning."

"Sorry, I wouldn't have sent her to you if I hadn't believed you could do the job. But you are going to put her before the others on your list?"

"I told you I would." She remembered what she had told Joe. Dedication and enthusiasm might work miracles for that poor child. "I know that you probably had a shock when you found that skeleton. It's never pleasant. But you have to remember that we can do something about it if we work together. We can find her parents, we can find the person who killed her."

"I wasn't shocked, ma'am. I was in Afghanistan, and I worked as an EMT several months before I went to work with law enforcement. There's nothing much I haven't seen." He paused. "And I told you yesterday that I know I can help her if you give me a face. I *know* it."

His voice was so passionate that Eve asked, "Really? And how do you know it?"

"Sometimes you just know. Sometimes you—" He stopped. "Or maybe I just want it so bad. I looked down at that little girl's skeleton all covered in dirt and mud, and I felt like she was calling to me. It was so damn strong, it rocked me. She was so . . . small and fragile. I wanted to pick her up and take her somewhere safe, where no one would ever hurt her again. Crazy, huh?"

"Not so crazy." All her impatience had disappeared with his words. When her own daughter had disappeared, she would have wanted someone like Nalchek to be hunting for her. It was a cold world, and men who cared were rare and to be valued. "What can you tell me about her?"

"Nothing much. We think she's nine or a little younger. She died of a blow to the head. She's Caucasian, and she's been buried for a good eight years or more. I've checked the missing persons reports at the time, and there's nothing that matches up to the location or the time frame."

"She might have been transported from almost anywhere in the state or beyond."

"I know that. You asked me what I knew. I didn't think you wanted guesses, ma'am."

"No, I don't." Nine years old. Buried eight years. If she'd lived, she'd have gone to high-school proms by now. She might have had a boyfriend or had a crush on some rock star or movie actor. She'd missed so much during those eight years. "Thank you. It may help to know something about her."

"I thought it might. I read a couple articles about you before I sent you the skull. You were quoted as saying that you liked to do anything that brought you closer to the victim. You said for some reason it seemed to make the sculpting process easier. The reporter made a lot of that remark."

"He was looking for a hook for his story. I made the mistake of giving it to him."

"It was a good hook. It was what made me send the skull to you. I liked the idea of someone's caring enough to want to get close to a victim."

"I feel sympathy for any victim, but the closeness of which I spoke only occurs during the actual sculpting process. That's really the only part of reconstruction that has the potential for creativity."

"And bonding?"

"You're putting words in my mouth."

"Maybe. I'm trying to make sure I did the right thing, sending her to you. I feel responsible."

"Should I send that skull back to you?"

"No, ma'am. I didn't mean to offend you. I'd appreciate it if you'd get right on it, please."

"No offense taken. You just seem very possessive about this skull."

"That's what I thought about when I researched you, Ms. Duncan. Two of a kind?"

"No." Though those words were eerily close to what Joe had said, she thought. "Perhaps I do feel a responsibility and closeness to my work while I'm doing a reconstruction, but I'd never feel possessive. I only want to set them free."

Nalchek chuckled. "I haven't gotten there yet. I feel like that little girl still belongs to me just like the minute we pulled her out of that grave. Maybe after you get me a face, I'll be able to let her go. Good night, Ms. Duncan. You'll let me know how it goes?"

"I imagine that you'll make sure I do," she said dryly. "Good night, Sheriff." She hung up.

Nalchek wasn't entirely what she had thought. She would still bet that he was young, but he wasn't inexperienced and had a toughness that made his insistence about her doing the reconstruction all the more puzzling.

A nine-year-old girl, buried over eight years.

I felt like she was calling to me.

"Eve." Joe was standing behind her in the doorway. He was carrying two cups of coffee. "Done?"

She nodded and took the cup he handed her. "For the time being." She moved toward the porch swing and curled up next to him as he sat down. She sighed with contentment as she gazed out at the lake. The fragrance of the pines, the moonlight on the lake, Joe beside her at this place they both loved. "Nalchek is very polite, very concerned. And he's going to be a thorn in my side until I finish her."

"Then don't take his calls."

"That's one solution."

A breeze was lifting her hair, and it made everything in this moment all the more wonderful. This perfect place, this perfect man for her.

That little girl had not lived long enough to have a perfect anything. That took time and searching and the wisdom to know it when you found it.

"Then do it." Joe put his arm around her. "Why not?"

"I'll think about it."

But she knew she wouldn't do it.

I felt like she was calling to me.

"So did your bone lady come through for you, Nalchek?"

Nalchek looked up as Deputy Ron Carstairs came into the office. He was a friend as well as coworker, and Ron had been riding him since the night they'd found the little girl. He was a good guy, and they'd worked together for five years, but he didn't understand why Nalchek hadn't just dropped this investigation and pushed it into the hands of the medical examiner. "She's not a bone lady. You're thinking of that TV show. She's a forensic sculptor and probably the best in the world."

"And she's rushing to give that kid a face just because you asked her to do it?" Ron dropped down in the visitor's chair. "Hell, then she couldn't be that good. We're small potatoes out here in the boonies."

"She's that good," Nalchek said. He tossed the Eve Duncan dossier to Carstairs. "Take a look for yourself." He pointed to the photo of Eve Duncan. Red-brown shoulder-length hair, hazel eyes, features that were more interesting than beautiful.

"She was illegitimate and born in the slums of Atlanta and had a baby of her own by the time she was sixteen. She named the little girl Bonnie, and the kid turned her life around. The kid became her whole life. She went back to school and then on to college. Then when the little girl was seven, she was kidnapped and killed. It was a terrible blow, and Duncan went into shock. But then she rallied and started to rebuild her life. Duncan went back to college to study forensic sculpting. Since then, she's become the most sought-after artist in forensic sculpting. She works for police, FBI, and private parties." He pointed to the dossier underneath Eve Duncan's. "That's Joe Quinn, ex-SEAL, ex-FBI, currently a detective with ATLPD. They've been living together for years."

Ron only glanced at the dossier. "I'll look at them later. Nice looking woman. Not my type. Too intense."

"She's my type. I want her intense." He grinned as he leaned back in his chair. "Though I'll probably stay away from Joe Quinn. His reputation is a little too lethal for me."

"You said he was a cop."

"There are cops, then there are cops. You know that as well as I do. He's supposed to be totally bonkers about Eve Duncan and very protective."

"Well, you shouldn't have to deal with either one of them now that you've turned the skull over to Duncan."

Nalchek's smile faded as he looked back down at the dossier. "Yeah, you could say that."

"Hey." Ron was shaking his head. "Drop it. Let it go, Nalchek."

"I have let it go. It's out of my hands."

"But not out of your mind. There's a lot of talk around

town about how weird you've been behaving since we found that kid's skeleton. We all felt bad about what happened to that little girl, but you overreacted."

"How can you overreact to the murder of a kid?"

"She's been dead over eight years. What are the chances we'll ever find her murderer?"

"Damn good if we try hard enough." He got to his feet. "And I'm trying hard, real hard. I'll find the son of a bitch. I've got Eve Duncan, and soon I'll have a face." He moved toward the door. "And right now, I'm going back to that grave site and take another look to see if I can find anything more."

"You've been out there five times. Don't you think it's a little excessive?"

"No."

I felt like she was calling to me.

He had said that to Eve Duncan, and he was still hearing that call even though the bones were long gone from that crime scene.

"You can never tell what you'll find if you look hard enough. Want to come along?"

"Waste of time." Ron grimaced. "Oh, what the hell." He got to his feet, grabbed the Duncan and Quinn dossiers, and followed him toward the door. "Why not?"

"Are you still going to wait up for that call from Jane?" Joe asked as he paused before going back to their bedroom. "Want company?"

Eve chuckled. "I've got company." She moved across the room to her worktable, where the FedEx box remained unopened. "No, you go on to bed. You've got to work tomorrow morning. I won't be too long. I'll just take care of the setup and

preliminary measuring, then come to bed after I get Jane's call."

"Sounds like a plan." He still didn't move. "Sure you're okay?"

"Absolutely." She started to unfasten the box. "Stop hovering. You're acting like a grandma with her first grandkid."

"I beg your pardon." Joe's voice was suddenly deep, silky smooth, and infinitely sensual. "Grandma? Me? I think we're going to have to address that insult when you come to bed."

She glanced up at him and suddenly lost her breath. Thigh muscles that were compact and yet sleek and full of leashed power. Tight stomach and buttocks. In this moment, he was totally male, completely sexual, and she could feel her own body respond. Even after all these years together, their sexual chemistry was just as explosive as when they had come together when he had been the FBI agent sent to investigate Bonnie's death. "I'll look forward to it," she said softly.

He grinned. "That was my intention. Anticipation is the name of the game." The next moment, he'd disappeared down the hall.

She stared after him for a moment before she ruefully shook her head. She was tempted to go after him, but he could just wait until she got the call from Jane. Anticipation worked both ways.

She looked back down at the box and completed opening it. Then she carefully removed the plastic ties that held the skull in place and the protective plastic wrap around the skull itself. "Let's see you," she murmured as she took the skull in her hands. She always talked to these lost children when she first started the reconstructions. It seemed to aid her in making a connection and helped her over the first painful shock of seeing their

remains. She never got used to that moment. She held the skull
under the light. "Small. You were small for nine. I wonder if
they were wrong about you . . ." Small, delicate features . . .
fragile. She looked so fragile and vulnerable. Nothing appeared
to be broken or devoured by animals.

If you discounted the crushed side of her right temple
where her killer had struck the fatal blow.

She'd have to repair that immediately, so that she could
concentrate on the actual reconstruction. Her fingers gently
touched the crushed bones. "Bastard." She felt a sudden surge
of rage that was as intense as it was unusual. She always felt sad,
but it was difficult to focus rage on a faceless predator. She was
having no trouble focusing now. This child's killer might only
have been a shadow-figure, but it was malignant and evil and
Eve felt as if she could reach out and touch him. "But I don't
think it could have hurt you for more than a few seconds.
That's a mercy. Though I'm sure he didn't mean it to be." She
tossed the box in the trash and spent a few minutes setting up
the skull on her worktable. "There you are. Now I'll clean
you up and start the measuring. I have to do a lot of measuring
before I can start bringing you back the way you were. Were
you a pretty little girl? Not that it matters. I've always liked
interesting more than pretty anyway. I've had two children of
my own in my life. My Bonnie was both pretty and interesting, and Jane is very beautiful. But they both know that it's
what's inside that counts." She was done with the cleaning and
tossed the cloth aside. "What's inside you? Maybe we'll be able
to see after I finish. Right now, it's difficult, but I've gone down
this road before. Okay, that's all. I just had to establish a sense
of what we have to do together to find a way to get you back
home. From now on, I just work and maybe you help a little."

She leaned back in her chair and gazed thoughtfully at the delicate skull. "One last thing. I always name my reconstructions. No offense. You can have your own name back once that sheriff finds out who you are. But I have to call you something besides 'Hey, you' when I talk to you or about you. It's just the way I work." She tilted her head. "What name . . . Linda? Penny? Samantha is a good name. It's got substance. Do you like it? Maybe too heavy. How about Carrie? Short and sweet. I kind of like that for—

Jenny. I . . . think . . . my name is Jenny.

Eve went still. Out of the blue, out of the darkness, those words had come to her. Weird. Imagination? Or had she been concentrating so hard on this little girl that the name had just popped into her head, and she'd mentally couched it in terms that the child might use. It didn't matter. The name was there, and she might as well use it. "Jenny. I like it. And it seems to suit you. Much better than Samantha." She opened the drawer of the desk and drew out her measuring tools. "And now that we've got that out of the way, it's time to get to work. Let's see if we can get the basic stuff done before I have to leave you and get to bed . . ."

Ringing.

Her cell phone was ringing, Eve realized vaguely with annoyance. She wished she'd turned it off before she'd started working as she usually did. She had just begun the mid-therum section of—

Shit! Jane! Three and a half hours had passed, and she hadn't even realized it.

She grabbed her phone from her pocket and punched the access. "Jane! Hello. Has your flight landed?"

"Yes, I'm in a taxi on the way to my apartment. It took you long enough to answer. I was beginning to worry."

"I was working. I just received a new reconstruction, and I was doing the preliminary measuring."

"I should have known. You cut down your schedule while I was there recuperating, and you probably had to make up for lost time." She paused. "I was a bother. I'm really sorry, Eve."

"I'm not." She got up from her worktable and moved across the room to the couch. "I loved every minute of having you with us. I wish you'd stayed twice as long. No, I wish you'd never go away." She added quickly, "But I know that's not practical. You have a career. So do I. We'll work it out." She changed the subject. "Good flight?"

"Smooth as glass. So is your new reconstruction a little boy or girl?"

"A little girl. Nine. Found in the vineyard country in California."

"And what did you name her?"

"Jenny." She looked back at the skull on her worktable. "I called her Jenny."

"Pretty name. I've always liked it."

"So have I. I guess. It just sort of fits her."

Jane chuckled. "How can you tell? It's a skull, for heaven's sake."

"I can tell." She added, "She definitely wasn't a Samantha."

"Samantha? Where did that come from?"

"You'd have had to have been here."

"And I'd just as soon not." Jane paused. "I don't know how you do it. So sad . . . Never being sure what you're doing is going to help those children's identities to be discovered."

"I've had a good percentage over the years."

"I know, and I admire you more than I can say. I call my-self an artist, but it's you who are the true artist, Eve. You create life from death."

"Only the semblance. But sometimes that semblance can cause the bad guys to be caught and revenge exacted." Her lips tightened as she looked at the reconstruction. "This little girl is so fragile-appearing. It makes you wonder how anyone could bear to hurt her. Yet that bastard crushed her head and—" She broke off. "For some reason, I couldn't do the measuring until I'd done a temporary cosmetic fix on that wound. I was going to wait but it . . . bothered me."

"Because you have a gentle heart. Why else would you have taken a street kid like me into your home?"

"Because that street kid was remarkable, and I knew that she'd light up our lives." She added, "And you're a very good artist, Jane. You have great vision. And it's not of skulls or death." She chuckled. "Far more socially acceptable. You must be close to your apartment. I'll let you go. Thanks for calling."

"My pleasure," Jane said. "Truly. Good luck with your Jenny. I hope you find a way to bring her home to those who loved her."

"I think I will." She added dryly, "She seems to have a young sheriff in California rooting for her. He says she wants to be found."

"A psychic?"

"No, he just has a feeling. Good night, Jane."

"It's morning here. Have a good day." She hung up.

Night here. Morning where Jane was living. It only pointed out how far apart they were.

Don't think about it. They were together in their hearts.

Time to go to bed. She wanted to get up with Joe and have a cup of coffee with him before he left to go to the precinct.

She washed her hands and dried them on the towel she kept at her worktable. She turned off the work light. "We made a decent start, Jenny. It will go faster later."

No answer naturally.

The fragile bones of the skull shone in the glow of the overhead light. Eve moved toward the hall leading to their bedroom, then impulsively stopped and looked back at the reconstruction.

She looked . . . lonely.

Imagination.

It was a skull, for Pete's sake. Eve had worked on hundreds of reconstructions, and she had never had that feeling with one before. Was she transferring her own sadness about Jane's departure to the death of this little girl? It was possible, but she wasn't going to look for psychological excuses for the strange feeling she'd had since she'd seen Jenny's skull.

Jenny.

I . . . think . . . my name is Jenny.

The phrasing was very odd.

Forget it.

She turned and started down the hall.

"Good night, Jenny," she said gently.

No answer from the darkness.

Of course there wasn't.

No answers.

No loneliness.

Not for the dead whose life had been snatched away.

That was for the people left behind.

She was suddenly filled with anger and rebellion and a desire to hold close to everything that life meant.

She opened the bedroom door. "Joe?"

"Present and accounted for." He held out his arms. "Come here."

"I have every intention." She was shedding her clothes as she crossed the room. "And you'd better account yourself well." She slipped into bed and wrapped her arms around him. "I need you." She kissed him and buried her fingers in his hair. "I really need you tonight, Joe."

"You've got me." He kissed her again and then moved over her. "Forever . . ."

"Good night . . . Eve."

The words were soft, hesitant, drifting to her in the darkness.

She was sleeping so hard after their hours of erotic lovemaking that she was barely conscious of the words. She was still half-asleep yet she knew she had to answer. "Good night . . ."

Joe kissed the tip of her nose. "I thought we'd said our good nights, sleepy head."

"Not you . . ."

"No? Who then?"

"No one really." She cuddled closer as sleep overcame her. "Only Jenny . . ."

"I don't like this," Ron said bluntly, as Nalchek parked the squad car at the edge of the forest. "I don't want to go blundering through those woods. You're being too damn— You're acting weird as hell, and they're going to tote you off to the funny farm. You're not going to find anything out there in the forest that forensics didn't find."

"Then why did you come along?" Nalchek grinned as he got out of the vehicle. "It's because you know I'm sharp, and I sometimes notice stuff that others don't. You wanted to be with me, so that I wouldn't be able to say I told you so later."

"I came along because for some reason I want to keep you from making an ass of yourself," Ron said sourly. "Imagine that."

"I'll try," Nalchek said. "But we've been together a long time, and you haven't seen me make an ass of myself yet." He grimaced. "Of course, there's always a first time. But I don't believe it's going to be here." He hesitated. "Look, you said you don't want to go with me to that crime scene. Why don't you stay here and keep an eye out for reporters and other folks who might think I'm as nuts as you do?"

"I don't think you're nuts," Ron growled as he got out. "I just think you've got this . . . thing about that poor kid, and you're not thinking straight."

"So stay here." He moved toward the trees. He smiled back at Ron. "It's okay. Keep yourself busy looking over those dossiers you brought with you. I'll be right back. Ten minutes. No more." He disappeared into the woods.

Ron got out of the car and moved to stand in front of the patrol car. Then he moved to the edge of the forest and gazed uncertainly down the trail. Maybe he should have gone with him, he thought. Not that he could have helped. Not that there was any more evidence to gather. But Nalchek was his buddy, and cops supported cops.

Hell, too late now. He'd wait and try to smooth over any feathers he might have ruffled when Nalchek got back. Maybe they'd go down to that bar down the highway and have a couple beers and he'd try to talk sense into—

Pain.

So intense that he didn't know where it came from.

Back.

Chest.

He looked down and saw the knife blade protrude from his chest.

He couldn't breathe. He could feel the blood pour out of his mouth.

He fell to his knees and pitched forward.

Darkness.

CHAPTER

2

"Who is Jenny?" Joe poured Eve's coffee and then his own.

Eve yawned. "I must have told you or you wouldn't know her name." She nodded at the reconstruction on the worktable. "Don't you remember? I gave her a name last night."

"It must have been after I went to bed. No, you didn't tell me." Joe sat down across from her. "You just said good night to her before you went to sleep. Not your usual custom."

"No." She was suddenly wide awake as that half-forgotten blurred memory came back to her. "Not my custom at all."

Good night . . . Eve.

"It's bothering you." Joe's eyes were narrowed on her face. "Why?"

"No reason, I guess." She took a sip of coffee. "I thought I was answering her. Crazy. I was half-asleep. Maybe I was dreaming."

"More than likely. You don't ordinarily have polite conversations with your reconstructions. At least, you've never mentioned it."

She shook her head. "Never. The conversation is all on my side. As I said, I must have been dreaming."

"And answered your Jenny when she wished you sweet dreams?"

"Sort of. I think she was actually answering me when I told her good night before I went to bed. She was just kind of . . . late."

"Maybe it had to sink home," he said solemnly. "She may be a little rusty. After all, being buried for eight years might do that to you."

"Stop making fun of me. If you hadn't worn me out last night, I wouldn't have been having weird dreams."

"As I recall, you had no complaints last night."

She grinned back at him. "Not one." She took another drink of coffee and then put her cup down. "Get out of here. You're going to be late."

He checked his wristwatch. "Yeah, I'll pour the rest of my coffee into a to-go cup." He got to his feet and headed for the cabinet. "I need the caffeine." He gave her a sly glance as he took down the thermal cup. "You kind of wore me out, too. Very aggressive."

She had been aggressive. She'd felt a desperate desire for life affirmation last night and there was no stronger affirmation than love and sex. "I wanted you."

"And I thank God for that." He tightened the lid on the cup. "Every day. Every minute. Come on. Walk me to the porch."

The sun was coming up over the lake as she followed him out on the porch. Beautiful . . .

He gave her a quick kiss and started to run down the steps. "You'll be working on that reconstruction today?"

She nodded. "The sooner I get it done, the happier Nalchek will be, and the sooner he'll get out of my hair."

"I looked him up while you were talking on the phone to him. John Nalchek isn't all that young, early thirties. He was in Afghanistan. Special Forces and he won a chestful of medals. When he came back, he worked for his grandfather in the vineyards for a while. Marcus Nalchek owned the vineyard and half the farmland in central California and was grooming his grandson to take over. But when his grandfather died, Nalchek ran for sheriff and won. His father had held the office before him and he must have grown up with a law-enforcement mind-set."

"And a massive determination. You should have heard him trying to be polite to me when I wouldn't commit to start work last night on Jenny." She called as he got into the driver's seat, "He said he felt she was calling to him."

"And when he went to bed, did she tell him goodnight?"

"I'm going to hit you."

"I'll look forward to it." His eyes were twinkling as he started the car. "We didn't go that route last night."

Eve shook her head ruefully as she watched him drive down the road. He was impossible but he always made her smile when he made the effort. He was probably trying to distract her from thinking about how empty the cottage might be with Jane gone.

Distraction was good. Time to get to work.

She turned and went back into the cottage. Fix toast and orange juice then get to work on Jenny.

Or maybe just check to see if the cosmetic repair on the wound on Jenny's temple was dry.

She moved over to the reconstruction and looked down at the skull.

Right as rain . . .

But there was nothing right about that wound that had taken a little girl's life.

"*But you were right, it didn't hurt.*"

Eve stiffened. "What the hell?" The words had come out of nowhere.

"*You said there was nothing right about it. If it didn't hurt, that was right, wasn't it?*"

She drew a deep breath and gazed around warily. "Not in the big picture."

"*I don't know about big pictures. I'm a little confused.*"

"You're not the only one."

Great. Last night Eve was talking to a skull. And now she was talking to herself?

Or was she? She looked down at the delicate bone structure of the skull. Poor child. But suddenly that skull didn't look as fragile to Eve as it had before. The bones were still delicate but they appeared stronger. It was as if she were changing before Eve's eyes.

Delusions and hallucinations. She had gone through that before, after Bonnie had been killed. But she had found Bonnie was not a hallucination. Just a spirit sent to comfort her.

But there was no reason to think that what she was going through now was anything but a hallucination. Jenny was not her own child as Bonnie had been. She was a stranger. Eve felt a chill run through her. This whole episode was strange and unsettling and she wanted it to go away.

"*I'm scaring you. I didn't mean to scare you. You're not ready. I thought—but I won't—I'm sorry. I won't do it anymore.*"

Eve felt as if she'd frightened a helpless doe and sent it flying away from her.

Okay, get control. What was happening? Assume it wasn't a hallucination. Stranger things had happened to her. Reach out.

"Jenny, are you trying to communicate with me?"

No answer.

"Because, if you are, we have to figure this out. I was caught off guard because this hasn't happened to me before. When I work on a skull, it doesn't usually want to have a conversation." She shook her head. "Well, that's not quite true, it did happen to me once before, and that may be why I got a little nervous. I was working on a very nasty, vindictive man who only wanted to bring me into his world and hurt me. I had to fight to get away from him. I know that's not what you want."

No answer.

The doe had truly fled and wasn't returning.

She should try again anyway to make sure that Jenny wasn't hesitating in the shadows, waiting.

"Look, it's not as if I don't believe that there are spirits among us. My daughter, Bonnie, comes to visit me, and she was one of the lost ones, like you, Jenny. It's just that I find it strange, and I'm a little at a loss. You'll have to help me." She paused. "If that's your choice?"

No answer.

"Okay, maybe I blew it. I hope I didn't if you need something from me." She sat down in her chair at the worktable. "But in the meantime, I have a job to do. I've got to return a face to these bones. I'll be doing a lot of things that will seem strange to you. Or maybe not. What do I know? You may be psychic and all-knowing and that kind of stuff, but somehow I don't think so. I measure, I stick markers in your face, then I start sculpting. You'll have to be patient."

And so would Eve.

Still no answer.

"Are you all right, John?" His father's hand grasped Nalchek's shoulder as the gurney with Ron Carstairs was rolled by them to the medical examiner's van. "Anything I can do?" He grimaced. "Stupid question. You'd think after working law enforcement for more than forty years, I'd know better. But you always want to find some way to help when it's a friend. Hell, he spent Thanksgiving at our house last year."

"Yeah." Nalchek could feel the moisture sting his eyes as he watched them put Carstairs into the van. "He didn't want to come out here with me, Dad. He thought I was crazy to spend so much time on this case."

"Your mom and I have wondered why you— Never mind. Water under the bridge."

"Which means you thought I was crazy, too."

"Nonsense. You had a rough time in Afghanistan, and it was natural that there were aftereffects that made you a bit edgy on occasion. I'm just grateful that it translated to sensitivity and not callousness."

Nalchek watched them close the doors of the van. "I should have been with him."

"You couldn't know there would be any trouble. Ron Carstairs could always take care of himself. Whatever happened must have been a complete surprise. You were the one in the woods and vulnerable to attack, John. Why would anyone think it necessary to go after Carstairs?"

"How the hell do I know?" Nalchek said roughly. "He didn't know anything about the case. He didn't even want to be here."

"And how do you know this has anything to do with that little kid you dug up? It's not likely, John. Who would be hanging around eight years after a killing? The murderer would think he was safe and go on his way. You always have to ask yourself why in a homicide. You said that someone had gone through Ron's pockets and stolen some petty cash and ID from his wallet. Why are you discounting theft?"

"It looks like someone is trying to throw a red herring. Why risk killing a cop for that little cash? Everyone knows we don't make that much money."

"Then maybe it's just someone who doesn't like cops and saw Ron out here by himself and took advantage of an opportunity."

John shook his head. "Weak, Dad. Very weak."

"He liked women. Maybe one of the girls he picked up in a bar got jealous and decided to—"

"No."

His father shrugged. "Just don't ignore other possibilities. You're the only one who thinks the discovery of that little girl's body is of any lasting significance in the scheme of things." He paused. "It's been a rough night for you. Why don't you come home with me, and we'll have a drink."

John shook his head. "I've got to go to see Ron's sister, Clara, and break the news."

"Later?"

"Maybe." He doubted if he'd do it. His father wouldn't be able to keep himself from sharing his own practical experience as sheriff, and usually John listened. But not this time. Practicality had nothing to do with what he was feeling right now, it was pure instinct. He looked away from him. "Thanks for coming out here when you heard about Ron. I appreciate it, Dad."

"What's family for?" He turned toward his truck, parked near the road. "If you need to talk, give me a call. Remember, the question is always why."

John watched him walk away. Why? He thought he knew why Ron was dead, but he couldn't explain or give reasons. No one believed that an eight-year-old murder of a child would cause this attack. Not even his own father.

But if it had anything to do with that kid, why would anyone attack Ron? He wasn't working the case. He hadn't even gone with him to the grave site.

He'd just have to think about it, and he couldn't do that now. He had to think how he was going to break the news to Clara that her brother was dead.

He opened the driver's door and got into the car.

And that wasn't going to be easy. Clara didn't have any family except Ron, and they were close. He wouldn't be—

He inhaled sharply.

Holy shit.

He went still as he looked down at the passenger seat and the documents placed with order and clarity on the dark leather. Every page had been unfolded and was by itself so that it was readily viewed and accessible. None of the dossiers were in the folder where Ron had so carelessly tossed them.

The dossiers he had told Ron to go over when he left him to go into the woods.

And on the first page, Eve Duncan's photo stared up at him.

"Eve?" Joe was standing at the front door. "Okay? I tried to phone you on the way home, and you didn't answer."

"What?" She shook her head to clear it. "I'm fine. Something must be wrong with my phone." She was having trouble fighting her way out of the intense concentration into which she'd been drawn. "You're home early."

"I'm two hours late." He came toward her. "That's why I called you. I wanted to tell you I was stopping to pick up Chinese." He picked up her phone on the worktable and checked it. "It's turned off."

"It couldn't be." She frowned as she took the phone. He was right, it was turned off. "I must have hit the button by mistake."

"That's hard to do." He was studying her. "You look . . . frazzled. And as if you're not quite with me. Did you have lunch?"

She tried to remember.

"You didn't." Joe pulled her to her feet. "Breakfast?"

"I was going to fix toast and orange juice. But then I got busy."

"I can see you did." Joe was looking over his shoulder at the reconstruction as he pushed Eve toward the kitchen bar. He gave a low whistle. "Good God, you've already got those depth markers that look like voodoo sticks inserted on her. It usually takes you another day to get to that point."

"Everything went smoothly. I had a little trouble with the orbital cavities but nothing major."

"Evidently not. I've never seen your work go this quickly."

Neither had Eve, she realized in sudden shock.

She stiffened, stopped short, and turned to look at Jenny.

As Joe had said, the depth markers looked like voodoo sticks.

Not only that, but she was almost done with the insertions. She was even further along than Joe knew to starting the actual sculpting.

There was no way she should be this far along.

Jenny, what are you doing to me?

No answer.

"Let's get some food in you," Joe said quietly. "I'll get the plates."

She nodded jerkily. "And I'll go and clean up a little. I'm not exactly a presentable dinner partner." She moved quickly down the hall toward the bathroom. "Five minutes, okay?"

Seconds later, she closed the bathroom door behind her and leaned back against it. Frazzled? The woman in the mirror definitely fit the word Joe had chosen. Her cheeks were flushed, her hair mussed, and she had a streak of clay on her throat.

And she had turned off her phone.

Forgotten about even minor sustenance.

And she had been driven to work like a proverbial demon to try to get that reconstruction finished.

Driven?

She was a workaholic, and she knew about driving herself. This didn't feel like that at all.

I believe we have to come to an understanding, Jenny.

And soon.

She stepped closer to the vanity and washed her face and hands thoroughly. She ran a comb through her hair, then turned out the light and opened the door.

"Better," she told Joe as she started toward the kitchen. "But not perfect. That's up to you and that Chinese dinner you brought home. I'm starving."

"You were hungry." Joe smiled as poured her coffee. **"At** least I'm not going to have to worry about your having an attack of malnutrition."

"You're not going to have to worry about me at all." She leaned forward and kissed his cheek before she jumped off the stool and gathered their plates and utensils. "You have your job, I have mine. Sometimes they both have a few weird quirks. We just accept them and go on. Right?"

"Weird quirks," Joe repeated as he watched her put the plates in the dishwasher. "Odd phrasing. Would you care to elaborate?"

"Not at the moment. Perhaps after I've worked a few of them out."

"Not accept, work them out. Opposites." He gazed at her thoughtfully. "Do I sense a battle in the offing?"

"You sense a tired woman who is going to head for the shower, then go to bed." She headed down the hall. "Care to join me?"

"Not going to work any more tonight?"

She stopped and looked at the reconstruction shimmering under the work light.

Waiting.

Dear God, she wanted to go back to work. The urge was so powerful, it was almost irresistible.

Almost.

"No." She turned. "I've worked enough today. Tomorrow is soon enough." She started down the hall. "Or maybe even the next day . . ."

She couldn't sleep.

Eve lay there in the darkness, hearing Joe's even breathing next to her.

She wanted to *work*, dammit.

No, she wasn't going to do it. What had happened had all the signs of control and manipulation. She didn't know if it was true, but she wasn't going to chance it.

But if she couldn't sleep, she could at least get a glass of water and go out on the porch until she was tired enough to try again. This tossing and turning would wake Joe.

She carefully avoided looking at Jenny's reconstruction as she passed through on her way to the porch.

"I'm not interested, Jenny," she murmured as she went to the rail. "Maybe tomorrow."

No answer.

There might never be an answer, she thought, as she raised her glass of water to her lips. Perhaps that contact had been rare and fleeting, not to be repeated. Perhaps it had only been imagination, which had been her first thought.

Not imagination. She had not only heard her, she had felt her as a person or entity or whatever.

But it was an entity who had driven her mercilessly today and had somehow managed to control Eve's own desires and disciplines. That couldn't happen again. She wouldn't permit it. It was far beyond what—

Her cell phone vibrated in the pocket of her robe.

Jane?

Not Jane.

Nalchek. She should ignore it. It was after three in the morning. But even Nalchek surely wouldn't call her at this hour of the morning unless there was a reason.

"Do you know what time it is?" she asked when she picked up. "If you want to check on progress, I don't work twenty-four/seven, Sheriff."

"I was going to wait until morning," Nalchek said. "But I didn't get the report until one, and I didn't want to— I thought I had to tell you."

"Tell me what?"

"My deputy, Ron Carstairs, was killed last night."

His voice was hoarse, strained, and she could sense the pain.

"That's terrible. I'm very sorry."

"I didn't call because I wanted sympathy. I thought you should know about it. I don't think you're in danger, but I don't know."

"Danger?"

"No one else thinks there's a connection, but I can see it. Just because she's dead is no sign that she's forgotten. They tell me a child is helpless, but there might be some reason that— You should know."

"How was your deputy killed?"

"We were out at the grave site. I was checking for additional evidence, and Ron was waiting for me at the car. He was stabbed."

"Dear God."

"The department thinks it's robbery or maybe something personal."

"But you don't?"

"I think someone was keeping an eye on the crime scene. I believe they wanted to know how the investigation was going. Maybe they saw me going out there a couple times and wondered if they'd left something that could incriminate them."

"After eight years?"

"I don't know. That's what everyone says. For God's sake, eight years isn't forever." His voice was suddenly passionate. "All I know is that little girl is dead, and someone should pay for it. She *wants* them to pay for it."

"You sound very sure of that."

"She was only nine. She had her whole life ahead of her. Of course I'm sure."

At least, he hadn't said that Jenny had told him that she wanted revenge, she thought wryly. Evidently, Eve was the only one who had been honored by her wish to communicate. "And why did you feel it was important to tell me about your deputy?"

"Because Ron had your dossier in the car on the way out to the crime scene. He tossed it on his seat when he got out of the car and walked with me to the edge of the forest."

"And?"

"When I got back in the car, the dossier was spread out on the seat, very organized, everything clear. No longer in the folder. That was on the floor."

"Maybe he went back to look at it."

"No."

"What are you thinking?"

"That all the information was spread out so that it could be photographed. That his killer had gone through the car to try to get a lead on what was happening in the case, what was happening to those bones."

She didn't speak for a moment, trying to rid herself of a sudden chill. "I suppose it's a possibility. If you had suspicions, did you have forensics go over the car for trace evidence? Fingerprints? DNA?"

"Of course I did. That's why I didn't call you right away. It took time to get the results."

"Which were?"

"Zero. Nothing." He added harshly, "But that doesn't mean that I'm not right. It just means he cleaned up after himself."

"And left those dossiers in full view for you to draw conclusions."

"Maybe he heard me coming back and panicked."

"You didn't draw me a picture of a killer who would panic."

"Or maybe he left them so that you'd be the one to panic and refuse to do the reconstruction."

"That's more likely." She paused. "And that's another reason why you didn't call right away. You wanted to give me time to work on Jenny before you scared me off."

"Jenny?"

"I had to call her something. It's the way I work."

"Jenny . . . Yeah, that kind of suits her."

"I'm glad you think so. I have no idea what suits her."

But Jenny had known.

Jenny. I . . . think . . . my name is Jenny.

"You're working on her?"

"Yes, I'm doing fairly well."

"When will you be finished?"

"I don't do estimates."

"I believe it would be safer for you if you'd do it very quickly."

"Because you think that your killer is going to go after me because I'm working to put a face on his victim?"

"Yes."

"But you're the only one who thinks that."

"I sent that skull to you," he said harshly. "I'm responsible. It doesn't matter what anyone else thinks."

She was silent. "I agree. It's between the two of us. And Jenny, of course." And Nalchek was in pain and still trying to do what he thought was right. She was beginning to like John Nalchek. "And I'll get you a face for Jenny as quickly as I can. It shouldn't be too long."

"Thanks," he said tersely. "And you won't take any chances?"

"I won't take chances," she assured him. "And I'll tell Joe Quinn what you've said if it will make you feel better. I'm sure that dossier you have on me stressed Joe's importance in my life. He's very good at eliminating threats, real or otherwise."

"I told Ron that Quinn was tough." He paused. "If you need me, I'll come there. Just call me. I don't like the idea that bastard could be on his way to you right now."

"Likewise," she said dryly. "But once I finish the reconstruction and get it back to you, I should be safe. Then it's up to you to find Jenny's murderer." She was looking out at the lake, and it seemed colder than a moment ago, the shadows of the trees darker, more threatening. If the deputy's death had happened early last night, then he might not be on his way to her, he might be here.

"Good night, Sheriff." She moved toward the door, and the next moment, she was inside the house. "I'll keep you posted." She hung up.

She drew a deep breath, locked the door, and set the alarm.

Whoever had killed that deputy wasn't stupid. The threat had been there, and it was aimed at her. There might not have been anyone out there in the woods tonight, but there might be tomorrow. Or any other night while she was working on Jenny.

That was the key. Jenny. As she'd told Nalchek, once she was done with the reconstruction, the threat was gone.

So do her job and let Nalchek do his.

As quickly and efficiently as possible.

She tightened the belt of her robe and went to get a cup of coffee.

"You didn't win, Jenny." She took her coffee over to the worktable. "But I'm going to work very hard, and you'd better help me. I've got to find out what you look like." She sipped her coffee and looked down at the skull. "You've already caused a good deal of trouble and hurt. Let's get this done."

No answer.

But . . . sorrow. Overwhelming sorrow.

Eve closed her eyes. "Okay, I guess I forgot for a moment that you're the victim here. You're so strong, little girl, that it's easy to forget. I got upset when I thought you were trying to control me. It brought back memories of that time I told you about when I had to fight off that monster whose skull I was working on."

Pain.

"Am I . . . a monster?"

She seemed to be constantly hurting this child, Eve thought in frustration. But at least Jenny was talking to her again.

"No," Eve said quickly. "I didn't say that. I just said it reminded me of— I was very defensive during that time." She grimaced. "And evidently I still have lingering aftereffects that make me—" She stopped and then said, "And I'm finding it awkward talking to you. I don't know whether I'm speaking to this skull or if you're a spirit floating around somewhere."

"I don't really feel any connection to that skull. But I'm not floating around, either. I'm . . . just here."

"But you didn't contact me until I took that skull out of the box."

"But I knew I was coming . . . to someone who was important. I knew that you were waiting for me." She paused. *"And I was waiting for you."*

"Because you knew that I could help that sheriff find out who you are?"

"I guess that was why. It's all coming back to me in bits and pieces. I only know what I have to do. But I . . . don't really know what your part is going to be."

"That's not very helpful. And what do you have to do, Jenny?"

She didn't answer.

"Okay. I may not need to know your motives. You told me your name was Jenny. What's your last name?"

"I don't remember. Only . . . Jenny."

"But you remember that you want to know more. That it's important to you that I finish this reconstruction."

"Yes. I have to know. I have to stop him. Because it's going to go on. When the sheriff pulled me out of that grave, I could feel him watching me."

"Him? Who?"

"I don't know. I just know . . . he was watching. And he was angry."

"The man who killed you?"

Silence.

"Surely you remember that, Jenny."

"I don't," she whispered. *"I'm sorry, Eve. It's all a blur until I came to you. I think it's supposed to come to me slowly. I remember being angry and telling myself that I mustn't show him I was afraid. He likes me to be afraid. I remember thinking that it had been a long time, and maybe I wasn't ready."*

"Ready for what?"

"What was coming. But nothing good can come until it's finished."

"Double talk. Until what's finished?"

Silence.

"Okay, I'm being impatient. Let's go through this slowly and logically. I'll ask you questions, you try to answer. You think your name is Jenny but you don't know the last name?"

"Yes."

"Do you remember your mother or father?"

"*No.*"

"Brothers? Sisters?"

"*No.*"

"A place, a house?"

"*No.*"

She hesitated. "You do know that you're not . . . as you were? That you're not the Jenny who was born in . . . You're a spirit, Jenny."

"*Yes, what they call a ghost. I've known that for a long time.*" She paused. "*But it confused me. Because I couldn't understand why. I was just there, in that place, and I was alone. All I understood was that I had to be patient. I had to wait.*"

"To find the person who took your life?"

"*That was a part of it.*"

"I would think it would be a big part." She stopped, hesitating again. She didn't want to go down this path. She was getting the impression that Jenny was being truthful but that the girl was lost and bewildered, and Eve didn't want to add pain to the mix. "You don't remember how you were killed?"

"*No.*" A pause. "*Am I supposed to remember?*"

"Perhaps not. My daughter Bonnie had no memory of the time she was killed. And I had no body to examine and tell her." She added, "There's a terrible wound in this skull. You said you didn't remember its hurting. You don't remember who did it? You don't remember the pain when he did it?"

Silence. "*I remember pain.*" Her voice was suddenly panicky. "*Not then. Not then. Before. Before. Not my head. Hands. Please don't do it. It will take it away. Please don't—*"

"Jenny." Eve was frantic, too. She had to stop that agony she was sensing in the child. Dear God, why had she even gone down this avenue? "I'm sorry. It's not here any longer. No pain.

All the bad things are gone. You don't have to remember him. We'll find him for you." She wanted to reach out and hold her in her arms, to comfort her, but how could she do that, dammit? "Forgive me."

"*Are you crying, Eve? Why?*" Jenny's agony was gone, and there was only curiosity.

She *was* crying, Eve realized. Two tears were running down her cheeks. "Because I screwed up." She wiped her cheeks on her work hand towel. "And I didn't mean to hurt you. I told you that talking to you is awkward for me." She drew a deep breath. "I don't know what's going to hurt you and what's not. It's all experimental between us. So I'd better be quiet and just do what I'm best at." She started to carefully remove the depth markers. "Because that sheriff who sent you to me gave me some very bad news, and I promised him I'd see if I could get him answers."

"*I know.*"

Her hand hesitated midway in the act of taking out another marker. "And do you know why I promised him?"

Sadness. "*His friend, Ron. I told you it was going to keep on, Eve.*"

She took out another marker. "Yes, you did. Was it the same man who killed—" She wasn't going down that road again. "Do you know because of some supernatural instinct or because I know?"

"*Because of you. I know what you know. I feel what you feel.*" She added simply, "*I like that, Eve. I don't feel as lonely.*"

Eve was touched, but she could see problems on the horizon. "Let's hope it's only until I finish this reconstruction. Then maybe we can find your parents." She took out another marker. "I'd like that, Jenny. To send you home is my main goal of doing this."

"*Home . . .* " Jenny said. "*I don't think that I—*"

"Hush, now." Eve's brow was wrinkled with concentration. "I've got to fill in the depth for accuracy and then we'll start to work together . . ."

CHAPTER
3

C offee." Joe set her cup on the worktable beside her. "I
don't suppose I can talk you into eating supper?"

"No." She took his hand and put it against her cheek.
"Thanks. Sorry I've been antisocial."

"That's an understatement. You were working when I got
up this morning, and you're still at it this evening." He kissed
her on the forehead. He took a step back and studied the reconstruction. "And if I'm not mistaken, you're approaching
the final stages. That's remarkable. I've never seen you work this
fast."

She rubbed the back of her aching neck. "It seemed the
thing to do."

"I can see why," he said quietly. "When were you going to
tell me there had been another death out there in California?"

Her gaze flew to his face. "I wasn't keeping it from you. I
was just so absorbed that I— How did you know?"

"I've been keeping an eye on the doings of your Sheriff

Nalchek on the Net. His attitude was unusual, and I don't like unusual when it's connected to you. Unusual can be trouble."

It shouldn't have surprised her. Joe was always protective, and he hadn't liked Nalchek's persistence. "It's clear he had a right to be concerned."

"Clear to you. Perhaps clear to me. But not so clear to any-one else. Have you ever run across a cold case like this in which the murderer after eight years was still hovering, ready to leap on anyone investigating the crime?"

"No, but that doesn't mean that it's not true." She paused. "Nalchek had my dossier in that squad car, and he thinks that whoever killed Carstairs took photos of it."

Joe went still. "There wasn't any mention of that on the Net. And it's something you should have told me."

"I'm telling you now." She inclined her head toward the reconstruction. "And that's an excellent reason why I should get Jenny finished right away."

"Yes." His gaze was narrowed on her face. "And is that the only reason?"

"No." She hadn't wanted to go into this right now. It was too involved. She needed to get back to Jenny. But she had to be honest with Joe. "Unless I've gone wacko, our Jenny is com-municating with me."

"What? How?"

She had to smile. "Only you would accept the fact and just want to know the method."

"You have me well trained." He was still frowning. "I've been living with you and your visits from Bonnie all these years. I've even had experiences with her. You have a bond with every child on whom you do a reconstruction, but they don't communicate. The bond just helps you to get an accurate resemblance. Why is this one different?"

"I have no idea." She held up her hand as he opened his lips to speak. "But she doesn't want to do me any harm. I know it. She's just bewildered and lonely. She's not sure why she's here."

"Because you're doing her damn reconstruction, and she needs you. Hell, we all need you."

"She's very strong, Joe. I guess I gave you the impression that she's clinging, but I can feel how strong she is. I don't believe she would have been able to reach me if she didn't have that strength."

"Good for her. I hope she'll find her home and Nalchek finds her killer. But I want to be sure that you're not damaged in the process." He looked down at the reconstruction. "Finish her. Send her on her way." He turned and headed for the door. "In the meantime, I'll take a look around the woods and make sure that we don't have any visitors."

The door shut firmly behind him.

She shook her head as she stared after him. Joe was definitely on the alert and moving with his usual efficiency.

"*He doesn't want me here,*" Jenny said. "*Why does he think I'll hurt you?*"

"He doesn't. He's just cautious. When you care about someone, you always want to be sure that they're safe. I'm sure your parents were like that with you."

"*I don't think so. I don't remember anyone's being like him.*"

She chuckled. "Because there is no one like him. He stands alone."

"*You feel . . . warm . . . toward him. Like standing before a fireplace and just toasting. It's nice.*"

"I feel many things toward him. And they're all nice." She thought about it. "Well, mostly nice. He's very stubborn, and that can be annoying."

"*But it doesn't stop the warmth.*"

"No, it doesn't stop that. Nothing stops that." She turned toward the reconstruction. "Now be quiet while I get back to work."

"*Okay. I was just curious.*"

And Jenny's interruption had the gentleness and familiarity of an old friend whispering in her ear. "Children are always curious."

"*I don't know if I'm a child anymore. Am I?*"

If Jenny had lived, she would be seventeen now. She had missed so much . . . "I don't know. My Bonnie says that she couldn't stand still when she crossed over, that she kept maturing. I imagine it might be the same for you. But that doesn't mean you might not be a little stunted as far as experiences are concerned. I guess that depends on what you've been doing for the last eight years."

"*Waiting. I've been waiting . . .*"

Waiting for what? To be brought home to the people she loved? To get justice for the terrible crime perpetrated against her? The words struck Eve as terribly sad, and again she had the urge to reach out and hold her.

Back off. Jenny was coming too close to her. She forced herself to go back to working on the depth markers on the reconstruction. "Then wait a little longer, Jenny. We're getting there. Just a little longer . . ."

The lights were burning bright in the cottage even though it was after midnight.

Walsh didn't dare get closer to the cottage than these trees across the lake, and it was filling him with frustration. But Joe Quinn had been out in the woods twice tonight, and he couldn't risk it. He'd read Quinn's dossier, and an ex-SEAL wasn't going to be taken by surprise like that deputy. He'd have to wait for an opportunity.

As he'd have to wait for the opportunity to go after Eve Duncan. But time was running out. She might be getting close.

Walsh could imagine that Duncan bitch sitting working on that damn skull and making that kid's face come alive again. Damn Nalchek. Any other small-town sheriff would have just let that skeleton be reburied somewhere and eventually filed the paperwork and let the little girl be forgotten.

But Eve Duncan wasn't going to let her be forgotten.

So Eve Duncan would have to be removed.

"Okay, here we go." Eve could feel the tension grip her muscles as she stared at the reconstruction. "I've done all the prep work I can. It's time we started working together on this."

No answer.

"Listen, Jenny, this isn't the time for you to opt out. Help me."

No answer.

Ignore the rejection and hope she would come in later.

Smooth the clay.

Such a small skull.

So delicate . . .

She had to be sensitive, gentle.

No mistakes.

She let the tips of her fingers move of their own volition.

Help me, Jenny.

The clay was cool . . . no, it was warmer now. As warm as her own fingers moving, molding.

Nose?

It had to be generic.

Instinct. Just use instinct.

Mouth.

Generic again. She'd measured the width but had to guess at the shape. A child's mouth, sensitive, because Jenny was so sensitive.

Eyes. So very difficult. No measurements, very few scientific indicators. Okay, study the shape and the angle of the orbits. That angle and the bony ridge above it would help her decide the shape. Keep them in mind but don't do the eyes yet. It always made her excited to see the eyes staring at her, and she might hurry the rest of the process.

Do the cheeks.

Fill in.

Smooth.

The other cheek.

Smooth.

She was going too fast. Slow down. Measurements were still important. Check them.

Nose width. Okay.

Lip height. Okay. No, bring the top lip down. It's usually thinner than the bottom.

There's a major muscle around the mouth, build it up.

But Jenny was a child and would have a child's fullness.

No, thin face.

Where had that come from? It didn't matter if it was instinct or Jenny.

Just go with it.

Mold.

Smooth.

Fill in.

Her hands were flying over that small face now.

Deepen.

Mold.

Smooth.

Fill in.

The chin.

More pointed.

Smooth.

Brows.

Winged.

Odd. Why?

Just do it.

Slow down. Her hands were too feverish.

No, they aren't.

Go ahead.

Smooth.

Mold.

Fill in.

But there was only a little more to fill in.

Smooth it.

Mold?

No, just the smoothing.

Fast.

Sure.

Let it come.

Let *her* come.

Blinding speed. Her heart was beating hard.

The reconstruction was only a blur.

Finished.

She leaned back, and her hands dropped away from the skull.

Only it wasn't a skull any longer.

It was Jenny.

No, not yet.

She reached into the drawer and drew out her eye case.

Eyes.

Jenny had to have eyes.

Eve looked down at the glass eyeballs. She usually chose brown, they were the most common.

She started to reach for them.

"*Green.*"

Eve stopped. "Now you appear. I could have used a little more help, Jenny."

"*I tried to help. It was hard to remember . . . It's not important here where I am now.*"

"Well, it's still important to me." She took the green eyes from the case. "And it's important to Sheriff Nalchek." She paused. "And it may be important to the person who put you in that grave."

"*But you did pretty well without me, didn't you? You must be very smart, Eve.*"

"Flattery? You must be fairly smart yourself, Jenny." She was inserting the right eye carefully in the right cavity. "Green eyes are very noticeable. That might help. Who did you take after? Your mother or your father?"

"*I don't know. They're not . . . I don't remember.*"

Distress. Veer away from the pain she sensed. "It doesn't

matter." She inserted the other eyeball and smoothed the clay around the orbital cavity. "What's important is that the eyes might trigger a memory that—"

She broke off and inhaled sharply.

Finished. The reconstruction was completely finished.

And the full impact of the work that she'd just done hit home to her.

"Jenny?"

She reached out and gently touched the cheek of the sculpture. She almost expected it to be warm with life. The little girl's expression seemed to radiate vitality and enthusiasm. Even those wide-set green eyes seemed to glow with a kind of wonder in that small, triangular face. Pointed chin, high cheekbones, and winged brows gave the child an elfin quality. But it was the vitality, the wonder, that held Eve spellbound.

And some monster had killed this?

She cleared her throat to ease its tightness. "Perhaps you helped me more than either one of us thought, Jenny. I believe you must have been a very special little girl. I'd bet you enjoyed every minute of your life. I'm sorry you don't remember more of it."

"*I don't have to remember. The joy has been with me while I was waiting. The most important thing I got to take with me.*"

"What thing?"

"*Why, the music, Eve. It's still part of me. It's still here.*"

"Music? What do you mean, Jenny?"

No answer.

"Okay, I guess I shouldn't expect more than one breakthrough at a time." She wearily rubbed the back of her neck. "And tonight I got a big one. I have a face. Tomorrow, I'll take photos and run it through my computer program for any matches. The program isn't as extensive as FBI and police databases, but I might get lucky."

"*You're happy. I like to see you like this.*"

"I did my job, and I came up with one great product. It gives me a sense of satisfaction to know what you look like. It's like solving a mystery. Now I know to whom I'm talking."

"*It's not only because of what happened to me?*"

"No, a whisper from the great beyond is better than nothing, but I'm a visual person." She looked back at the reconstruction. "You know, sometimes I don't even do brows but you must have been insistent." She got to her feet and arched her back. "And now I'm going to shower and go to bed. I'll see you in the morning." She had a sudden thought. "Or not. Maybe you'll disappear now that I've finished your reconstruction."

"*I'll be here.*"

"Oh." Why did she feel this relief? "You and the music?"

"*You're smiling. I'm sorry I can't explain about the music. It's just that—*"

"You don't have to explain anything unless you want to. We're just ships that pass in the night. I don't have to know. You've been hurt, and you're in a place I can't possibly understand."

"*Ships that pass . . . I don't think so, Eve.*"

"Time will tell."

"*You're going to bed with your Joe again?*"

"Absolutely."

"*You were very happy at what he was doing to your body that first night I came. Are you going to do that again?*"

Her mouth fell open. "What?" Then she shook her head. "Never mind. Jenny, I had no idea you were— Do you know what a peeping Tom is?"

"*Yes.*"

"That's what you did when you watched me and Joe—" But did she watch? Was she just attuned to Eve and aware of her feelings? "Whatever you did, that was a private moment and not to be shared without invitation. Do you understand?"

"*But I liked it. It was . . . happy and excited.*"

"Yes, it was." And a happiness Jenny would never know. So many experiences she would never know. "But it's still private, and you shouldn't intrude. Okay?"

Silence. "*I guess.*"

Reluctant at best. Eve wasn't sure that she either understood or would comply. "Thank you."

"*You're welcome.*" Still that thread of wistfulness. "*But I didn't mean to hurt anyone . . .*"

"I know you didn't. And you didn't hurt me, Jenny. It's just the way people feel about—" Oh, give it up. She didn't even know how much a nine-year-old Jenny knew about sex. She was glad that she didn't seem to feel anything horrific connected to it. It was always a fear in a child's murder. "Good night, Jenny."

"*Good night, Eve.*"

"Is she finished?" Joe asked drowsily as Eve climbed into bed forty-five minutes later.

"Yes." She cuddled close. "It turned out exceptionally well. She has a very memorable face. She kind of reminded me of a young Audrey Hepburn. Unusual . . ."

"Everything about her has been unusual." He brushed his lips across her temple. "But I'm glad that she'll be out of your head soon."

But would she? Eve wondered. Jenny was full of mysteries and contradictions, and Eve was irresistibly drawn to try to solve them. "I suppose I'll be glad, too."

"Suppose?"

"Jenny is appealing. She . . . touches me. Do you know, I've been wondering if there's some reason why I can communicate with her. That maybe I was meant to help her."

"You are helping her. You did her reconstruction."

"Maybe I was meant to go a step further."

Joe was silent, his arms tightening around her. "I'm not going to argue with you. You'll do what you think is right." He added harshly, "But I don't like it, dammit."

"I'm not sure I do, either. And I'll probably send her off to Sheriff Nalchek tomorrow. He can do more than I can to find out who she is. It's just . . ." She wearily shook her head. "She's become too close to me. I feel as if I'm responsible for her."

"Eve."

"I know. I know." She suddenly chuckled. "I wish Bonnie would drop in and have a chat with me. I could use a little advice from the other side. Jenny isn't nearly as integrated there as Bonnie, and she seems to be missing key memories. Maybe Bonnie could help her out."

"Send your Jenny to Nalchek," he said firmly.

She nodded. "You're right." She turned in his arms and clasped him tightly. "I can't be responsible for everyone. I have to pick and choose." She kissed him. "And I choose you."

"And I humbly thank you." He raised himself on one elbow and smiled down at her. "Does that choice offer fringe benefits?"

"You bet it does." She kissed him, long and deep. She felt the familiar stirring, the hot need that never changed and yet was forever new. She pulled her sleep shirt over her head and tossed it to the floor beside the bed. "All you have to do is put in a request." She climbed on top of him. "Or not."

He chuckled. "Consider it entered." His smile faded, and he was suddenly intense. "And then let's do a little more entering." His hands were on her breasts. "And I'll prove you didn't make a mistake in making that choice."

And would Jenny be aware that they were making love, Eve wondered suddenly. It was possible. She was curious. She had liked the warmth.

"Eve? Something wrong?"

And what difference did it make, Eve thought recklessly. There was no shame in the love she and Joe shared. It was beautiful, and the warmth that Jenny had noticed lit up both their lives.

"No, nothing is wrong. Everything is right." She leaned down and whispered, "I love you, Joe Quinn."

"I see what you mean." Joe was looking at the reconstruction on the worktable when she came out of the bathroom the next morning. "She's extraordinary. You're right, unusual. You usually get the resemblance right but she looks . . . alive. And there's an amazing joi de vivre."

"Yes." She went to the cabinet and poured a cup of coffee. "My first thought was how could anyone kill anyone who had that much joy in living. She's almost . . . alight."

"And that made you think that maybe you should be doing something more."

She nodded. "But Nalchek can do it. I've done my part."

"She goes off today?"

"This afternoon. I'll do the photographs and the computer input this morning." She followed him out to the porch. "Then I'll call Nalchek and FedEx."

"Good." He gave her a quick kiss, then glanced over his shoulder as he started down the porch steps. "And keep the door locked until you get that FedEx box on its way. Okay?"

"Sure. But you said there was no sign of an intruder yesterday."

"That doesn't mean that there might not have been one. It just means that he could have been very good." He got into the car. "Better to be safe. I'll call you later and see how it's going."

"Joe, it's going to be fine." She blew him a kiss. "I'm almost at the end of this job. I'll see you tonight."

She watched him drive away, then stood a moment looking out at the lake. She wasn't as confident as she'd let Joe believe. Joe believed it his duty to be suspicious in order to protect her. She only had instinct.

And that instinct was making her uneasy.

She would definitely keep the door locked today.

And she didn't want to keep standing here and staring out at the lake and the woods.

She went back into the cottage, closed the door, and locked it.

"*He's worried about you,*" Jenny said. "*And you're worried, too.*"

Eve's gaze flew to the reconstruction across the room.

"*No, not there. I keep telling you that I don't really have a connection with that skull. I'm here, Eve.*"

Eve slowly turned and gazed at the couch.

Jenny.

Sitting on the couch, wearing a long white eyelet dress with an empire waist and long, bell sleeves. She had black, patent-leather shoes on her small feet and her long, shiny, black hair was tied back away from her face with a white satin ribbon. She looked younger than nine except for that remarkable face and a brilliant smile that Eve would not even have attempted to capture in the reconstruction.

"Well, this is a surprise." Eve was a little breathless. "No, more of a shock. I wasn't expecting this, Jenny."

"*But you like it?*" Jenny asked eagerly. "*You were so happy when you could see my face at last. I want you to be happy, Eve. I thought if I concentrated, I could do this and it worked.*"

"It certainly did." Eve smiled. "And, yes, I'm very happy to see the entire product. You're all dressed up as if you're going to a birthday party. Very elegant. What was the occasion?"

She shrugged. "*I don't know. It wasn't a party. I think I wore this dress a lot.*"

"It's very pretty. *You're* very pretty." Her smile faded as a thought occurred to her. Had Jenny been killed in this white eyelet dress? Bonnie always appeared to Eve in her jeans and Bugs Bunny T-shirt she'd worn when she was taken. Forget it. Accept that Jenny had appeared in an outfit that she'd worn while alive to please Eve and let any sadness go. "Thank you for being so thoughtful." She lifted her cup to her lips and took a sip of coffee. "I just wish that you could remember a few other things besides that dress."

"*I'll try.*" Jenny was smiling eagerly. "*Things are coming back to me all the time. But this did please you, and it's easier than the rest. There are all kinds of confusing stuff that I don't think I'm supposed to know yet."* She tilted her head. *"Maybe we're supposed to find out together."*

"I don't think so, Jenny. Sheriff Nalchek has better ways than I do to find out what happened to you. I'm sending your reconstruction back to him today."

Her smile faded. *"I know that's what you said. I thought maybe you'd change your mind."* She lifted her chin. *"But that's all right. I know you're busy, and you have Joe. I'm sure everything is going to work out fine. I just don't know how right now."*

And Eve was having that now-familiar urge to comfort and hold her. "Neither do I. But I'll be in contact with the sheriff, and he'll give me progress reports on what's going on with you. He's a good man and he cares what happens to you."

Silence, then a wistful, *"But he's not you, Eve."*

What was she supposed to say to that?

"I've upset you. Don't worry, I'll be fine." Jenny added quickly, *"There's always the music."*

The music again. It seemed to be Jenny's safe haven when she was upset or afraid. "Yes, you told me it was always there. What kind of music?"

"All kinds. I like Chopin best. He makes my heart sing. Though Brahms soothes and takes away the pain."

And it was breaking Eve's heart that she was the one who had caused that pain. She moved toward the reconstruction. "I have to do the computer program on the reconstruction now. But you might remember something else, that there are always the memories of you that are held by the people who loved you." She added, "Who still love you, Jenny."

No answer.

Jenny was gone.

And Eve was looking down at the reconstruction of that little girl who had worn her pretty white dress to please Eve and make her happy.

She blinked back the stinging moisture and started to set up her computer.

It's the right thing to do, Jenny.

12:40 P.M.

"Sorry, I was a little late, Ms. Duncan. I know you requested a morning pickup." Ted Donner, the FedEx driver, was entering her package onto his computer. "The company had me pick up a few packages on another route."

"No problem. I had some computer work to do anyway." She smiled. Donner had been covering this route for the last four years, and he'd always been reliable. "Just so it gets to California tomorrow. I have a sheriff out there who will be on my case if it doesn't."

"We'll get it there." He turned and ran down the steps. "Have a nice day."

"You, too, Ted."

Eve stood there watching the FedEx truck drive away from the cottage and down the road. Usually, she felt relief and sat-isfaction at a job well-done when she saw her reconstructions depart her custody.

Not this time.

She was feeling sad and a nagging sense that she had failed Jenny.

Nonsense. She had done exactly what Nalchek had asked

of her. It was possibly the best reconstruction she had ever done. Any emotional backfire had to be caused by the fact that she had begun to be too close to the little girl. It had been logical and practical for her to send that skull and the other information to law enforcement, who had the means to take the search a step further.

Logical.

Almost from the beginning, there had been nothing logical about her approach to Jenny's reconstruction. She had that in common with Nalchek. They had both been swept away by the mystery that surrounded Jenny. That might have been a good thing because it had caused both of them to exert all their efforts to solve that mystery.

But now her part was over, and logic had to rule. She'd feel better after she called Nalchek and told him that Jenny was on her way to him.

She turned and went back into the cottage.

Empty.

Of course, it was empty. Joe was at work.

And she was done with Jenny and had told her that she was now in Nalchek's hands.

She took out her phone and dialed Nalchek. "I've just FedExed the reconstruction to you," she told him when he picked up. "I think you'll be pleased. She has a very memorable face and should be easy to ID if you're able to get cooperation from the media. I'm doing a last check of the computer photos, and I'll be e-mailing them to you later today."

"Great." Nalchek's voice was sharp. "And you overnighted that skull?"

"Of course. She should be there before ten tomorrow."

"Sorry. I've been under a lot of pressure." He paused. "And

I just got back from a memorial service for Ron Carstairs. It was hell."

"They usually are. And I'm the one who is sorry for your loss. I hope when you get the reconstruction, that it will help you to feel a little better."

"Thanks," he said curtly. "But that may take a long time." He hung up.

So much for calling Nalchek to make her feel what she'd done was worthwhile. It had only reinforced how wrong everything had gone on Jenny's case.

She found her gaze wandering over to the couch where she'd last seen Jenny.

Of course, she wasn't there.

Work.

Finish up the photos.

That would distract her.

She put her phone on her worktable and opened her computer.

2:45 P.M.

One more adjustment . . .

Eve zeroed the computer camera in on Jenny's delicately pointed chin that she'd sculpted on the reconstruction.

And her cell phone rang.

Joe calling to check? She'd tell him she'd call him back.

Not Joe.

FedEx.

Dammit, had she forgotten to fill out one of those many boxes on the form?

She punched the access. "Look, did I make a mistake? Can we correct it on the phone? That box has to be in California in the morning."

"No mistake, Ms. Duncan. This is the dispatcher, we just wanted to make sure that the driver picked up your package. We show he did, but you're the last one before we lost contact."

She stiffened. "Lost contact?"

"I can't talk to you any longer. I was just authorized to check. We have the police and a company representative who will be on their way to—"

"Police? What the hell are you talking about?"

"An accident," he said quickly. "Our FedEx driver had an accident."

"What? Where?"

"On Quinn Road, a few miles from the expressway. That's why we were almost sure he'd made the pickup." He paused. "But we can't locate the package. Don't worry, I'm sure that we will. And, as I said, a company representative will—"

"Can't locate the—" She jumped to her feet. "This is weird as hell. And why would anyone send the police with that FedEx rep?" She was heading for the front door. "You're not telling me the truth." She slammed the door, locked it, and ran down the porch steps. "Let me talk to your supervisor." No, that would just be adding to the red tape. "Never mind." She hung up and called Joe as she jumped into the Jeep. Voice mail. "Joe, something crazy is happening with that FedEx I sent out a couple hours ago. I'm on my way to check it out. Call me."

Her foot pressed the accelerator, and the Jeep leaped forward.

•   •   •

She saw the white FedEx truck a mile before she approached the expressway.

But there was no sign of a crash or another vehicle. Yellow crime-scene tape was barricading the area around the truck. Police squad cars, a forensic van, and an ambulance were parked along the road.

Not good.

She parked behind the barricade and jumped out of the Jeep. She lifted the tape and ducked beneath it.

"I'm sorry, ma'am, you'll have to go back." A young policewoman ran forward. "This is an investigation and you're not allowed to—"

"What kind of investigation?" She looked at the woman's badge. "Officer Maddox. I just received a call from the FedEx dispatcher to tell me that I'd be receiving a visit from the police and the FedEx rep. Why?"

"I'm sure that one of the detectives will be able to tell you what you need to know. But you really do have to get beyond the tape and let us get your statement. It's not—"

"Eve, what the hell are you doing here?" Detective Pete Salyer had come around the truck. "I just called Joe and left a message for him. He's with the captain and the mayor at some council meeting. I thought he'd want to know."

She breathed a sigh of relief. She'd known Pete for years, and she liked and trusted him. "Know what?"

"A murder practically on his doorstep would interest him."

Shock surged through her. "Murder?"

"The FedEx driver was shot at close range. No one heard the shot, so we think the weapon had a silencer." He looked around at the trees lining either side of the road. "No houses. So far, we have no witnesses."

"Murder," she repeated numbly.

"She said that the company dispatcher phoned her about the truck," the police officer said. "We wouldn't allow that, would we, sir?"

"No way," Pete said flatly. "What's happening, Eve?"

"I have no idea." She shivered. That pleasant young man to whom she'd given the reconstruction only hours ago was dead. "The man who phoned me said he was the dispatcher and there had been an accident. The package I'd given the driver was missing."

"No accident. And we haven't had a chance to determine if there was anything missing from the truck." Pete turned and headed for the truck. "But I think it's time we checked it out. I'll talk to one of those FedEx bigwigs and see if they can pull up the info."

Officer Maddox grimaced. "Look, I'm sorry that I wasn't more helpful. I was just trying to do my job."

"And you did it," Eve said. "I must have looked pretty wild when I jumped out of that Jeep. And my story was just as improbable. Don't apologize."

Pete came back fifteen minutes later. "A record of a package being sent by you at 12:42 P.M. No package in the van. We'll go through the entire van later for other missing packages but that's a positive."

"I don't believe you'll find any other missing packages," Eve said. "I think he got what he wanted." Her phone rang. "It's Joe."

"Are you okay?" Joe said the instant she picked up.

"Yes, I'm not the one who got shot. It was that poor driver."

"Yeah, I got Pete's message. Right before I got yours. It

scared the hell out of me. I'm on my way," he said tersely. "Are you at the crime scene?"

"Yes."

"Stay there. Stay with Pete. Twenty minutes." He hung up.

CHAPTER

4

Joe arrived in fifteen minutes, and he fought his way through the police and media crews that had just arrived to where Eve was standing in the trees. "Talk to me." His expression was grim. "Tell me everything."

"There's not much more to tell." She went over the entire phone conversation in detail. "He said he was a dispatcher. At first it sounded legitimate, then it got weird. It bewildered me. And all that about the police and FedEx reps coming to see me didn't sound right. I've been standing here trying to piece it together."

"And what did you come up with?"

"That he wanted me to be suspicious. He wanted me to suspect something wasn't as it should be." She met his eyes. "He wanted me to go try to find out the truth."

"And you did it." His jaw tightened. "He could have ambushed you, too. Just as he did that FedEx driver."

"You know I keep a gun in the glove box." She added, "And I was already suspicious. I wouldn't have been that easy."

"No, you wouldn't." His hand reached out and gently touched her cheek. "But I think you wouldn't have been so eager to run out of the house if your precious reconstruction wasn't in danger."

"I don't know if I would or not." She could feel the fury that she had been trying to subdue start to rise. "I do know I'm angry as hell that Jenny's reconstruction was stolen. All I have now are those computer photos that I—" She stopped. "The photos." She whirled away from Joe. "The photos, Joe. That's the only documentation I have on the reconstruction. I was going to send them to Nalchek later today, but I—"

"You were interrupted." He took her elbow and strode toward his car. "And you weren't ambushed because the killer had something more important he had to do first."

There was a squad car in their driveway, and the front door was wide open.

"It's okay," Joe said, as Eve tensed beside him. "At least, this part is."

"This part? What's happening?" Eve asked.

"Don't panic. I phoned ahead when I was on the highway and told one of the officers at the crime scene to check out our house and surrounding area to make sure that—"

"You could have told me." She got out of the car and headed quickly for the steps. She *had* panicked when she'd seen that open door.

And the panic didn't abate when she saw the face of the gray-haired officer who met them at the door.

"Officer James Kiphart, ma'am. You're Ms. Duncan?"

"That's right." She looked beyond him to her workstation. "Dammit, where's my computer?"

"It's missing?" the officer asked. "I was hoping that we'd scared the thief off before he was able to steal anything. The lock was broken, and the door was wide open, but nothing appeared to be missing."

She ran over to the worktable. The place that her computer usually occupied was vacant. The notes and measurements she'd used to reconstruct Jenny were no longer in the binder on the dais.

"Would you like to fill out a report?" Officer Kiphart asked.

"Not now." Joe was standing beside her. "Maybe later. You checked out the other rooms?"

"Clean as a whistle. Like I said, I hoped that I'd scared him off." He was looking sympathetically at Eve's stricken expression. "Maybe your home insurance will cover the computer."

"Maybe," Joe said. "We'll look into it. Thank you for coming so promptly, Officer. I'll help with the paperwork and give you a statement when I get back to the precinct."

It was a clear dismissal, and the officer nodded and headed for the door. "I'm sorry that I didn't get here in time to catch your thief, Detective Quinn. I'm afraid you'll have to replace that lock." He nodded at Eve. "Good day, ma'am."

"Good day." She was still looking at the place on the worktable where her computer had been and paid no attention to the door closing behind the officer.

"How bad is it?" Joe asked quietly.

"Bad," Eve said. "He took all my notes on the reconstruction. And he made sure the photos couldn't be copied by stealing the entire damn computer." She swallowed. "And I don't have the actual reconstruction of the skull. He took care of that when he killed that FedEx driver." Her hand was shaking as she brushed a strand of hair back from her face. "I have nothing left of Jenny. She's gone."

"God, I'm sorry, Eve. Look, you know exactly what she looked like. Can't you draw a sketch and send it to Nalchek?"

"Yes, but that wouldn't be enough without the reconstruction. Nalchek wouldn't be able to persuade any of the media to act without proof it was based on the actual skull. It would just be my word, and it's a damn cynical world."

"It was a great reconstruction." He pulled her into his arms. "I know how hard you worked, how glad you were that you had something concrete to send to Nalchek."

And Jenny had been so much more to her than that. The spirit of that little girl had reached out and touched her, stirred her curiosity, her sympathy, and something . . . deeper. "I've lost her, Joe." She nestled her head in his chest. "It's all crazy. Why would anyone be so paranoid that he'd kill someone just to get his hands on that reconstruction? She was only a nine-year-old little girl." She had a sudden aching memory of Jenny in that white eyelet long dress smiling at her across the room. "I *hate* this. I can't stand feeling this helpless." She stepped away from him. "That call I got had to be from him to lure me away from the cottage. He'd gotten his hands on the reconstruction, but he had to have the complete package."

"That's my take on it."

"Why? Why does Jenny have to remain lost?"

"You'll have to ask him."

"Him? I don't even know if it's a male or female. I just instinctively call him he."

"The biggest percentage of little girls are killed by males. Sexual predators go after—"

"I know that. I don't want to hear it again. I don't want

percentages. I want Jenny's killer to be tied up and sent to the electric chair." She whirled away and headed for the porch. She felt stifled in this room. "Can you get forensics out here right away to test for trace and prints?"

He nodded. "No problem." He started down the steps. "And I'll take another look around the cottage grounds just to make sure that he didn't leave any evidence. Stay here where I can see you."

"I'm not going anywhere." She pulled out her phone. "But I have to call Nalchek to tell him he won't be getting that reconstruction . . . and why."

He nodded and disappeared around the side of the cottage.

She could hear him moving through the brush, and she knew that he was doing that so that she'd feel safer. Joe was usually panther-silent courtesy of his SEAL training. He needn't have bothered. She wasn't frightened, she was only angry.

She punched in Nalchek's number. "You won't be getting the reconstruction," she said jerkily when he picked up. "You can't be sorrier than I am." She briefly went over the events of the afternoon. "You were right, the killer came looking for that skull."

"Are you all right? You're not hurt?"

"I'm not hurt. But as I told you, that FedEx driver is dead." She was looking out at the lake. "And I have no idea where that computer and reconstruction are going to end up. They may be at the bottom of the lake right now."

Nalchek was cursing beneath his breath. "There's nothing that you can do?"

"Not unless you can find that skull. I can go back and re-create the reconstruction, but I can't do it out of air. No one in the media will touch it without proof that I used that skull to do it. And what are the chances of that killer's not destroying it now that he has it?"

"Zero. Unless he's a trophy collector."

"Then he wouldn't have buried the skull in the beginning. No, he wanted her lost forever." Another wave of anger poured through her. "And I won't let it happen. He's not going to win, Nalchek."

"You just told me you couldn't do anything."

"I told you I couldn't do the reconstruction again. But I'm not going to let him get away with this. I'll make sure he won't stay free and gloating over killing that little girl." Her voice was shaking. "There has to be a way, but I'm not thinking straight right now. I'll call you after I go over everything and see what my options are."

"Very sparse, I'd say." He paused, then said harshly, "I can't deny I'm disappointed as hell. But whether you can do anything more or not, thank you for what you've already done. You've been the only one in my corner since the night I found Jenny. Maybe they'll believe me and move on this after that driver was killed."

"Maybe. Good-bye, Nalchek. I'll get back to you." She hung up.

She doubted if Nalchek would get anyone to push forward on a cold case when they didn't have proof of identity. It had been her experience that any excuse was good enough for manpower-strapped law-enforcement departments to file away the records in a bottom drawer and look the other way. But they'd had a chance with that reconstruction, dammit. She defied anyone to look at that face and turn away.

I won't let it matter, Jenny. I won't let what he did make a difference.

Somehow, I'll make it work.

"You're very quiet," Joe said as he pulled her closer in bed that night. "Depressed?"

"Yes." She stared into the darkness. "And angry. I can't let him get away with it, Joe."

"I knew that was coming." He paused. "We have a chance. I found tracks of a vehicle near the road and sent the imprints to the lab. That may help, but what else are we going to do about it?"

"We? It's my job."

"Not with a killer out there."

She would feel the same way about him. "And I don't know what I'm going to do yet. I'm trying to put something together. I feel as if the rug's been jerked from beneath me." She was silent. "I was so sure that I was doing the right thing sending the reconstruction back to Nalchek. I wanted desperately for Jenny to find her family. She seemed so . . . lost."

"Lost?"

"When Bonnie first came back to me, she wasn't like Jenny. She was just the way she was when she was alive. Oh, she had things she didn't know, like about where she was, and a few lapses of memory about how she died. But she knew me, she knew what we were together."

"And Jenny isn't like that?"

She shook her head. "She doesn't remember her parents. She doesn't remember anything about who killed her. She has only fleeting memories about anything connected to her life.

As for her afterlife, that's terribly vague. She only knows she's been waiting."

"Waiting to know who killed her?"

"I don't know, Joe. Maybe waiting for her parents to bring her home? Though I think that things were starting to come back to her." She paused. "That last day I actually saw her."

"What?"

"I saw her. I'd said something about how happy I was that I knew what she looked like after I finished the reconstruction. And later I saw Jenny in her white dress and black, patent-leather shoes. She wanted to please me. She was so sad when I told her I was sending her away."

"You actually saw her? The way you see Bonnie?"

She nodded. "I was surprised, too. She said that she'd thought she might be able to do it, so she tried. I think that she was exploring, stretching . . ."

"Since she was no longer lying in that grave, waiting," he said bitterly.

"I don't believe that's what she meant."

"You'll have to forgive me. Your Jenny is a little out of my experience."

"And mine." She closed her eyes. "Hold me tighter, Joe."

His arms closed around her. "There has to be some kind of cosmic justice for kids like Jenny. I don't believe God would saddle you with that responsibility. She's kind of out of our jurisdiction."

"How do you know? Jenny was *sent* to me. Maybe that's a sign that I'm the one who should help her. Oh, I know I did my best with that reconstruction. But it wasn't enough, was it? She's back with that monster who killed her." She shuddered at the thought. "And that's not justice, cosmic or otherwise. That's a horror story." She opened her eyes as a thought occurred to her. "Or maybe it's payback time. I had a miracle come into my life, and her name was Bonnie. Even when she was taken from me in the cruelest way possible, she was allowed to come back and visit me. That was a miracle, too. Perhaps I'm being tapped to return the favor."

"Perhaps you are." His lips brushed her temple. "In any case, you've convinced yourself that it's possible. Now go to sleep, and we'll start planning what to do in the morning."

"Okay." She nestled closer. She doubted if she could sleep, but she mustn't keep Joe awake. She'd try to persuade him to go to work in the morning. It was foolish to expect him to hold her hand while she was trying to think of a way to trap that bastard. "When is the report on those tires supposed to come in?"

"Tomorrow sometime. As soon as I get it, I'll try to match it to a vehicle, then visit the properties on our road and the farms to the north and start questioning. He was operating in broad daylight today. Someone must have seen him."

She could only hope. The lead was flimsy at best.

But at least it was a lead. Not someone creeping up in the dark woods to kill, then vanishing as it had happened in California.

And she'd take whatever she was given.

Because it just might take her to Jenny.

It was chilly sitting here on the porch swing. Eve tightened the belt of her robe and stared out into the darkness. It was a little after four in the morning, but there was no light on the horizon.

No light on the horizon. It seemed a fitting phrase at this particular moment.

No, dammit. She wouldn't accept that defeatist attitude.

If she couldn't see a break in the darkness, she'd blast one through herself.

How?

Joe was relying on tried-and-true police work, and that was sensible and logical.

But she wasn't Joe, and she had only one asset that Joe didn't possess.

Jenny.

This was all about Jenny, who was once more a victim.

And her reconstruction and computer photos that were in the possession of that murderer.

If they hadn't already been destroyed.

Assume it hadn't happened yet. Assume that Jenny had gotten a break in that cosmic justice scenario Joe had talked about.

There was only one way to be sure.

Try to reach Jenny.

Again, how?

She had never tried to reach out and contact. Jenny had just been there.

"Jenny?"

She concentrated. Thinking.

Nothing.

The skull. Think about the face that she'd been so close to during the reconstruction.

Nothing.

The little girl in her white dress smiling at Eve across the room.

She tensed. Something different was there.

Something . . .

Bewilderment. Darkness.

But no fear.

"Jenny?"

"Here!"

"Jenny, listen to me. I don't know what's happening with you, but I want to help."

"Sent me away . . . "

It *was* Jenny.

Excitement surged through Eve. "I know, and I was wrong. I thought it was for the best, but it didn't turn out that way. We have to make it right."

"He won't let us."

"Who?"

"Walsh."

Darkness. Evil. Fear. So much fear.

"Who is Walsh?"

"He's here with me now. He shot that driver." Ugliness. Evil. Fear.

"Is he the man who also killed you?"

"Yes. He hates me. He wants me back in the dirt where he buried me. He keeps thinking about it. He's angry with you, angry at the police who found me." She paused. *"But most of all, he's angry with me. He's scaring me, Eve."*

"You don't have to be frightened. He can't do anything to you, Jenny." She added gently, "It's all been done. All the fear and suffering is over."

"I don't think so. But I can't let him see he's scaring me. He likes it too much. I have to pretend to him, just like I did before."

"Before?"

"It's not the first time. I told you, I think . . . he's the one."

The one who had killed her. The one who had thrown her into that grave. "How do you know that man's name is Walsh, Jenny?"

"*That's what he signed on the credit card slip at the gas station. He scrawled it, but it was clear enough to read the last name. He bought groceries and smiled at the girl behind the counter. She thought he was nice. He's not nice, Eve. He was thinking terrible thoughts about what he'd like to do to her.*"

"You can tell what he's thinking?"

"*Sometimes. It goes in and out. I don't want to know. I have to force myself. It scares me.*"

She could tell that from her voice. Try another path.

"Where are you now, Jenny?"

"*Car. Trees. Lake. Dirty. Not pretty like your lake, Eve.*"

"You're aware of all that?" She tried again. "Why are you still with him? Is it because of the reconstruction?" She held her breath. "Does he still have it?"

"*Yes, he put the box in the backseat.*"

Yes.

"And the computer?"

"*I think so.*"

But Jenny was certain about the reconstruction. She asked again, "Is it because you have to stay with that reconstruction that you're still with him? Because it's part of your earthly body?"

"*No, why should I have to do that? That's kind of silly. I don't believe that makes any difference any longer.*"

"If it doesn't make a difference, why did you follow that skull to my home? Why did you appear to me after I created that reconstruction?"

"*I told you, I didn't know you wanted to see me.*" She was troubled. *"And I didn't follow the skull. I just came to you. I knew I had to come to only you."*

"And tried your best to ram that reconstruction through at record pace."

"I thought maybe that was what I was supposed to do, why I was there."

"Then if you don't have to stay with the reconstruction, why are you still with that killer?"

"Because that's what I'm meant to do. That's the one thing I've always known. Everything else is still confusing, but I was sent to stop him." She added simply, *"Besides, you sent me away."*

"To Nalchek, to someone who would help you, not to that monster."

"But I'm not important now. Every minute makes that more clear." She paused. *"But I'm glad you're here, Eve."*

"I'm glad I am, too." She drew a deep breath. "And I'm a little confused myself. But I know we have to work together. Will you help me, Jenny?"

"I'll always help you, Eve. What do you want me to do?"

"The reconstruction. I don't want it to be tossed away or destroyed. It's important. I think that he'll try to do that."

"I think he will, too. He took it out of the box and looked at it. He hates it as much as he hates me."

"It could be proof of who you are. I'm surprised he hasn't done it already."

"He keeps thinking about burning it. He sees it burning, Eve."

"But he'd have to have time to do that. It takes a long time to completely destroy bones by fire. Maybe he's waiting until after he's far enough away from here that he feels safe. We can't let him do it. I *need* that reconstruction." She paused. "If he tries to do it, you have to stop him, Jenny."

"I don't know how to do that. How could I stop him?"

"Big problem. As far as I know, spirits can't use force to make their displeasure known. At least, in my limited experience. Let me think a minute." She was silent, going over options in her mind. There weren't many.

But there might be one possibility.

"Jenny, when you appeared to me in that pretty white dress, you said you thought you could do it, so you tried. And then you managed to do it. How?"

"*I just knew. I concentrated, and it happened.*"

"Because it was me and we've become close?"

"*No, I don't think so.*" Silence. "*I guess it could be, but it felt . . . right. It had something to do with why I'm here. It's a gift. Like the music.*"

"Do you think, if you concentrated, you could make Walsh see you?"

"*Why would I want to do that? I don't want him to see me. It would be like that other—*" She stopped. "*I feel safe where I am now, Eve.*"

"And you almost remembered something that wasn't safe at all," Eve said gently. "I hate having to remind you of that time. But you think that there's a reason that you're with Walsh now. You said you have to stop him. If there's one thing I've learned from Bonnie, it's that she doesn't believe anything is random after you cross over. There's a kind of order."

"*I don't know about that.*" She was silent a moment. "*But he does have to be stopped. Why would letting him see me help to keep him from burning the reconstruction?*"

"Most people are frightened of ghosts. I think Walsh would be afraid of you, particularly if you're his victim. Maybe you could intimidate him into not destroying that reconstruction."

"*He'd be afraid of me?*" she asked doubtfully. "*I don't believe he was afraid of me before. I'm just a kid.*"

"Not just. And you've grown more mature during those years. Reach down inside yourself for strength. You probably have a few powers that you didn't have in life. Use them."

"*I don't even know what they are.*"

"Stretch. Think. Feel your way."

"*I'll . . . try.*"

"That's all I ask. I don't know how much time we have."

"*Time,*" she repeated. "*Yes, it's all about time. He wanted to kill you, but there wasn't time. He kept thinking how you'd interfered with him. He's intending to go back to you . . . afterward.*"

"After . . . what?"

"*The little girl . . .*"

Eve felt a chill. "What little girl?"

"*I don't know her name. He just thinks about her as the little girl. But she's special to him. He keeps thinking of her as 'the one.' He's been searching for her for a long time, and now he thinks he may have found her. Special. Not like the others who are all the same to him. Not important. With them, it's what they make him feel that's important.*"

And eerily similar to the psychological philosophy of every serial killer she'd ever heard about. "Jenny, is this little girl still alive?"

"*Yes.*"

"And what does Walsh intend to do to her."

"*What he always does,*" she whispered. "*It's always bad things. He had it all planned before they found me. He was thinking that she might be the one, and he was excited that the hunt was almost over. He was in Carmel, then he had to drop everything and rush back to the forest to make sure that he was still safe. He was in a panic because no one should ever have been able to find me. It was important I never be found. He'd be in trouble if they knew about it. He was scared and angry."*

"So angry he abandoned a potential victim?"

"He didn't totally abandon her. He couldn't. He has to go back to Carmel because she's on the list. He's marked her."

"Marked?"

"I don't know what he meant. But she's one of the reasons why I have to stop him. She may be the most important reason."

"I don't understand about this . . . hunt and why Walsh was disappointed."

"Neither do I. All I can tell you is what he was feeling. That's all I know about her, Eve."

And Eve knew far more than she wanted to know.

Except that little girl's name.

Except a way to save her.

"Do you know how many . . . little girls . . . there have been, Jenny?"

"I don't know any numbers. Lots and lots. And not only children. He likes them best, but it's the kill itself he likes. Do you have to know?"

"No, of course I don't."

"But one of them was me?" A pause. *"Then why can't I remember it? You'd think I'd remember."*

"Perhaps . . . mercy?"

"I guess so." A silence. *"There are so many things that I don't know. I suppose you're impatient with me, but things are becoming clearer. The longer I'm with Walsh, the more memories are coming back to me. I'm changing, Eve. I can feel it inside. It's as if I was asleep, and now I'm beginning to wake. You woke me, Eve."*

"The reconstruction?"

"No. Oh, maybe, a little. But I felt as if I were meant . . . " She

stopped. "*There's so much I have to learn. It's all coming at me now like a giant wave. I'm getting stronger and stronger. That little girl . . . If she was the reason that I've been waiting. Maybe I was meant to help her, Eve?*"

"I don't know." Yet Eve had said much the same thing to Joe about Jenny. "If that's true, I do know it's worth doing. But Walsh has to be caught first, or that can't happen." She added, "And I'm not forgetting you. We've got to bring you home to your parents. You're important, too, Jenny."

"*Am I?*" Her voice was fading away. "*I told you, I don't think so. Not yet . . .* "

"Jenny, I'm losing you!"

"*I can't . . . help it. As I said, I'm in and out . . .* "

She was gone.

Eve drew a shaky breath. Those moments had flown by, and yet she had to go back and try to remember every word that had been uttered. As Jenny had told her, she was learning, changing, moving back and forth from child to adult, from weakness to strength. And Jenny wasn't the only one who was learning every minute.

And the primary thing Eve had learned from that conversation was a name.

Walsh.

"Walsh," Joe repeated. "No first name. Initials?"

"Don't be greedy," Eve said. "We have a name. What are databases for?"

"Not generally to be used by ghosts searching for their murderers. You're sure that your Jenny got it right?"

"I'm not sure about anything. But it's our best bet." She thought about it. "Yes, I'd trust her."

"General location?"

"Unknown. But I'd think he was going back to California."

"Because he was going to try to find the evidence he'd left at Jenny's crime scene?"

"And because he had another victim in mind." Her lips tightened. "He'd marked her. Whatever that means. He wouldn't just have gone on to another kill."

"Then I'd better get down to the precinct and start running this name through the databases with emphasis on California." He got to his feet. "And the chances of Walsh being his real name are slim to none. But if it's the one he's been using most recently, we might get lucky. What are you going to do?" His brows lifted. "Try for a séance?"

"Very amusing. I've told Jenny what I need from her. I'll just have to see if she can do what I asked." She took out her phone. "And I have a few calls to make myself."

"Nalchek?"

"That's one of them." She started to dial. "And the other is to a friend who came through for me a few months ago. I've just got to hope she's still in California . . ."

"I'm not sure where you can find Margaret Douglas," Kendra Michaels said. "I think she's still in California, but you never know with Margaret. She's something of a gypsy."

"I thought she went to California because you were there," Eve said. "But she's not answering her phone. I was hoping that you might still be in touch."

"I tried, but Margaret marches to her own drummer."

"Like several other people in our circle," Eve said dryly.

Including Kendra Michaels, who was sometimes a music thera-
pist and sometimes worked with the police and FBI. She was
truly an original since she had been blind until her twenties and
had learned to use all her senses with incredible accuracy. "No
idea where Margaret could be?"

"She worked as a volunteer at the San Diego Zoo," Kendra
said. "But it wasn't challenging enough, so she moved on.
Maybe she went back to Summer Island to work with those
dogs in that experimental program."

"I'll check with them and see if they've heard from her. But
it would be difficult for Margaret to go back there when she
has no papers."

"That's never stopped her before. Margaret is an expert at
jumping over obstacles like a lack of ID."

So Eve had been told. But she had never questioned Margaret about it, and neither had Joe. They had been too grateful
for Margaret's help in finding Eve when she had been kidnapped
months ago. Jane, who had brought Margaret into their lives
when she had taken her dog, Toby, to Summer Island to be
treated for ingesting a rare poison, had told them that Margaret
was incredibly gifted with animals. It hadn't mattered to Jane
that Margaret apparently skipped around the world under the
radar and no one knew anything about her. All she cared about
was that Margaret had saved her dog because she had the ability to bond with animals.

And Margaret might have saved Eve's life because of that
same gift.

"Am I allowed to ask why you want to get in touch with
Margaret?" Kendra asked. "And why I can't help instead?"

She had known this was coming. "You have many talents

but not the one I might need. Margaret lived for years in the woods near her home as a child after she ran away from her father. That makes her uniquely qualified since I need someone who is woods savvy."

"That's not me. But I'm told I make it up in other ways that are—"

"No," she said firmly. "This is my problem. I'm grateful, and if I need you, I might call on you. But not unless I run into a blank wall."

"You just did," Kendra said.

"Not yet."

Kendra was silent. "I'll make a few calls. Margaret made a lot of friends while she was here. She might have mentioned something to someone. How much time do I have?"

"We need her as soon as possible. Joe and I will be arriving in Sonderville tonight."

"Sonderville. That's wine country."

"It's the woods north of town, not the vineyards that I'm concerned about."

"I'll see what I can do."

"Thank you, Kendra."

"Don't thank me until I find her. Why do you have to have someone who is woods savvy?"

"I need to find something that was lost or hidden in the woods eight years ago."

"Eight years." Kendra gave a low whistle. "Definitely not my area of expertise. I don't even know if it's Margaret's."

"I'm willing to take a chance." Eve paused. "It may lead me to a killer, and there's a child's life on the line. I don't know where else to start."

"Start with me. Okay, okay, I know you're not going to

budge. Let me get off the phone and see if I can find Margaret."
She hung up.

Typical Kendra. Eve found herself smiling as she hung up.
Sharp, honest, and beneath that brusqueness was a treasure
trove of warmth and loyalty. If Margaret could be found, Kendra
would locate her.

"You couldn't reach her?" Joe asked as he came in from the
porch. "Then why are you smiling?"

"Kendra." She shrugged. "She's being . . . Kendra. And I'll
bet she'll find Margaret for me."

"No bet," Joe said grimly. "But whether you manage to get
hold of Margaret or not, you're not going to go into those woods
without me. I'm pretty woods savvy myself."

"Yes, you are. But eight years is a long time and you—" She
stopped. How could she tell him that it wasn't his competence
but her own fear that she'd be responsible for something happening to him? Joe was like a force of nature when he was on
the hunt. "I know this is a long shot, Joe. But Walsh was keeping an eye on Nalchek while he was searching those woods, a
deputy died while Walsh was lurking there like some kind of
ghoul. Whatever he's looking for is making him desperate. I'm
just reaching out and trying to find something, anything, that I
can grab hold of before Walsh gets his hands on another victim.
Those woods where Jenny was buried may be a way to do it."
She shook her head. "Or point me in the right direction."

"You've been thinking about this. Anything else?"

"If we find out who Jenny was, we may be able to make a
connection that will help us find Walsh. I've been going over
the things Jenny has said to me since I started the reconstruction.
I'll check with Nalchek and see if I get anywhere with them."
She got to her feet. "And then I'll pack a bag for both of us and

make reservations for San Francisco while you're checking out Walsh in those databases. I'll call you to tell you when to meet me at the airport."

Joe's brows rose. "We're in that much of a hurry? You're not giving me much time to process all those databases. I may have to go international, too. Let's leave tomorrow morning."

She shook her head. "Suppose I leave today and check into a hotel and do the preliminary work with Nalchek. That would save some time. You can fly in tomorrow."

He frowned. "I don't like your going alone."

"Joe, it's one night, and I promise I won't do anything that doesn't concern Nalchek."

He was silent. "Okay, but I still don't see why you're in such a hurry."

"I don't know, either." She reached for her phone again. "I'm just not sure how much time we have."

Or how much time that little girl in Carmel had.

CHAPTER

5

Get rid of her. **He had to get *rid* of her.**

Walsh could feel the hatred sear through him as he stared at the FedEx box on the seat beside him. He'd built a huge campfire in the woods and was tempted just to throw the damn box into the flames. But he couldn't do that, he had to be sure. He had to know that Eve Duncan wasn't just playing Nalchek for a fool.

He had to look at that bitch, Jenny's skull.

Get it over with.

He reluctantly took the box and slowly opened it.

He couldn't see anything, dammit. The skull was secured to the box. He started to undo the fastenings.

His fingers were tingling, burning.

Imagination.

There, he was finished. He'd take the skull out to the fire and get ready to toss it.

He grabbed the box, got out of the car, and strode over to the fire.

The flames were leaping high, the fiery shadows reflecting off the leaves of the surrounding trees.

One more minute and you burn, bitch.

He grabbed the skull and pulled it out of the box and held it high so that he could look at it.

Only it wasn't a skull.

It was *her.*

He felt as if he'd been kicked in the stomach.

Same pointed chin, same winged eyebrows.

And those green eyes, blazing at him, as bold as they had been the night he had put her in that grave. She had been afraid, he'd known she was afraid, and yet she wouldn't admit it to him. That night was suddenly right here before him.

"You're going to die, little girl." He cradled his bleeding hand where the little viper had bitten him. *"Die, then I'm going to throw you in the ground where no one will ever find you."*

"They'll find me." Her eyes were glittering in her pale face. *"Because you're stupid and cruel, and they'll want to take you and throw you in a jail where they put people like you."*

"Stupid?" He lifted his hand and struck her in the face. Her head jerked back from the blow, but when she lifted it, there was still no fear in her eyes. It filled him with rage. *"You bit my hand. Let's see how you like to have your hands hurt."*

Fear. For the first time he saw fear in her. *"Not my hands. I can't let you—"* She lifted her chin defiantly, and the fear was gone. *"It won't matter. They'll fix them."*

"They won't bother. You'll be dead." He took her hand and bent back the first finger. *"Tell me what I want to know. Tell me where they are. If you do, I'll stop the pain."* He pressed the finger back until he knew it was agony. *"Tell me."*

She whimpered.

Why didn't she scream?

She had never screamed.

Not even when he'd lost his temper and taken the crowbar and struck her on the temple.

He couldn't see that wound on her temple on this damn reconstruction now. Duncan had carefully erased it. He held the skull higher.

It was as if the blow had never happened.

And those green eyes were blazing with defiance at him as they had when he'd broken her fingers.

No, they weren't. Glass eyes. They were only glass eyes. But how had Duncan known that little girl had green eyes? How had she known about that pointed chin, those eyebrows?

Guess work. It was only a lucky guess.

And in another moment, all her work would be devoured in these flames.

"No, they won't. I won't let you."

He froze.

Her voice.

His eyes widened in shock, his gaze locked with the green eyes of the skull's reconstruction.

Ignore it.

He was hearing things.

He had been concentrating so hard on that long-ago night that he had only thought he'd heard Jenny speaking to him.

Hallucination.

As soon as he got rid of the skull, he'd be fine.

"No. I told you that you were stupid. You'll never get rid of me."

The voice wasn't coming from that skull. It was coming from his left, over in the trees.

Don't look.

"Are you afraid of me? I'm not afraid of you. You can't do anything to me that you haven't already done. But I'm only learning everything I can do to you. Look at me, Walsh."

His head slowly turned.

And then he saw her.

White dress, black, patent-leather shoes, and those eyes as green as the glass ones in this damn skull.

Those eyes that had wept but never held fear.

He could feel his heart pounding and the cold sweat break out. "I'm looking at you, bitch. You're not real. You're dead. You're only a damn hallucination. Once I settle this, I'll forget you just like I did before."

"And go on and kill that little girl in Carmel? Isn't that what you're thinking?"

"I'll do what I please. And you don't know what I'm thinking."

"Then how did I know about the little girl? What's her name, Walsh?"

"See, I told you that you didn't know anything. If you were Jenny, you'd know. Go *away.*"

"So you can toss my skull into that fire? I can't let you do that." She took at few steps closer. *"I haven't decided what I'm meant to do with you, but I won't let you destroy Eve's work."*

"Let me? What can you do about it?"

"Try it." She took a step closer, her eyes glaring into his own. *"You can't let it go. You remember when I bit your hand? I didn't. Not until it all came rushing back to you, then I remembered. There are all kinds of things I don't remember yet. But I think it will*

all come back to me. Except the pain. I may not ever remember that entirely. But I can make you remember your pain. Your hand will start to hurt just as it did that night, only the pain won't go away until you take the skull back to the car."

"I *will* drop it." He started to release the skull into the flames. Pain!

He screamed.

He backed away from the fire.

The pain lessened but didn't go away.

"No, Walsh, I won't let you destroy me all over again."

Green eyes staring at him, golden skin gleaming in the firelight, lips tight.

He was cursing. "It's not you. You're not real. I'll get over this; and then I'll burn this skull. Then I'll find wherever they've put your skeleton and burn every bit of you until you're ashes." His hands were shaking as he shoved the skull back in the FedEx box. "And then I'll throw them into the ocean for the fish to eat."

"You won't get over it. Every time you try to burn this reconstruction, I'll be there. It will get worse and worse." Her voice followed him. *"And maybe by that time, I'll find out what I have to do with you. How you have to be punished . . . "*

"You're not *real*." He didn't look over his shoulder as he jumped into the car and threw the box with the reconstruction on the floor of the backseat. But he couldn't resist one last glance after he started the car and pressed the accelerator.

She was still standing there by the fire.

Her dark hair shining in the firelight, her eyes staring at him with that fearless boldness that made him want to kill her all over again.

Not real. Not real. Not real.

But his hand still throbbed and hurt the way it had when she'd bitten him.

He had to get away from her.

His foot stomped on the accelerator, and the car lurched forward. He wanted to throw the damn reconstruction out the window, but he couldn't do it. Too dangerous. It mustn't ever be found.

Get rid of it later.

Get away.

He'd show her.

But maybe not tonight.

"At last," Eve said impatiently, as Nalchek finally picked up her call four hours later. She hadn't been able to get past Nalchek's voice mail until now, when she was on her way to the airport. "I've been trying to reach you."

"Sorry. I was in a town meeting trying to soothe down a bunch of very nervous citizens. In this town, everyone knows everyone else, and Ron Carstairs's death sent everybody into a tailspin."

"I can see how it would. First, you find a murdered little girl, then a deputy is killed. Any developments?"

"No," he said tersely. "What can I do for you?"

"I just wanted to tell you that Joe and I are going to be on our way out to Sonderville today."

Silence. "Why?" he asked warily. "You can't do anything that I can't."

"That's what I've been telling myself since I started the reconstruction. It's not working for me any longer."

"It's true. You did your job, and it's not your fault that you lost that reconstruction."

"Well, then why does it feel like my fault?" she asked fiercely. "I should have been able to do something. I shouldn't have just waved good-bye to that FedEx truck and thought everything would work out. I was uneasy when I did it, and I should have paid attention to instinct."

"And I'm paying attention to instinct, and everyone in town thinks I'm nuts," he said dryly. "I know my job, Ms. Duncan. I don't need you wandering around my town and searching for that bastard who killed Ron. You stay where you are and let me do it."

"Too late. I'm on the way to the airport." She paused. "You're afraid I'll get in your way."

"You're damn right."

"I won't do that. I'll be careful not to step on your toes. I'm bringing Joe Quinn, and he has a tendency to take over, but I won't let that happen. However, you must have some knowledge of Joe's capabilities. He'd be an asset to you."

"I don't need a big-city detective to barge in—" He stopped. "I sound like a belligerent ass. I guess I'm being defensive." He was silent. "Yeah, he'd be an asset as long as he doesn't try to pull rank."

"It's your town, Sheriff. And you might find I could be an asset, too."

A very skeptical silence. "Not without a skull to re-create that little girl's face."

"That's still a possibility. We don't know that the killer destroyed the reconstruction."

"If he took it, he destroyed it," he said flatly. "Nothing else makes sense."

"Killers aren't always sensible or logical." She added bluntly, "And we need to work together if we're going to blow him out of the water. I have a couple things to ask you about Jenny's body."

"Her body?"

"I saw the wound on her temple; did she have any other wounds or signs of torture?"

"Why do you ask?"

"What does it matter? Is there any reason why her hands would hurt?"

He was silent for a moment. "Yes. The bones on the fingers of her right hand were all broken. The pathologist said that they'd been bent back until they snapped."

Dear God, poor Jenny. Eve felt sick. "Bastard."

"Yeah, that's what I thought." He paused. "How did you know?"

"If I'd known, I wouldn't have had to ask." She wasn't about to tell him about that moment when Jenny had told her about the pain to her hand. He might believe in instinct, but that was entirely different from embracing the concept of ghosts. "Maybe you have a leak."

"And maybe I don't."

She changed the subject. "You said you've spent a lot time looking for any clues in those woods where Jenny was found. Have you found anything at all?"

"No."

"Then why keep looking?"

"Sheer frustration," he said. "I told you I felt like she was calling to me. I interviewed everyone in the neighborhood about that killing that took place over eight years ago. Nothing. No one missing a child, no one who even remembers a nine-year-old child in the neighborhood who wasn't fully accounted for. The only things I had left were you and the crime scene."

"And I failed you," Eve said. "I'll make it up, Nalchek."

"Bullshit. I told you that I didn't expect more of you than you gave me. What were you supposed to do? Hand-carry the skull out here?"

She chuckled. "You're right. And I won't make it up to you, I'll make it up to me." Her smile faded. "But your friend was killed near that crime scene, and that means that the killer was watching it. Have you found any signs of anyone besides you wandering around that area?"

"No, if there was anyone, he was damn good about covering his tracks. I grew up in those woods, and I know them like my right hand. I was in the Special Forces, and I've been trained to observe. I saw signs of my men and the forensic crew. Nothing else."

She hesitated. "Maybe you need a fresh eye."

"What the hell are you talking about?"

"I don't doubt that your Special Forces training made you very savvy, but there are all kinds of other people with specialized talents that might prove valuable."

"You have someone in mind?"

"Maybe." She went on quickly, "Isn't there just a possibility that you might not see—"

"If there was something there, I would have seen it." His voice was cool. "Is that all?"

"Just one other thing. What clothes was Jenny wearing when you took her out of that grave?"

"What? Why do you want to know that?" He went on impatiently, "Never mind. Everything she had on was in such tatters that it was hard to tell, but we decided that she was wearing a long white dress. Black, patent-leather shoes. Kind of dressy. She looked like she might have come from church. But I sent

men around to all the churches within a hundred-mile radius, and they came up with zilch."

Eve felt a surge of disappointment. Nalchek had already covered the only lead that she had thought might be a possibility. Which only proved how sharp and competent he was. "If not a church, where else would a little girl wear a fancy dress? A party?"

"Search me. I'm still looking."

The music.

"I have a suggestion. Little children sometimes have musical recitals. They dress up for them."

"That's reaching. But I'll check it out."

"You're obviously not going to give up." She was turning into the airport. "Neither will I, Nalchek. I have to hang up now. I'll call you when I arrive in San Francisco and have picked up our rental car. Can you give me the name of a decent hotel in your area?"

"Sonderville doesn't have more than a few hotels. Martello's Vineyard is pretty nice." He sighed. "If you're still set on coming, I'll make your reservations."

"I'm still set on coming. Thanks, Nalchek." She hung up and drove into long-term parking.

The call had not been entirely satisfying, but she knew what she had to face now. Nalchek would cooperate but might be surly. He didn't want to have anyone getting in his way. She could deal with it. It didn't matter as long as he was committed, and he was certainly that.

And she had confirmed that the dress in which Jenny had appeared to her was the one she'd worn the night she'd been killed or taken. Where had she gone that night?

And Jenny had suffered that night. Dear heaven, what pain

she must have gone through when that monster had broken her fingers.

She drew a deep breath and tried to fight down the anger that was searing through her. Jenny hadn't remembered the deathblow, but she'd remembered the pain of her hand. Even in the great beyond, that memory had lingered.

Forget it, Jenny. If you can, let it go.

But I won't let it go. I'll remember what you went through.

I promise you.

SONDERVILLE, CALIFORNIA

1:05 A.M.

It was damn chilly in the woods tonight. There might be frost by morning.

Nalchek zipped up his leather jacket and moved a little faster down the trail toward the grave site. He could hear the leaves crackle under his feet, Hell, why was he even here at this hour? He hadn't been able to sleep and had given up after a couple hours of turning and twisting in his bed.

And it was Eve Duncan's fault. She had made him doubt his ability, and he'd been drawn back here to make sure that he was right, and she was wrong. It had been hard for him to give her the politeness she deserved when he was so frustrated. He didn't need to begin thinking he might be making mistakes. He had learned in Afghanistan that that could lead to disaster. You just barreled ahead after you decided on a course and went after the objective.

If you knew the objective. It was only a vague—

Movement.

Up ahead.

He stopped.

A light step but not an animal. Two-footed. And the rhythm was different.

And he was headed for the grave site.

Nalchek glided forward, listening.

Not much to hear. That step was very light, and the brush was scarcely moving as he passed.

And then the movement stopped.

He had reached the grave.

Nalchek stopped, too.

No sound.

What was the bastard doing?

He glided forward until he could see the grave beyond the trees.

A figure in jeans and a dark hoodie was kneeling by the grave, reaching, digging through the dirt.

Shit!

"Halt." He barreled through the trees and dove down in a low tackle. "You're under—" He stopped as a fist crashed into his lower lip. To hell with it. Read him his rights later.

Just take him down.

He grappled him over on his stomach and grabbed his wrists to cuff him.

Him?

He stiffened. Those wrists were too delicate, that body he was straddling was not—

A woman? Either that or a teenage boy. He'd bet on its being a woman.

He finished the cuffing and flipped her over on her back.

He shined his flashlight down on her face.

Maybe not quite a woman. A girl not over nineteen or twenty.

Her sun-streaked hair had tumbled from beneath the hoodie, and she had glowing, healthy skin, and her blue eyes were very wary.

"I'm not a threat to you." She moistened her lips. "Are you a threat to me?"

"Maybe. It depends on what you tell me in the next few minutes."

"I can't see you. It sounded like you were starting to say I was under arrest before you got rough with me."

"I didn't get rough with you. You would have known it if I had."

"You have on a leather jacket. I felt it when I was struggling with you. It had some kind of insignia on it. Cop?"

"I could be one of the Hell's Angels."

"Yeah. I'm hoping for cop. Let me see you."

He turned the beam on himself. "You might be better off with the motorcycle gang. I don't like people messing around my crime scenes. Are you some college kid who's hazing for a sorority?"

"No." She was studying him with narrowed eyes, her gaze going from his broad shoulders sheathed in the black leather jacket to his muscular body garbed in the tan uniform and down to his black boots. Then it traveled up to his close-cut dark hair, to his craggy cheekbones, square, defined chin, and deep-set blue eyes. "I think maybe you're right. You look . . . formidable. I might be better off with a Hell's Angel."

"Now that we agree on that score, let's find out who the

hell you are. You're not a college kid. Curiosity seeker? Do you belong to one of those phony witch covens and are trying to get ritual dirt for one of your spells?"

"You do have an imagination. Why don't you just let me answer you?" She tilted her head. "You're the local sheriff? What's your name?"

"John Nalchek." He pulled her to a sitting position. "And I was giving you the benefit of the doubt. My next question was going to be what you had to do with the killer who murdered the little girl who was buried in that grave."

"Nothing. I was just examining the grave and seeing if I could tell if—" She studied his face. "You're very tough and you're not ready for explanations yet." She suddenly gave him a luminous smile. "But maybe you could take these handcuffs off me. Then you could take me to the diner I saw down the road and give me a cup of coffee until you are ready."

He started to pat her down for weapons. "Or you could tell me your name, and I'll phone it in and get your record."

"My name is Margaret Douglas." She made a face. "And my way is better for all of us. Do you know anything about me?"

"No, but I will after I phone it in. Give me your driver's license."

"That's kind of difficult. I don't have one."

"Then how did you get here?"

"I hitchhiked from San Francisco, then walked the rest of the way after I reached Sonderville. You've never heard of me?"

"Why should I have heard of you?"

"I thought Eve might have paved the way. I guess she wasn't sure that I'd show up."

He stiffened. "Eve?"

"Eve Duncan. She sent word through a friend that she needed me."

"Why?"

"She thought I might be able to help." She added simply, "I know pretty much about woods and animals and stuff like this."

"Son of a bitch."

"You're upset. That's why she didn't tell you about me. I'm kind of hard to explain."

"Because you're a kid who looks like she's barely out of high school and supposed to be better at tracking and recovery than I am? Yeah, that's damn hard to explain."

"And your pride is hurt?" She studied him. "I wouldn't think that your ego was that fragile."

He finished searching her. "You don't know anything about me, Margaret Douglas."

"No, but I think I'd like to. You're very interesting. But you can see I'm not much of a danger to you. That patdown was very intimate, and you have to know I don't have any weapons."

"Not while I have you down and under control. You could have stashed them somewhere in the woods. You might look like the girl next door, but that doesn't mean anything. When I was in Afghanistan, a young woman not much older than you came running toward my unit screaming for us to save her. When she was close enough to do damage, she pressed a button and blew herself to pieces, together with four of my buddies."

"I'm sorry," she said quietly. "That must have been terrible for you. No wonder you frisked me down so thoroughly." She sighed. "Now why don't you call Eve and tell her that you've captured and cuffed me and see what she says. If you don't trust me, you'll trust her. Everyone always trusts Eve."

"Because she's not a flighty kid wandering around the woods and sniffing the soil around graves."

"She would if it was part of her job. I imagine she does lots of things that would scare most people off. Call her. I could use that cup of coffee."

He hesitated. "She's not going to appreciate a call in the middle of the night. She probably just checked into her hotel." He started dialing. "What the hell. She's the one who sent you and started all of us spinning in circles."

"Spinning? That's a good word. Yes, she did, didn't she?" She crossed her legs Indian fashion. "Tell her that I would have called her, but I wanted to have something to tell her before I made contact."

"Tell her yourself." He spoke into the phone as Eve answered. "John Nalchek. I apprehended a young woman in the woods tonight at the crime scene. She identified herself as Margaret Douglas. I assume you're familiar with her?"

"Margaret?" Eve repeated. "I didn't know she was on her way. Apprehended? That sounds . . . is she okay?"

"Do you mean did I hurt her? No, but it could have happened when I caught her snooping around that grave." He added deliberately, "She had no business there."

"Where is she now?"

"We're still in the woods."

"Tell her to bring coffee," Margaret said, "I'm freezing."

"She wants coffee," Nalchek said sarcastically. "I guess she expects you to provide it."

"I'll be right there." Eve hung up.

"She verified your identity," Nalchek said as he hung up. "So now we sit and wait."

"You could take me to your car. It would be warmer."

"No, I think that we're fine here. You shouldn't be trekking through the woods in nothing but that hoodie if you're worried about the cold."

"Punishment?" She shrugged. "Fine. But I thought that I'd be moving around and be able to keep warm." She got to her knees. "Will you take off the cuffs and let me do that? I'm not going to run away."

"How do I know—" He muttered a curse and reached behind her and unlocked the cuffs. "Stay close. I'll be with you every step."

"Okay." She moved toward the grave and fell to her knees. "Just keep out of my way." She picked up the soil and began to sniff it. She put out her tongue and delicately tasted it.

"What are—"

"Hush." Then she got to her feet and moved into the surrounding brush. "Don't worry, I'm not trying to escape the unfriendly arms of the law. You can come along."

"Thank you." His eyes were narrowed on her. "But I can't ask questions?"

"You're not ready. And you disturb my concentration." She finally stopped beside a huge oak tree. "Here. He likes it here."

"Who?" Nalchek snapped.

"I don't know his name or if he has one." She sat down beneath the tree. "If you'll be quiet, maybe I can find out."

Nalchek opened his lips to speak, then closed them again.

Watch.

Listen.

Collate all information.

She might be a screwball. She might be some kind of con artist. But he wouldn't know if he didn't stop protesting and start analyzing.

He dropped down beside her and focused on her every move.

CHAPTER

6

"Margaret!"

"That's Eve." Margaret got to her feet. "It's only been thirty minutes. Her hotel must have been close." She moved out of the forest toward the grave. "Here, Eve. Did you bring my coffee?"

"Yes." She handed her the paper cup. In the process, she touched her hand and gave a low whistle. "You're ice-cold. Why didn't you wait in Nalchek's car?"

Margaret gave Nalchek a glance. "I was so busy, I didn't notice the chill. Neither did the sheriff, or I'm sure he would have offered to bring me out of the cold." She chuckled. "Or is that an espionage term?" She took a sip of coffee. "That's so *good*. I've spent so much time in the islands that my body temperature tends to plummet. I was fine as long as I was in Southern California."

"I didn't offer because I was pissed off," Nalchek said bluntly. "And I don't need you to make excuses for me.

You shouldn't have been here if you object to facing the consequences."

"I'm not objecting," she said quietly. "I believe in consequences. It's nature's way of balancing the order of things."

"When your friends don't take a hand." He turned to Eve. "This isn't how I expected to meet you. I don't like your coming here anyway, and I certainly don't appreciate your sending this weird kid into my woods."

Eve's brows rose. "Your woods?"

"My jurisdiction." He paused. "My hometown. My county."

"You're waving all your credentials at us," she said shrewdly. "You must really not want us here."

He was silent. "You'll get in my way."

"No, I won't." She met his gaze. "And I'll vouch for Margaret."

"Not good enough," Margaret said soberly. "He thinks that I might be trouble. He had a bad experience with a woman in Afghanistan who blew up a couple of his buddies and herself along with them."

"Really?" Eve shook her head. "Just look at her, Nalchek. Anyone could see Margaret is no threat."

"Because she looks like a college kid? The woman in Afghanistan had a baby in her arms when she blew herself up." He gestured dismissively. "And I don't need to make any judgment about her if I don't accept her value to my investigation."

"She will have value." Eve turned to Margaret. "I'm sure you haven't had much time, but can you help me?"

"Maybe. He let me look around a little after he called you." She suddenly smiled. "I don't know if it was because he was curious or that he wanted me to have enough rope to hang myself. Maybe a little of both?"

"I'd say you managed to give me plenty of ammunition. As a woods expert, you leave much to be desired," Nalchek said dryly. "Did you know she eats dirt, Eve?"

"No, I don't recall hearing that," Eve said. "But I'm sure she has a good reason." She glanced at Margaret. "Do you?"

"Not what he'd consider good." She took another drink of coffee. "It's just my way of analyzing trace evidence. And I didn't eat it, I merely tasted it."

"That makes all the difference," Eve said solemnly.

"Yes, it does." She chuckled. "Though I would have eaten it if it had been necessary. It turned out that it wasn't."

"I'm through here," Nalchek said shortly. "And so is she. I might have accepted your expert if you could have proved she would contribute but I'm not wasting my time."

"Proof." Margaret's smile faded. "That's difficult for Eve. She has no firsthand information about me or what I can do. She has to trust her daughter, Jane, and a few other friends who have put their trust in me."

"But I wouldn't have asked you to come if I hadn't believed in you," Eve said. "Jane told me that your knowledge of those wolves in the forests of Colorado helped to save me."

"Wolves?" Nalchek was frowning. "What the hell—"

"Another time. Not important now," Margaret said quickly. "It would just get in the way." She finished her coffee. "And this has nothing to do with a wolf." She frowned. "Or maybe it does. I'm not really clear on it. I didn't have much time before you got here, Eve."

"Enough to kneel by that grave like a ghoul communing with a demon," Nalchek said grimly.

"A demon?" Margaret broke out laughing. "You don't really believe that. You're just uneasy and trying to get a handle on what makes me tick and why a smart woman like Eve would be taken in by me." She got to her feet and moved toward the grave. "No demons." She fell to her knees as she reached the taped-off area. "Actually, it may be the opposite."

Eve had followed her and was gazing down at the grave. "This is Jenny's grave?" She blinked back tears. "All those years she was here, Nalchek?"

He nodded. "So the medical examiner says. He says that she was killed in these woods and buried. She wasn't transported from any other place."

"Jenny?" Margaret repeated. "Jane told me that you named all the skulls you work on, Eve. You call her Jenny?"

Eve nodded.

"It's a pretty name." She tilted her head. "It has a sort of . . . cadence. Musical."

Eve stiffened. "What? It's a nice name, but I never thought it was particularly musical."

Margaret shrugged. "Everything strikes people differently."

Eve was silent. "Yes, it does. So what did you mean about the opposite of demons?"

"I believe the grave might have been protected."

"What?" Nalchek said roughly. "Why would you think that? She was in that grave for eight years until we took her out of it. It was left to the elements and buried so deep, we might never have found it if there hadn't been flash floods in the area that eroded the dirt so that some Boy Scouts eventually found her."

"That doesn't mean that the grave wasn't protected." Margaret made a face. "I guess I have to explain. You're not ready, but then, no one is really ready for me." She shot a wary look at Eve. "I could have avoided this if I hadn't come here tonight. Mistake?"

"No, if anyone made a mistake, it was me," Eve said quietly. "I asked you to come. But it wasn't a mistake. By all means, explain to the sheriff that you may be weird, but not anything like what he faced with that crazy woman in Afghanistan."

"I can hardly wait," Nalchek said sarcastically.

Margaret nodded. "Okay, here goes. Ever since I was a kid, I've been able to communicate with animals. I can kind of merge and read them."

Silence. "Read them?" Nalchek repeated. "Read their minds?"

"No, not usually. Oh, sometimes. It depends on the species. I have real trouble with serpents. Of course, that might be my fault because I have problems with their lack of—"

"Wait." He held up his hand. "This is bullshit."

"No, it's true. I found out that I had the knack when I was just a little kid. My father didn't believe me, and I was beaten whenever I tried to tell anyone I was communicating with their dog or cat or whatever. Later, it got pretty bad, and I ran away from home and lived in the woods for a couple years." She met his eyes. "I learned a lot while I was there."

"A real nature girl."

She ignored the sarcasm. "Something like that. But it was mainly survival, just like it was at home. Survival and learning to adapt and come out on top." She stared him in the eye. "You know about survival, don't you?"

"Yes, but I never claimed to learn it from a wolf or not-wolf, or whatever."

"There are all kinds of wolves in the world. All kinds of

animals. And the worst is the one who put that little girl in that grave. I think maybe you believe that, too."

"And what about your precious balance of nature?"

"Sometimes it becomes unbalanced when a rogue comes along."

"He's not believing you, Margaret," Eve said impatiently. "Drop it. I need to know your impressions."

"I'll give it to you. It was just easier to face the obstacle than avoid it."

"And I'm the obstacle," Nalchek said mockingly. "Of course I am. But by all means proceed."

"Because you're curious," Eve said. "And you want all the help you can get, or you would never have sent me Jenny's skull." She asked Margaret, "Who was protecting the grave and how do you know?"

"I'm not sure." She frowned. "I keep getting flashes of a dog or wolf or . . . something. But I don't think that it was either one. But he's near, he's close, he thinks he has to stay close."

"Why?"

"He needs to protect the grave. Even though the bones are gone. He still has to do it. Though I don't believe he knows why."

"Why would any animal feel obligated to—"

"I don't know. I'm only getting flashes of what he's feeling in connection with the grave. But it's very strong. I felt it the minute I came near the grave. He's been here all along. Since the night she was put in that grave, he's been standing guard over it."

"Guard?"

"I know. I know. But that's what he's feeling. He doesn't

like it, but he thinks he has to do it." She grimaced. "That's all I know right now. Maybe when I get closer to him."

"Or he comes closer to the grave?" Eve asked.

"Possibly."

"How do you know he was protecting the grave?" Nalchek asked bluntly. "Maybe he wanted to devour the remains."

Margaret shook her head. "That was my first thought. It would be a natural reaction for most wild animals. But not for this one, not in this case. He has memories of chasing off predators who were digging at the grave. He was definitely on guard all these years."

"That's the most unbelievable part of your entire 'impression,'" Nalchek said. "And makes any other aspect of the story suspect."

"Yes, and you didn't have to go very far to discover reasons to discount it," Margaret said. "You're both cynical and suspicious because of your profession and your background. I know that what I do and what I'm telling you is hard to comprehend for anyone. I've faced that all my life. It would be incredible if you believed my story with no proof." She thought about it. "And I can't give you proof, but I might give you cause to question."

"By all means."

"This animal saw Jenny buried. He has a good memory because he still recalls it."

"If he wanted to guard her, why didn't he stop her from being killed?"

"I have no idea. Maybe he wasn't there for the actual killing. I know you're trying to trip me, but it doesn't work that way. May I go on?"

He shrugged. "Why not?"

"Jenny was buried very deep in the ground. That should have made her safe from most predators that would generally dig her up and tear her body to pieces. It wouldn't happen right away, but over the years, the odds of her skeleton's remaining intact would be very slim." She glanced at Eve. "Do you agree?"

"Yes."

"And Eve would know. She deals with skeletons and skulls all the time." She turned back to Nalchek. "But her initial burial kept that from happening, and there was a double safeguard later, when no predators were allowed near Jenny's grave. Only time and the wear and tear of nature caused her to eventually be found. Right?"

"So it would seem," he said warily. "But it wasn't as if she was in pristine condition. She was a skeleton, and her white dress and black slippers were in tatters."

"What about the green plastic tarp she was wrapped in?"

He went still. "Tarp?"

"Green plastic tarp," she repeated. "What kind of shape was that in?"

"Tarp," Eve repeated. "You never mentioned a tarp, Nalchek."

"You didn't ask me. You asked what she was wearing."

"Was the tarp still intact?" Margaret asked.

"Better than her dress," Nalchek said. "How did you know about the tarp? We never released any details to the press."

"He saw Jenny wrapped and put into the ground with it around her."

"We're talking about your mythical guardian animal?"

"I think we should consider him entirely Jenny's guardian," she said. "Don't you?"

"I'm not swallowing any of this. You could have talked to someone who was at the scene when we found her and saw that tarp."

"That's true. But I just found out about all this today and very few details. Would I have had a chance to look up witnesses and question them?" She shook her head. "And you could find a reason for anything else I happen to tell you about that little girl. I'm through with trying to prove myself to you. You'll have to take me or leave me."

"No, he doesn't," Eve said. "*I'm* taking you, and he'll just have to put up with it." She put out her hand and helped Margaret to her feet. "Now, unless you're going to have any other revelations, I'm going to take you back to my hotel and let you get to sleep after a nice hot shower."

"Wonderful." Margaret smiled. "I left my knapsack at the edge of the forest. We'll have to stop and pick it up. Okay?"

"No problem." She turned to Nalchek. "I don't mean to be discourteous. I know this is your case, and you're doing your best, but I asked Margaret to come and help, and I intend to make it as easy as I can for her." She grimaced. "I'm not like you. I've found that sometimes you have to look beyond the obvious of so-called reality to find answers. I believe her."

He was silent. "I believe that she thinks she's telling the truth. And, for your information, Eve, I've batted around the world and run into a lot of things that have no basis in reality. I might not have spent years in the woods hiding out from a son of a bitch of a father like she did, but I know enough to realize that nature in all its forms can be unpredictable as hell. Though a wild animal that guards a grave for eight years like a hound dog grieving for his master is really reaching. Which means that she could be completely delusional, and all this is bullshit. You'll have to prove it to me." He turned away. "I'll walk you back to your vehicle."

"And then what will you do?" Margaret asked curiously as she fell into step with him as they started to follow Eve.

"Do what I meant to do when I found you trespassing. My job as sheriff."

"Which includes wandering around in the forest in the middle of the night?" She tilted her head. "Are you guarding that grave, too?"

"I'm just trying to find additional evidence, anything we might have missed."

She gazed searchingly at him. "No, I think there's more to it than that."

"My deputy was murdered here. I think it was by the same person who killed that little girl. There's always a possibility that he'll come back."

"And you want to be here."

"I'm going to be here." His lips thinned. "And tonight, I'm going to take soil samples and see what or who has been messing around that grave. Then I'm going to examine the area around that oak tree for any signs of animals or humans that might tell me anything."

Margaret's eyes widened. "You do believe me."

"No, but I never discount anything." They had reached a silver-gray Toyota and he watched Eve unlock the car. "Call me when you get back to the hotel, Eve." He added grimly, "And don't come back here without letting me know you're going to do it."

"I won't. I didn't intend this to happen." She said, "Margaret evidently can be impulsive."

"I was curious why you'd want me," Margaret said as she got into the passenger seat. "And I thought I'd get a head start. It was a beautiful night, and I wasn't tired." She looked at Nalchek. "If you find out what animal is guarding that grave, will you tell me?"

"Maybe."

"You're still angry with me?"

"No." He gestured impatiently. "Okay, I'll let you know. Why not?" He added sarcastically, "After all, it might help you to communicate with him."

She beamed. "My thought exactly. I knew we were getting on the same page."

He jerked his thumb. "Out of here."

"We're going." Eve quickly started the car and pressed on the accelerator. "Good night, Nalchek. I'll call you tomorrow."

"No, not tomorrow." He was walking back into the trees. "I told you to call me when you get back to the hotel."

"Of course, it slipped my—" She stopped. Nalchek had disappeared. "It appears he's washed his hands of us for the moment, Margaret."

"No." Margaret was looking back over her shoulder. "He stopped when he reached the trees, and he's watching us leave."

"You can see him?"

"No, I can *feel* him. And the birds flew out of that tree where he's standing only seconds ago. He'll probably stay there until he's sure we're well on our way back to the highway." She turned around and leaned back in the seat. "He's very protective. It's no wonder he's in law enforcement. And when he lost those men in Afghanistan, it must have torn him apart. Even if he's irritated with us, he can't stifle that instinct."

"You like him?"

"I think he's one of the good guys. But that doesn't mean he won't cause us trouble." She turned around and faced the road. "He likes to be in charge. He's learned he can get hurt if he trusts other people. These days, he tends to bulldoze over anyone who gets in his way."

"Like he bulldozed you?"

She chuckled. "He tried. But he was smart enough to step away when he had an inkling he was facing something he didn't have a complete handle on. Not many people would do that."

"Particularly when confronting you."

"Yes." She glanced back over her shoulder. "Do you think he's gone back to that grave?"

"Sure; Nalchek is obsessed with everything connected with Jenny."

"And so are you?" Margaret asked softly, her gaze on Eve's face. "Not your usual M.O. where your reconstructions are concerned?"

"That FedEx driver was killed because someone wanted that reconstruction. That act throws ordinary out the window."

"But that isn't all?"

Eve shook her head. "I won't lie to you. I'm like Nalchek, I feel . . . differently about Jenny."

"So does that creature who was protecting her grave." She smiled faintly. "Fascinating. I can hardly wait to learn more." She shook her head as Eve opened her lips to speak. "No, I'm not going to nag you to tell me stuff you're not ready to talk about. I can see that you're hesitating. That's okay with me. I've been there."

"I'm sure you have," Eve said dryly. "Does that mean you'll help me?"

"Of course. I wouldn't have come if I hadn't intended to find out what you want to know." She grinned. "But it helps that everything is so interesting. When can I go back to the woods?"

"Tomorrow. You need to rest, and we need to let Nalchek adjust to your being here to help. You heard him—he doesn't want us in his woods without him."

"Which would probably not mean anything to you if you thought it was urgent."

Eve nodded. "But I promised Joe I wouldn't go off on my own without Nalchek until he could get here. Tomorrow is soon enough."

"And you keep your promises to Joe Quinn."

"Always," Eve said as she pulled off the road at the driveway leading to a charming redwood building, overflowing with flower boxes filled with geraniums. "I was feeling guilty about running out in the middle of the night when Nalchek called me. That might not have met the letter of the promise I made to him."

"Close enough." Margaret grinned. "And it was a lifesaving operation. I was fading fast without that hot coffee."

"Considering your affinity toward animals, perhaps I should have sent a St. Bernard to rescue you."

"Nalchek wouldn't have understood." She opened the car door and looked up at the hotel. "Nice place. Cozy. But I don't have any credit cards and only twenty bucks. You'll have to lend me the money."

"My treat," Eve said as she came around the car. "I'm putting you on retainer. I wouldn't expect you to do this for—"

"It's a favor, Eve," Margaret interrupted. "I take all kinds of jobs to survive but not from my friends. Just pay the bill, and I'll send you the money next time I have it."

"That's not what I—" She shrugged. "We'll work it out."

She took Margaret's arm and pulled her toward the front entrance. "Come on. I need to get you to bed."

"You're treating me like a kid." Margaret's eyes were gleaming with amusement. "I've been taking care of myself for a long time, Eve."

"Since you *were* a kid. That doesn't make it right."

"And you suddenly had a maternal flash of your Jane as a child trying to survive on the streets." She chuckled. "She did very well, and so did I."

"Again, that doesn't make it right." She opened the glass door. "And I'll treat you the way I wish to treat you. Okay?"

Margaret nodded slowly. "Okay." Her smile was brilliant. "Like you said, we'll work it out. I can handle it."

"There's Joe," Eve waved across the terrace at Joe, who had just come into the hotel restaurant. "He made good time," she told Margaret. "It's only a little after noon."

"Protective." She ate a bite of her salad as she watched Joe make his way through the tables toward them. "Like Nalchek. He was probably on edge about your being out here without him."

She was right, Eve thought. She'd talked to Joe early this morning when he was getting ready to go to the airport, and he hadn't been pleased with her.

"Hi." Joe pulled out a chair and dropped down onto it. "Good to see you, Margaret. Though I could wish that you hadn't exploded on the scene with such enthusiasm."

"You mean recklessness," Margaret substituted. "And no one would have ever known I went to those woods if Nalchek hadn't been out there. I would have done what I had to do, then called Eve and told her I was on my way to her hotel."

"And she would still have left the hotel and come to pick you up."

"I can't argue with that," Margaret said. "She's as protective as you are."

"I can argue with it," Eve said. "Drop it, Joe."

He smiled. "It's dropped. Just wanted to draw her attention to my take on it."

"Loud and clear," Margaret said cheerfully. "Everyone in the world has to take care of Eve, or they'll be facing Joe Quinn's wrath."

He nodded. "Something like that. And she's staring very disapprovingly at me at this moment. I think it's time I changed the subject." He turned to Eve. "I got word from the Interpol database right before I got on the plane. They may have come up with a match." He grimaced. "Though it took long enough. Walsh is a fairly common name. I was bouncing back and forth between Interpol and the FBI most of the night. One dead end after another. This one came closest, and the location seems right." He took out his phone and dialed up the report. "James Bradford Walsh. British subject, fifty-seven, last-known address in Sacramento, California. That's not his real name but one of his most-frequently-used aliases." He paused. "No current warrants, but he's a very ugly customer. His prime area of expertise is as enforcer. He's worked for various mobs both in London and the U.S. His last-known employer was the Castino Cartel in Mexico City. He fit right in with them. His record reflected burglary, drugs, suspicion of human trafficking, suspicion of murder. In short, he did anything that was demanded of him by the Castino family."

"What about children?" Eve asked. "Is there anything about violence toward children?"

"Some of the human trafficking involved children but not exclusively."

"Anything about 'marking' his victims?"

Joe shook his head. "No details. Either he's not our man, or he's very clever. I'm searching other European Web sites to see if he's mentioned."

"It's pretty vague." Eve's hands clenched. "You didn't get anything from any other Web sites?"

"Only a Paul Walsh who was located in San Antonio, Texas. But he's been serving time in Huntsville Prison for the last three years. And the FBI came up with Ronald Samuel Walsh who looked promising until I realized he had no history of violence. So were back to James Walsh."

"Damn. Photo?"

He punched a button and pushed the phone toward her. "Looks pretty ordinary."

"So did Ted Bundy." She looked down at the photo. Thin, brown hair, high forehead, full lips. Deep-set, dark eyes. As Joe said, ordinary.

Or was he? There was something about the set of those lips . . . His eyes were so without expression they had a kind of blankness, but those lips were . . .

She knew from her sculpting experience how they could change, betray, transform. Sometimes she had to struggle to give the lips no expression in her reconstructions. An indentation at the corners, the faintest curl could change everything.

And Walsh had made no effort to keep his lips from betraying what was beneath his impassiveness.

Ugliness.

Which didn't mean he was a child murderer.

And that didn't mean he wasn't.

"Eve."

She looked up and pushed the phone back to him. "I don't believe he's ordinary. I think he may be the one. I want to know more about him. What made him such a great enforcer?"

"Total ruthlessness and he trained himself into a top-notch executioner. Guns, knives, explosives; he was an expert with all of them. And he had no trouble with decapitation. Every week or so, one of Castino's enemies would be seen hanging headless on one of the local bridges."

"You say he lived in Sacramento for a while. Can we find out anything from the police department or maybe his former neighbors?"

"I'm already on it. I called the Sacramento PD after I landed at San Francisco."

"I should have known."

"May I see?" Margaret asked as she took the phone. "Walsh . . ." She gave the phone back to him. "I can't tell anything. Human killers are much more difficult to judge than animals. There are all kinds of signals broadcast by the big cats or rattlesnakes." She looked at Eve. "Is it okay if I go to the grave site now that Joe is here? I'm not accomplishing anything here."

"And we're boring you?" Eve said. "By all means, I'll call Nalchek, and we'll all go."

"I've already called him," Margaret said as she got to her feet. She checked her wristwatch. "I told him I'd meet him at the grave site at one thirty." She smiled. "And you can introduce him to Joe and get them on the same page. That will give me the chance to look around without Nalchek hovering."

"You have it all planned."

"Not really. I just want to know who was guarding your

Jenny and why. It's been nagging me since last night. May we go?"

Eve nodded. "I admit I'm curious."

"So is Nalchek." She zipped up her hoodie and started across the terrace. "He was entirely too willing to let me go into his woods again today. I thought I'd have a battle . . ."

Nalchek was standing by the grave, and he only nodded curtly to Margaret. His gaze went beyond her to Joe. "You're Joe Quinn. I've heard about you. I'm John Nalchek."

Joe nodded. "I've heard about you, too." He glanced at the grave site. "Eve says you're obsessed."

Nalchek stiffened. "Does she?"

"Yeah." He looked back at him. "But that doesn't mean anything. She's obsessed, too. It won't bother me unless you start causing her problems."

"Joe," Eve said.

"He should know," Joe said. "I think I can probably work with him, but he has to know the limits." He met Nalchek's gaze. "Got it?"

"Got it. Understood." He paused. "And I'll let you hang around unless you get in my way." He smiled faintly. "I won't cause Eve any problems because she's on my wavelength." He turned away. "But I don't promise I'll work with Margaret Douglas. She's a little too—" He stopped and muttered a curse as he looked around. "Where the hell is she?"

"She's slipped deeper into the woods while you and Joe were exchanging words and sizing each other up," Eve said. "She warned me she'd probably do it. She didn't want you around to get in her way."

"The hell she didn't." He strode toward the trees. "I have no intention of letting her run her own show."

"Too bad," Joe said as he started after him. "Margaret has a tendency to close everyone out. Natural enough, since most people can't follow where she goes anyway."

"Literally or figuratively," Eve said. "Back off, Nalchek. Give her a chance."

He glanced over his shoulder. "Is that an order?"

"Only if you insist on pushing it," she said. "I want to work with you. But I have to see if Margaret can put us on the fast track. I'm afraid we don't have much more time."

"Why not?" His eyes were narrowed on her face. "You know something you haven't told me."

"No, I don't *know* anything. We may have a few leads that might prove promising."

"And you're dangling them in front of me in exchange for what?" he asked grimly.

"Cooperation. Help Margaret. Don't interfere. Then I'll be glad to share whatever Joe found out about a man who might have killed your deputy."

"You're interfering with a murder investigation."

"No, she's just not helping with it." Joe paused. "Yet."

Nalchek stared him in the eye and didn't speak for a long moment. "I want that information immediately."

"You'll get it," Eve said. "As soon as you give me your word that you'll work with us and not by yourself to try to catch him." She smiled. "And Margaret gets her chance. I want your word."

Another silence.

He nodded curtly. "Okay. As long as you don't endanger

my men or the investigation. If I see any sign of that happening, no deal."

"You won't see it happening," Joe said. "We may want that son of a bitch more than you do." He gestured to the trees. "Now, shall we join Margaret?"

Nalchek didn't answer but strode ahead of them into the trees.

"Not pleased," Joe murmured to Eve as he fell into step with her. "Can't blame him. I'd feel the same way."

So would Eve, but she couldn't let it matter. How close was Walsh? Would he come here or go to Carmel? "Nalchek will have to get over it. He can't have everything his own way."

"He's probably thinking the same thing about us," Joe said dryly. "Let's hope Margaret isn't being too radically Margaret when he reaches her."

Evidently, Margaret was moving fast, and it was taking Nalchek time to catch up with her.

It took Eve and Joe another ten minutes before they caught sight of Nalchek. He was standing still in the center of the trail in the densest area of the forest. He turned to face them. "She's right up ahead," he said. "She's sitting by that stream, and she's not trying to avoid us any longer."

"She probably wasn't trying to avoid us before," Joe said. "She just didn't want to have us disturb her concentration."

"You sound as if you're familiar with the way she operates."

"He is," Eve said. "More than I am. He was on hand months ago, when Margaret was trying to find me in the woods. I could have died except for her."

"And you believe all of this crap, Quinn?"

"It's hard as hell for me. I'm a pragmatic bastard." He was

silent. "Yeah, I believe something is going on with Margaret. I'm willing to go along with her."

Nalchek shrugged. "We'll see." He moved ahead of them down the trail.

"Hi." Margaret smiled at them as they came into view. "Isn't it pretty here?" She was sitting cross-legged on the bank of the stream as they turned the bend of the trail. "It's like a secret garden. Not like the one in the book. A sort of misty green haven. I bet you've been here before, Nalchek."

"A couple times."

"I thought so. Since you said it was your grandfather's land."

"Even though he owned it, I wasn't given any more privileges than the town kids. He treated this forest as open land, and anyone who respected the environment was allowed to use it."

"Sounds like a nice guy." She looked at the stream. "I like it here."

"You covered a lot of ground to get here," Nalchek said without expression.

"I was tracking. I didn't know where he was going to lead me."

"Who was going to lead you?" Eve asked quietly.

"Can I make a guess?" Nalchek asked.

Margaret smiled. "Tell me."

"A coyote."

Margaret chuckled. "You did take those soil samples."

He nodded. "I put a rush on them, and they came back genus *Canis latrans*. Coyote. Not that it means anything."

"No, because it's not quite accurate," she said. "Sajan is half-coyote, half-wolf. The two don't mate very often, but it happened in this case. Though I think Sajan considers himself a coyote. Coyotes are fairly solitary animals. But when he hunts in a pack, it's with coyotes."

"Sajan," Joe repeated. "Your coyote has a name."

"Maybe. In a way. It's how he thinks of himself. Or how I interpret it." She looked back at the stream. "He likes it here. He often hunts small rodents and stays here by the stream for days."

"When he's not guarding the grave?" Nalchek asked.

"You're having trouble with that," Margaret said soberly. "So am I. So is he."

"Yeah, you said he didn't know why he was still guarding the grave after Jenny's bones were removed," Eve said. "And he didn't see Jenny die?"

"No, only afterward, when her killer was digging the grave and placing her in it. I believe he felt . . . drawn. It confused him. He didn't know why he was there. And afterward, it would have been natural for him to just wander away." She shook her head. "That didn't happen. He stayed close to her. He protected the grave. He thought it might have something to do with the man, the killer."

"What?"

"Because he kept coming back here."

"To the grave?"

"Yes. It went on for years. He wouldn't come for months at a time, then he'd be back."

"No other reason? He was just checking on the grave?"

"Yes, it made Sajan nervous. He didn't know what he was supposed to do if the killer started to disturb the grave. But he never did. That's it. I've told you all I know. All he knows." She made a face. "It's not much, is it?" Her gaze shifted to Nalchek. "But it might tell you why Jenny's killer was nervous about your wandering around the woods looking for evidence and was keeping an eye on you."

"You're saying he might have not been sure that he hadn't lost something that might have incriminated him?" Nalchek said.

"I'm not saying anything except that he was on guard while he was in those woods. Perhaps he was worried you might find something that would have given you a hint about Jenny's identity."

"Then he might be back," Joe said. "Maybe all we have to do is wait."

Eve shook her head. "We don't know what he's going to do. That might not be at the top of his agenda."

"The little girl . . ." Margaret said. "You believe he'll go after her first?"

"What little girl?" Nalchek said sharply. "What the hell are you talking about?"

"I'll tell you in just a minute," Eve said. "It's part of—"

"Tell me now," Nalchek said fiercely. "I've played your game. Now you play mine. Talk to me."

Eve could understand his anger and frustration, and it wasn't fair not to concede. He had certainly gone beyond the limits with Margaret. But it would have to be in a way that he would accept. Okay, dive in and go for it. "I'm not arguing. You're right, it's time that you know everything that we know. We found a confidential informant who gave us certain additional information regarding the name of Jenny's possible killer . . ."

CHAPTER
7

W alsh," Nalchek repeated after Eve had stopped speaking. "The whole thing sounds flimsy as hell to me. What's the name of your informant?"

"Confidential," Joe said. "But reliable, very reliable. Very close to Walsh."

"Then let's go pick him up and question him."

"And put my source in danger?" Joe asked. "Not likely. But I'm checking with both Interpol and the FBI and gathering other information."

"I want the name of your informant."

"No way. Will you trust me when I tell you that there's nothing you could find out from the informant that we haven't already learned?"

"I'm not big on trust."

"It's true, Nalchek," Eve said. "I promise you."

He gazed at her. She could see his frustration. "You'll tell me if you learn anything else?"

She nodded.

He turned away. "Then I'm going to start a search in local records for anyone of that name. He may be a British citizen, but we may still have something. Right now, I've had enough, and I'm going back to my office." He looked back at Margaret. "I only half believe you, and I'm not going to tell you to keep me informed. Coyotes aren't my idea of confidential informants, either."

She smiled. "I believe we won't hear anything from Sajan unless Walsh comes back here. I'll keep tuned in to him for you."

He grunted, and the next moment, he'd disappeared around the bend.

"Poor guy. It's very difficult for him." Margaret jumped to her feet. "Too bad. I like him." She looked at Eve. "I told him the truth. There's nothing much I can do right now with Jenny's coyote. What else do you want me to do?"

"Stay close. You'd know if Walsh returned to these woods?"

"Sajan would know, then I'd know."

"Then stay at the hotel and monitor him while Joe and I go to Sacramento and see if we can find out anything about Walsh."

"And that's all I can do?" she asked, disappointed.

"That's more than enough. You've done your job. You've told us that it wasn't over for Walsh when he'd made the kill. That he was on guard and worried that she might be found. Or that something else might be found to tell us her identity."

"Evidently you knew that already."

"You confirmed it. Now we have to find out why that was so important to him. We'll drop you off at the hotel on our way out of town." She turned to Joe. "Let's go."

"I'll be with you in a minute," Margaret said as she sat down again and reached for her tennis shoes. "I have to dry my feet and put on my shoes . . ."

Margaret tied her tennis shoes and got to her feet.

She stared thoughtfully after Eve and Joe as she tucked her shirt back into her jeans.

Pity.

Eve had obviously written off her help in anything but a minor manner. She thought Margaret had done her part and didn't want to jeopardize her any more than she had already. Eve was protective and independent and wanted to do everything herself. Margaret understood that concept but couldn't accept the application where she was concerned. She couldn't see herself lazing beside the pool at that pretty little hotel waiting for something to happen.

She turned and stared at the dense trees on the other side of the stream.

Are you there, Sajan?

No answer.

But that didn't mean that the coyote didn't understand. He was a mixture of emotions where people were concerned. He wanted to live his simple, solitary life, yet he had been pulled into monitoring and guarding this forest, this grave. He couldn't understand it, and he didn't like it. He wanted it to all go away.

Maybe it will soon. I don't know why, either. But sometimes we're guided in strange paths.

Like this one for her. From the moment she had entered this forest last night, she had felt a sense of rightness. She had known that she could help Eve, known that she could help that child who had been thrown in that grave.

"Margaret?" Eve called.

"Coming."

She started down the path after them.

But she couldn't help that child who was targeted if she played the waiting role that Eve had chosen for her. She would have to do what she did best and ignore everything else.

She could learn this forest and the creatures who inhabited it. She didn't necessarily need Sajan. She just had to be here.

And she would be.

CARMEL, CALIFORNIA

"Come on, Cara." Heather Smallwood wrinkled her nose. "You know you hate getting on those school buses as much as I do. It's only ten blocks to the apartment building, and we can stop off at that delicatessen and get a soda."

It was very tempting, Cara thought wistfully. Heather was cool. She was funny and popular and always wore neat clothes. Cara hardly got a chance to see her except at school. They lived in the same apartment building, but Elena had strict rules about Cara's visiting other kids in the neighborhood. Elena had strict rules about everything.

"I'd be grounded for a month if I didn't ride the bus home. My aunt says it's not safe to walk home."

"Oh, for Pete's sake. You're almost twelve, and there would be two of us," Heather said in disgust. "I've walked it lots of times by myself. I just thought it would be fun to have you with me."

"It would be fun." She hesitated. "Let me talk to her. Maybe next time."

"Yeah, sure." Heather turned away. "It won't happen. You can't ever do anything. I don't know why I even tried."

"I'll talk to her," Cara repeated. "And you're not going to convince me by making me sound like a wimp. My aunt worries a lot, but she can't help it. It's probably all those creepy news stories on TV." She headed for the bus. "I'll see you tomorrow, Heather."

"Yeah." Heather stood looking at her for a moment, then turned toward the street. "Tomorrow."

The young girl with the blond ponytail and green plaid skirt would be so easy, Walsh thought.

Even from where he was sitting in his car down the street, he could tell that Heather Smallwood was one of the confident ones who thought nothing could ever happen to them. There was a bounce to her step that was almost a swagger, and she had obviously been trying to convince Cara Delaney to come with her. Too bad she had failed. Successful repetition bred that confidence, and after a while, Cara might have been lured to try to take more chances.

And then she would have been his.

But instead she was safely on that yellow bus going home to sweet, steady, interfering Aunt Elena.

He smothered the surge of anger that exploded through him at the thought of that betrayal. Calm down. It was only a postponement. The important thing was that he had found the child, the one they called Cara Delaney. He leaned forward, his gaze focused on her face as she looked out the window at her cocky, little friend walking down the street swinging her book bag.

Yes.

He had been right to mark Cara. It had been a long time, but he'd finally found her. But seeing her in the flesh had erased any hint of doubt.

Because this time there was no mistake.

She was the one.

He took out his phone and dialed Salazar. "I've found her."

"You've said that before and failed me. Why should I believe you now?"

Arrogant bastard. "Then don't believe me. But I'm going after her anyway. I'd suggest that you be prepared to send someone to help me dispose of this particular body in case it might cause you extreme discomfort." He paused. "And deposit that money in my account in the next few days. I may have to move fast."

"Without proof that I'm going to get my money's worth?"

"I'm sending you a photo I just took." He pressed the button on his phone. "Proof enough?"

There was silence. "It . . . could be."

"And the kid has an Aunt Elena. Elena Delaney. This time I went after *her* photo at the Department of Motor Vehicles. Last name different from our Elena Pasquez, but the first was the same. I suppose it was easier to change the fake ID. And the face was definitely our Elena. It took me a load of bribe money and weeks of going through their records before I found a picture of the bitch. Then all I had to do was stake out her apartment until I saw the kid."

"What about the kid's name?"

"Marnie? Come on, Elena wouldn't be that stupid. She knows the kid has to enroll in school. She's calling her Cara now. But, put it all together, and I'm much closer than the other marks I removed on pure speculation. You agree?"

"I agree that she might be a likely prospect," Salazar said cautiously.

"Then send me the money. If you double the price, I'll arrange for the body disposal." He added, "Unless you want the head. That could be arranged."

"I don't want to wait for a few days. I want you to be done with this job and out of the country," Salazar paused. "Because I think you blundered all the way on this job. Jenny wasn't supposed to be found, and after they did find her, you should have made sure that there was no possibility she'd be recognized."

"You're wrong," he said impatiently. "You don't know what you're talking about. Okay, they found her, but that was because of some freak rainstorm. After Nalchek called in Eve Duncan, I blocked her as soon as I could. I made sure that Jenny wouldn't be recognized. I did everything right."

"Then why did I get a report that Eve Duncan has just shown up in Sonderville?"

Walsh's hand tightened on the phone. "What?"

"You heard me. She and Quinn checked into a local hotel and made contact with Nalchek. She spent some time with him. So she evidently doesn't consider herself blocked. Why didn't you get rid of her at the same time you took the skull?"

"You don't understand. There were difficulties. It wasn't the right time. I was going to do it later."

"All I understand is that you let her get finished with that damn reconstruction, then left her alive to talk about Jenny. I wanted her forgotten . . . except by her father. I wanted to see him roasting in the hell I created for him."

"She will be forgotten. You won't have to wait long before I—"

"I've waited too long already. Eight damn years. It was

supposed to be a simple job. You put my ass on the line, and I've been walking a tightrope, thinking every minute I'd fall off and have her father come after me."

Walsh opened his mouth to spit out his defense and thought better of it. He should tone it down. Salazar was not a force to take lightly. He didn't need him to send one of his soldiers across the border to try to gut him. Not that he would succeed. No one was better at either surviving or the kill than he. "None of the delay was my fault. And I've been trying hard to rectify it since it happened."

"If you hadn't, I would have had you very painfully removed that first year after Jenny."

"Do you think I don't want to move faster? But I have to move carefully if I want to finish this up, so that it's safe for you."

"I don't feel safe, Walsh."

He lost his temper. "Then it's your fault. You've been tying my hands for too long. Do you know what lengths I've had to go to, pussyfooting around to keep you safe? The minute that I got that tip from the bank officer that Elena was still in California for at least the first year after I killed Jenny, I never stopped searching for her and that brat. I went the extra mile in making sure you couldn't be hurt no matter where it led me."

Silence that was laden with menace. "Extra mile? And so you should have. And I don't care if I've made it difficult for you."

No, of course he didn't. "Well, now it's the end of the road, and I'm in control. Send me my money and be prepared to get me help for the disposal."

Silence. "Excuses, again. We'll see who is in control, Walsh." Salazar hung up.

Bastard.

But Salazar was smart, and he wouldn't take the chance of having Walsh exposed and himself with him. He'd get him help. He'd send the money.

Because he'd seen what Walsh had seen in that photo.

Cara Delaney's bus was leaving the school parking lot now. Soon, she'd be safe within the doors of her apartment house.

And he was feeling frustrated and hungry. He'd scoped out her setup and knew that it would be hard to get to her. There were alarms, the little girl was very careful. It might take days of stalking before he could safely pounce.

But the pretty blonde with the ponytail who was so sure nothing could happen to her? She wasn't careful at all.

He thought about it.

No, he decided reluctantly, he didn't want any red flags that would alert Cara Delaney or her dear aunt Elena. He enjoyed the child kills, but he could control it.

He'd have to be patient and wait for Cara . . .

And he'd get her. Just like he'd put that bitch, Jenny, into the ground. Only this time, with Cara, there would be nothing to reconstruct. There wouldn't be a skull with glittering green eyes that made him writhe with fury.

No, he would not think of that skull. He had thrown that reconstruction into his trunk so he wouldn't have to look at it again. It had to be his imagination that had caused him to think he'd seen Jenny. Out of all the lives he'd taken over the years, why would Jenny be the only one who had come back to torment him? He didn't believe in ghosts, so it had to be stress or some kind of weird primitive instinct because he was getting near to Cara.

So prove it to *himself.* Prove that Jenny had no power to stop him from doing whatever he wanted to do.

Get rid of the skull.

Yes, that would do it. Lately, he'd been thinking of keeping it or sending it to Salazar as a trophy. That would show her.

Do you hear me, Jenny? You're *nothing.* You can't stop me from killing Cara. You can't stop me from destroying the last part of you that would prove you ever lived.

And destroying that interfering slut, Eve Duncan, along with her. He would show her that she couldn't make him look like an amateur to Salazar. She'd be sorry that she'd decided to track him down. He couldn't move on Cara Delaney yet, but he could go after Duncan.

How? It had to be a completely satisfying kill that would make him forget the frustration of the past days. Something . . . spectacular . . .

He didn't even look back at the yellow school bus as he started his car and headed down the street.

"Hi." Elena Delaney looked up with a smile as Cara walked into the apartment. She had on her black work pants, but she was wearing a pink T-shirt with a cocktail on the front that was the same color as the pink streak running through her brown hair. She was somewhere in her midthirties, but all of Cara's friends thought she was younger. "Just in time. I just finished the spaghetti and meatballs. Put in the garlic bread for me, will you?"

"Sure." Cara dropped her book bag on the chest by the door. "But you should have waited for me. I could have done this. You don't like to cook."

"Maybe I was having a couple guilty twinges." Elena made

a face. "You do all the cooking and cleaning, and you're just a kid."

"I don't mind. Someone has to do it, and you're too busy." She headed toward the kitchen. "I didn't expect you to be here, Elena. You said you worked today."

"Night shift. Don't have to go in until seven. I thought we could have dinner together."

"Great." Cara got the garlic bread out of the freezer and turned on the oven. "We haven't been able to do that all week. You've been working double shifts."

Her aunt shrugged. "Pays the bills." She glanced at Cara. "You okay? No trouble at school?"

Cara nodded as she put the garlic bread in the oven. "I'm okay. School's fine; boring, but fine." She suddenly smiled. "Now that you've done your duty and asked me, can we forget about it? Once every few months you decide you just have to check on me. I'd tell you if I had any problems. I promised you that I would."

"I know, but you don't . . ." She wrinkled her nose. "I know you're smart, probably smarter than me, but I'm always afraid that I should be helping you more."

Cara shook her head. "You work all the time. You told me we had to share the load. I understand that, and it's not bad. I clean up the apartment and do my homework. Later, I get to play my violin. I'm doing good, Elena." She looked in the refrigerator and took out a bottle of cranberry juice. "Better than Heather, and she's got a mom and dad and a brother to help her."

"Oh, yes, Heather." Elena looked away as she got down the plates. "She seems nice, but a little . . . spoiled. What do you think, Cara?"

"I like her." She drank her juice. "Is that what this is about? You want to talk about Heather? Is that why you're working the night shift tonight?"

"I told you that you were smart," Elena said. "It's just that I have to leave you alone a lot, and I wanted to make sure that you weren't—"

"I don't break the rules," Cara said quietly. "Sometimes I want to, but I don't."

"Good. That's a relief. It's so easy to just . . ." Elena gave her a quick hug. "But those rules are important. We both know that, don't we?"

Cara nodded. "I know it." She stepped back and hesitated. "But maybe I could just bend . . . Heather wanted me to walk home with her today."

"No," Elena said sharply. "You can't do it, Cara. The bus is safer."

From the safe bus, to the locked door of the apartment that Cara was never to open. "Maybe it is safe now. Maybe something has changed." She whispered, "Maybe he's not out there anymore."

"And maybe he is," Elena said gently. "I know what your life is like. I wish I could tell you that you could take the chance. But I can't do that." She looked her in the eye. "Think about those nightmares you have. Do you think it's worth the risk, Cara?"

Running through the darkness.

Blood.

Screams.

Jenny!

She jerkily shook her head. "No." She turned and went to the cutlery drawer. "I'll set the table."

"Cara."

"It's okay." She didn't look at her. "You're right. Heather is spoiled. I don't need her to tell me what I should do. She doesn't understand . . ."

SACRAMENTO, CALIFORNIA

"I shouldn't be long, Eve. I just want to question a few detectives and check out the records on Walsh." Joe pulled up in front of the Sacramento Police Department precinct. "Do you want to come in with me?"

"No, I'll leave that to you. I want to check the forensic records on Jenny to see if it triggers anything." She grabbed her computer and got out of the car. "But I'll go across the street to the park and find a bench with a bit of sunshine. I've had a chill from that wood where Jenny was buried ever since we went there. I want to see sunlight and hear birds singing."

He nodded. "I'll call you when I finish. Then we'll go to the apartment where Walsh lived for a while and question the neighbors."

"Right." She nodded. "I doubt if we'll find anything. You said he had a fairly clean record here."

"Which means he's being very careful. Or that he was incompetent while he was in the U.K." He added grimly, "But he wasn't clean while he was in Mexico. Maybe that was his training ground." He turned and walked toward the front entrance. "But everyone slips, we've just got to find where Walsh made his."

Eve watched him disappear into the precinct before she turned to cross the street. She knew he was right, but so far,

Walsh had not made a slip. He had killed that officer from the Sheriff's Office and the FedEx driver. He had stolen Jenny's reconstruction.

He had killed Jenny.

And, as far as she could see, there had been no errors.

That didn't mean they didn't exist.

She entered the stone park gates and dropped down on a green bench several yards down the path. There was a fountain sparkling a few feet away, and she could see a children's playground in the distance.

Two good, bright things to balance the darkness.

So don't think negative.

"That's right, Mama. You always find a way to get around the bad things."

Bonnie.

Eve felt a surge of pure joy as she saw her little daughter sitting on the edge of the fountain, dressed in her usual jeans and Bugs Bunny T-shirt, the spray in the background framing her riot of red curls. She hadn't realized until this minute how frightened she'd been that Bonnie hadn't appeared to her for so long. "It would be easier not to be negative if I'd had a little help from you, young lady. You're not a very reliable ghost. Where have you been?"

"Here and there." Bonnie's small face lit up with her brilliant smile. "It's hard to explain since you haven't been here. You know that I can't be with you all the time."

"And I accept it." She paused. "But you scared me the last time you came to me. You said that you might not be able to come to me again. I'm glad you came to your senses."

Bonnie chuckled. "And you told me you wouldn't have it. As if you could do anything about it."

"I can be very persuasive. Maybe somebody up there likes me."

"Everybody likes you, Mama," she said gently. "That's why I got to come to you in the beginning."

"Well, there's no reason why you can't keep up with the status quo. Why change anything?"

"It wouldn't be my choice. And it may not happen. But things are going to change, and I don't know how that's going to affect us."

"Not at all," Eve said flatly. "Go tell them that."

"Yes, ma'am." Bonnie's eyes were twinkling. "I'll do my best. But I haven't been here long enough to have much influence."

"Then tell them that I need you. You told me that the reason they sent you is that they knew I needed you. That hasn't changed. I was just thinking the other day that I needed you to come and help me understand—"

"Jenny," Bonnie said. "You're having trouble understanding what's happening to you."

"So is she. She's not like you. You have trouble now and then with blanks. But Jenny doesn't seem to know anything about who she was or what's happened to her. At least not the details."

"It's coming back to her. Soon she'll know everything. I think they wanted a blank slate when she came to you."

"Why?"

Bonnie shook her head.

"Does that mean you don't know?"

"I'm getting glimpses now and then. I don't know everything."

"And you don't want to tell me."

"I always want to tell you everything." She added gently, "Sometimes I can't do it."

"Then tell me why Jenny. I've never before had a reconstruction who actually appeared to me. Why Jenny?"

"She needs you."

"And those other poor children didn't?"

She shrugged. "Choice."

"You're being very unsatisfactory. Evidently, you didn't come to answer questions." She held up her hand. "And that's okay. You know that's not what I need from you, what I want. You're what's important. Love is what's important."

Bonnie nodded. "You always knew that, Mama," she said softly. "From the moment I was born, I knew you would always love me. It's your special gift."

"Not unusual. Most parents love their children."

"But not the way you do. You glow with it. And Jenny's parents didn't love her. She was cheated of it. Maybe that's why she was sent to you for help. There's a certain balance. Not all the time. But sometimes, it's there for us."

"How do you know Jenny's parents didn't love her?" She shook her head. "No more questions. I remember Jenny said that she didn't remember her parents. I'd hope she'd remember them if there was love between them."

Bonnie nodded. "Love should always be there."

Eve swallowed to ease the tightness of her throat. "It always is for us. And I don't know why her damn parents wouldn't love Jenny."

"I know you don't," Bonnie said. "I told you, that's why she was sent to you."

"To punish that bastard who killed her, to bring her home."

Bonnie was silent. "Yes, to bring her home, Mama."

"We'll find a way. Joe is working on it now. And Margaret will be a help." She paused. "There's another child involved. Can you help us find her?"

"Jenny will help you."

"I hope so. Jenny's help seems to be fading in and out." She leaned *back on the bench. "But we'll work it out. Right now, I don't want to think about anyone but you. We never have enough time together." Her gaze enveloped that beloved little figure. "I wanted sunlight when I came here. You are sunlight, Bonnie. The light is reflecting off the water and touching you with a kind of radiance." She smiled. "Did you arrange that for me?"*

"Sure." Bonnie grinned. "Why not? Anything for you . . ."

"You're looking very serene." Joe tilted his head as he strolled toward the bench where she was sitting. He glanced around the park. "Found your sunshine?"

"Yes." She smiled. "And Bonnie."

He went still. "She came to you."

"Yes." She made a face. "Though she wasn't very informative. I think she came because she sensed how scared I was."

"And still are," he said quietly.

"She keeps saying things are changing. I want them to stay the same."

"No, you don't. You want the best for everyone you love, and that could mean change."

She nodded. "Maybe I just mean that I want to find a way to keep them with me."

"You don't have to search to find a way to keep me with you." He reached out and gently touched her hair. "I'm not going to wander away to try to find myself like Jane. Or be involved in that final great adventure like Bonnie. Even then, I'd find a way to make them change the rules like you did with Bonnie. You're stuck with me."

"Thank God." She took his hand and brought it to her cheek. "I said something of the same to Bonnie, and she laughed at me."

She kissed his palm. "But I do think if you want something this badly, there could be some kind of special dispensation." She tilted her head. "What's happening with Jenny is . . . different. Do you suppose that she wanted something so desperately that she was allowed to come back and try again? She thought maybe it was to stop Walsh from killing that little girl."

"Why don't you ask her?"

"Compared to Jenny, Bonnie is a font of knowledge about the afterlife. Besides, I tried to reach her last night, but I got zilch. She told me that she was fading in and out with both me and Walsh." She shrugged as she released his hand. "So it's up to us to work it out for ourselves. What did you find out from the detectives at the precinct?"

"Not much. They had Walsh under surveillance for nearly two years at the request of Interpol before he moved out of Sacramento. But they came up with nothing."

"Nothing?" Eve frowned. "He killed Jenny, and from what she said, he liked it and had done it before. He wouldn't have just taken a two-year break. Serial killers can't resist the surge of power they get from the kill, he wouldn't have been able to resist it."

"Unless he isn't the usual serial killer," Joe said slowly. "Unless he has an enormous amount of control and the ability to channel and focus."

"Focus on what?"

"The final goal. Maybe he was keeping an eye on Jenny's grave while he searched for another target. Remember, he stuck around for years near the place where he killed Jenny. You would have thought that he would have moved on and not taken the risk. What was so important that he was willing to do that?"

"And he wasn't only a murderer. You told me he was involved in all kinds of ugliness, from thefts to human trafficking. Surely the police picked up on some of those?"

"Not here in Sacramento. He lived in a palatial apartment on the south side with no obvious source of income. He told his landlord he had private means."

"From previous criminal activity, no doubt," Eve said grimly.

"It's one explanation." He paused. "There are others. Maybe . . . blackmail . . . Or it's possible Walsh was still on someone's payroll."

"Doing what?"

"We'd have to find out. But he didn't set up here in Sacramento until after Jenny's killing. Before that, the last report was that he was working for that cartel in Mexico City. It would be logical to assume that his presence here could have something to do with the murder."

"No charges brought against him during that entire period?"

"Nothing significant. A complaint of possible trespassing from the owner of a photography studio. But the charges were dropped when no theft was found to have taken place."

"A photography studio?"

"Memory Lane Studios. It's a small outfit near Sutter Elementary School."

She tensed. "Elementary school? Maybe he wasn't interested in that photography studio as much as the kids at that school. Was there any report of—"

Joe was shaking his head. "No. There were no stalkings nor any reported attacks on any of the children."

"Then there had to be something he wanted from that

studio." She got to her feet. "Let's go see if we can find out what it was."

He smiled. "I've already called Nick Dalkow, who owns the studio, and told him we'd be on our way."

CHAPTER

8

I haven't got much time," Nick Dalkow said impatiently, as they walked through the door of his shop. "I have to be across town in twenty minutes to photograph a high-school football team."

Dalkow didn't look much more than a high-school student himself, Eve thought. He was small, thin, with wild red hair that was spiked with mousse. He was dressed in jeans and an orange T-shirt. His left earlobe sported a tiny rhinestone earring. "I believe we can meet your schedule. It shouldn't take long." She glanced around the studio. A few landscapes, but most of the photos were portraits of children and teenagers. "You do very good work."

"You bet I do. But you're not here to hire me, are you?" He glanced at Joe. "You want to know about that creep who came here and wasted my time." He scowled. "Just like you're doing."

"You're talking about Walsh? How did he waste your time?"

"He came in here and wanted to see examples of my work.

He said that he was thinking of opening a studio of his own and might want to hire me part-time. He looked at everything in sight. Then he asked me to pull out examples of past work." His lips curled. "He was lying. He didn't know anything about photography."

"He didn't specify anything in particular?" Eve asked.

"He said he'd heard I specialized in school pictures and that there was good money in it. He wanted to see all of those."

"And you showed him?"

"Some. Then I threw him out."

"Why?"

"I told you, he was a creep." His lips tightened. "Look, I may not look like what you'd call— I'm my own person. I go my own way. But I take good photos, and those kids are safe with me. I know there are lots of sickos out there, and I didn't like Walsh's poring over all those school photos. Particularly the young kids."

"And you reported him to the police?"

"Not then. What grounds? Suspicion? I just threw him out." He shook his head. "But two days later, I came out of the dark room and found him going through the photos in my file cabinet. That's when I called the police." His lips twisted. "I thought that Walsh was going to go for me. Ugly. Real ugly. But then he apologized, said that he didn't think I'd mind, and walked out. But I still reported him to the cops when they came." He looked at his wristwatch. "Sorry, I've got to go."

"One more thing. Which school pictures was Walsh looking at in that cabinet?" Eve asked.

"Brownroot Elementary." He shook his head. "I told the cops that was where he was digging. And I kept an eye out to see if there was any fallout from his coming here."

"No fallout?"

"Nope." He headed for the door. "Come on. You'll make me late. I have a reputation."

And he also had scruples and integrity, Eve thought. She could see why he was able to overcome that bizarre appearance to become popular in his profession. "I wouldn't think of it." She moved toward the door. "But we may have to call you if we run across anything on which we need help."

"Yeah, whatever." He was locking the door. "I didn't like Walsh. I hope you put him away."

"So do we," Joe said. "But first we have to find him. You don't have any idea where he is?"

"He said he lived here in Sacramento." He turned toward his van. "But he showed me a couple of his photos, and they weren't cityscapes. They were just pretty vineyards and rolling hills."

"Vineyards?"

"Uninteresting, and the composition wasn't even that good."

"Sonderville," she murmured.

"I don't know, and I don't care." He jumped in the van. "All that matters is that I protected those kids from him."

"Yes, that's what matters." Eve watched the van go down the street before she turned to Joe. "I think we need to go back to that precinct and look through those records again. Walsh was obviously interested in locating a child or children in the area. You said that there was no sign that any child at Sutter Elementary had been targeted. But what about Brownroot Elementary? He was looking at those photos when Nick caught him in the act."

"And he may not have found what he was looking for." He took her elbow and propelled her toward their car. "And, if he did, he might not have acted. But we'll definitely check it out."

"There's nothing here," Joe said in disgust as he shut down the precinct computer two hours later. "The captain was right. No sign of any serial killings or child attacks of any kind in the city during the period that Walsh was here."

"No." Brownroot Elementary had been a complete failure, so they had meticulously gone through the other elementary and private schools in the area. They had found zilch there also. "I'm going to start calling other photographers and see if they had visits from Walsh."

Forty-five minutes later, she struck pay dirt.

She turned back to Joe, excited. "Josiah Tierney Studios. Four weeks after Walsh was almost arrested, he tried again. The Tierney Studios aren't in the city. They're in a small town, Milsaro, north of here. Walsh asked Tierney the same thing that he asked Nick. Class pictures. Tierney wasn't as careful as Nick. He didn't see any harm in letting him just look at the photos." She swallowed. "My God, I hope he was right."

He reached for his cell phone. "Did he give you the names of the elementary schools in Milsaro?"

She nodded. "There were only three. McKeller, Davis, and Campbell. I'll take McKeller."

"No, I'll have to identify myself and maybe tap one of the local law authorities to get the information I need from them. Not everyone in the school systems is as trusting as that ass Tierney."

She leaned back in her chair and watched him go into high gear. She didn't like this. It was driving her crazy not to be busy and help. She wanted desperately to know what mischief Walsh had been up to and was equally frantic to know that he had not been successful.

That there had not been another Jenny.

There were lots of them, Jenny had said.

But maybe in his past, maybe not here in this sunny California town.

She jumped to her feet. "I'm going to get a cup of coffee. I'll bring one for you. Call me if you need me."

She stood at the coffee machine a long time, sipping black coffee and thinking about Walsh. Nick had thought he was an ordinary pervert, but there was nothing ordinary about him. Why had he been looking at all those photos? Did a certain feature appeal to him when he chose a victim? That could be it. She knew that some killers were drawn to a hair color or the color and shape of the eyes. There was no telling what physical feature might draw them. What had Walsh been looking for when he had taken that second risk after Nick had almost had him arrested?

"Eve." Joe was standing in the doorway.

Her hand tightened on the cup as she saw his expression. "You found one?"

"Maybe. I can't be sure."

"What do you mean?" She followed him back to the desk. "Why aren't you sure?"

"Because there was the death of a child shortly after Walsh examined those school photos Tierney took." He pulled up the report on the computer. "An eight-year-old student from McKeller Elementary School three weeks later." He nodded at the report. "But no foul play was suspected. Donna Prahern drowned in the pond in back of her house early one Saturday morning."

"Then it was a coincidence. Poor little girl."

"Except that she could swim like a fish, and no one could figure why she'd be walking along the edge of the pond by herself. The consensus was that she'd slipped on the edge of the pond and hit her head on the rocks bordering the water."

Her gaze narrowed on his face. "But you have doubts?"

"You know what a suspicious bastard I am. It was too close to the time that Walsh was doing his search." He was typing into the computer. "So I decided to check and see if there were any other curious coincidences." He pulled up another report. "Candace Julard, another eight-year-old girl. Another unfortunate accident. She died of smoke inhalation a month after Donna Prahern's death, when Candace's mother's house caught fire from faulty wiring. Again, no foul play suspected; her mother also died in the fire."

"Candace went to the same school?"

"No, she wasn't even from the same town. I went a little farther afield to Fillmore, seventy miles south. Candace went to Douglasville Elementary."

"But we don't even know if Walsh made the effort to search for her out there."

"No, I haven't gotten that far yet. But there's a good chance that he'd hit the local photographer in that town, too."

"Why?" She impatiently shook her head. Hadn't she just been thinking that some serial killers were prone to go after certain physical types? "Walsh went to a hell of a lot of trouble. Definitely not victims of opportunity."

"Neither was Patsy Danver."

"Another one?" she whispered.

He nodded. "Same town. Seven months later. Eight years old. Car accident with her father, brakes failed, and they went off the side of a cliff."

"Good God."

He nodded. "But every one could be an accident."

"Yes, and none of them bear the signs of the usual serial killer. Most of those killers are into power and the attacks are close-up and personal. Except for possibly the first child, he wouldn't have even touched those little girls."

"And there was no indication of abuse even with her." He paused. "If it was Walsh, he only wanted them dead and was willing to give up any personal satisfaction to make the kills safe and appear unconnected and go virtually unnoticed."

"Then why did he want them dead? What did they have in common?"

"They were all little girls. Eight years of age. They all had type O blood. They all had dark hair, green or hazel eyes." He bent over the computer. "And one other similarity. I'll pull up the school photos for you. It's only slight but enough so that even I noticed . . ."

The three photos were suddenly before Eve, staring out of the screen at her. Smiling at her with all the vitality and adorable beauty of children. Dark-haired, green eyes . . .

She inhaled sharply. "Dear God, they all look a little like Jenny."

Joe nodded. "Only a little. The same arched brows, but the cheekbones aren't that pronounced. Still, they all bear a faint resemblance to that reconstruction I saw on your worktable that morning."

"So he killed them all because they looked like Jenny?" She lifted her shaking hand to her temple. "Not only the same type, but an actual resemblance?"

"It's a possibility. But we can't rule out that it could be a family resemblance and that tie could be significant. Providing we accept the premise that these seemingly accidental deaths were murders committed by Walsh."

"I'm close to accepting it." She shuddered. "Though the idea of his going through those photos and picking out three innocent children just because they reminded him of one of his former victims is totally macabre."

"Maybe more than three."

Her gaze flew to his face. "What?"

"I didn't have time to go any deeper into the search yet," he said quietly. "It appears he might have confined his killing to this area of California, but how do we know that he limited his hunting ground to these few towns?"

"We don't."

"*There were lots of little girls.*"

She felt sick.

Joe nodded. "Then we'd better find out what we have to deal with." He dropped down in the chair again. "We know what we're looking for now. Let me get to work. It may take a few hours."

And he wasn't suggesting that she help him. He was trying to protect her from being pulled any deeper into this horror.

But it was her horror, too.

And so was the terrible anger that was beginning to flare within her.

"Maybe not if we do it together." She pulled out a chair and logged into the computer. "Eight years old. Accidental death. Right?"

LAKE TAHOE, CALIFORNIA

Everything about these mountains was knife-sharp, Walsh thought.

Pale blue skies, sharp wind whipping the rental car almost off the curves as he drove up the road.

He knew these mountains. He had been sent to hunt down an escaped target in the next valley. That was a long time ago, but he remembered that day with pleasure.

As he would remember this day with pleasure.

That little bitch, Jenny, had not really been at that campfire in the woods that night. It had only been a hallucination.

But everything up here was sharp and clear, and he felt in control as he had told Salazar.

I'm going to destroy you once and for all, bitch.

Try and stop me.

He was at the top of the mountain, and he pulled over to the side of the road with a screech of tires. The wind tore at his hair as he jumped out of the car and went around to the trunk. He grabbed the FedEx box and stuffed it in his knapsack, trying not to look at it.

Not that he believed that skull meant anything but what it was. Proof that he had triumphed and crushed that defiant girl who had fought him and stared at him with those eyes that seemed to see right through him.

Because the dead did not return once he'd killed them.

As Eve Duncan would soon learn.

He moved to the edge of the cliff and gazed down at the glacier lake that was Tahoe. Blue and cold and over a thousand feet deep. The man he'd been hired to find and punish was still down there beneath those waters. He'd had difficulty getting that weighted body down the cliff to where he'd managed to push him into the lake. But he'd regarded it as a challenge, and he'd needed to prove himself after Jenny.

No one was ever going to find that body.

So why not just hurl that skull from the cliff? He could weight it and then—

"*No.*"

He stiffened. He would not believe it was her.

"*You can't destroy it. I won't let you.*"

He could feel her staring at him. He would not look over his shoulder; he kept his eyes on the water below.

His hands were suddenly burning as they had that night when he'd held the skull over the flames.

"That's all you know," he muttered as he started down the narrow trail toward the cliff edge. "I'll do what I want, bitch."

She wasn't real.

It was his imagination.

When he killed, they stayed dead.

"*Walsh.*"

"I don't hear you." He looked straight ahead and smiled recklessly down at the ice-cold waters below. "But you can come along if you like and watch the show. It may not be what you expect . . ."

"**We've got to stop, Eve.**" Joe's gaze was raking her face. "You're pale as a ghost. We'll come back to it later."

"Just give me a few minutes," she said wearily as she leaned back in her chair. She felt as if she had been beaten. All those eager faces in the photos. All those smiles and expressions of hope and wonder.

All those deaths.

"We'll come back to it," Joe repeated firmly. He stood up and pulled her to her feet. "Let's get some air."

She nodded jerkily and let him lead her out of the precinct. The sun was going down, but the air was clean, fresh, and still possessed a lingering warmth that felt comforting against her face. She needed that comfort.

"You should have stopped when I asked an hour ago." Joe was leading her across the street toward the park. "I should have made you stop."

"*He* didn't stop," she said numbly. "He just went from town to town and killed and killed again."

"Yes, he did."

"And nobody knew. How many were there, Joe?"

"I'm not sure."

"You're always sure about things like that. How many?"

"Twelve." He pushed her down on the bench. "If there were no real accidents in the mix."

"I doubt it. They all looked like . . ." She drew a shaky breath. "I don't understand it. What kind of satisfaction did he even get out of it? Some of those boat and automobile accidents were completely without visual or physical contact. If there was any power rush for him, it was definitely remote."

"Then we look for a different motive than pure pleasure. We've been looking at Walsh as a child predator. What if he's not?"

"I don't know." She rubbed her temple, trying to banish

the ugliness of the past hours. "Okay, why did he target those little girls? The first half a dozen or so we located were the same age as Jenny. Then, as time passed, the ages escalated as well. Nine. Ten . . . Maybe he was bored with the younger children. Same color eyes and hair." She stopped. "Blood type was the same as all the other children. O. What about Jenny?" She grabbed her phone and dialed Nalchek. "Nalchek, what was Jenny's blood type?"

"Just a minute, and I'll check it." He came back on the line. "B negative. Is it important?"

"Maybe not. I'm not certain."

"You sounded urgent. Is there something I should know?"

Yes, he should probably be told about those children, but she wasn't up to it at the moment. "It's not urgent. I'll call you tomorrow." She hung up and looked at Joe. "That's one thing that wasn't the same. B negative."

"What are you thinking?"

"Not thinking, grabbing for something to hold on to. Okay, that was one thing different. Though it may not have any significance." She gazed at the fountain. Only hours before, she had sat here with Bonnie and tried to make sense of Jenny and her own connection with her. Now she knew there was no sense to the violence that had rocked the world and destroyed that little girl. But there might be reasons, and they had to find them, so they could find Walsh. "So many deaths. What a monster he must be." Her hand clenched her phone. "And we haven't even scratched the surface. Who knows how high the body count is going to rise." She straightened on the bench. "We should go back. We've been following his trail through all these small towns in northern California watching him decimate and destroy with a kind of morbid fascination. It's time we accepted what he's doing and pull away and try to stop him from doing it again." She moistened her lips. "Jenny said when he was thinking about the girl he was targeting, he was excited because she was 'the one' at last. I didn't realize what that could mean, but I'm beginning to see now. She was supposed to live in Carmel. But we looked at Carmel records and didn't find any photos of anyone resembling Jenny. Maybe Jenny was wrong."

"You believe he was going to try to arrange another 'accident' in Carmel or wherever?"

"It may not have to seem like an accident. How do we know? He might be planning to allow himself a sudden explosion of pleasure. Maybe this girl is the finale he's been working toward." She repeated, " 'She's the one,' remember."

"How could I forget?" He helped her to her feet. "Okay, we'll skip to a few towns near Carmel and go looking for little girls who meet the same criteria as the ones we've located." He paused. "But, as you noticed, the ages changed with the dates of the kills. The last one in Silicon Valley was last September and she was ten years old. We should probably be looking for a ten- or eleven-year-old."

Eve nodded. "We'll check for both." She started for the gates. "And what did he mean, 'She's the one'? I'm beginning to have a terrible feeling that I have an idea about—" Her cell phone rang, and she glanced down at it impatiently.

No ID.

But it could be someone from Nalchek's office.

She answered it. "Eve Duncan."

"You're very interfering, you know. You've caused me a good deal of trouble. I don't like the idea of having to deal with you twice."

She went rigid. She knew that voice. She pressed the speaker.

"And you think killing an innocent FedEx driver is just trouble?"

Joe's eyes narrowed as he leaned forward.

"Ah, you remember me? I thought you might. You're very sharp."

"Why shouldn't I remember you? You didn't even try to disguise your voice when you were pretending to be that dispatcher, Walsh."

Silence. "Walsh? Now I wonder where you got hold of that name."

"Perhaps you're not as clever as you thought you were. Joe is a very competent law-enforcement officer and terrific at searching databases. Why would you think that you might not have managed to let something slip along your very ugly career?"

"Because I'm not that careless."

"But you do compartmentalize, and you evidently felt very comfortable with the Walsh identity. Was it because you were so adept at fading in and out when you were taking all those children's lives?"

Silence. "I don't know what you're talking about."

"Do you want me to reel off the names and numbers of your kills? It started with little Donna Prahern in Sacramento, didn't it? No accident. None of them were accidents."

"Why, I have no idea of what you're accusing me." He paused. "And I have no intention of listening to your raving about crimes that have nothing to do with me. That's not why I called."

"Why did you call?"

"I'm very irritated that you interfered with me. You had no right. I believe you have to be punished. You should have hung up on Nalchek when he phoned, begging you to help him."

"It's what I do. Identify and then find a way to put monsters like you in a prison or gas chamber." Her tone hardened. "And I'll do that, Walsh. No one deserves it more."

"So dedicated," he said softly. "Do I detect a touch of possessiveness? Let's put it to the test. You were very bitter when I took the reconstruction of that sweet little girl, weren't you? How badly do you want her back?"

She didn't answer for an instant. "Are you offering?"

"I might be. How much do you want her?"

"Money?"

"Now I'm sure you know that's not in the cards. You'd have to earn her."

"And for all I know, you've already destroyed my reconstruction."

"True." He added, "But as it happens, I haven't gotten around to it yet. You still might have a chance. Why don't you come and get her?"

"When you've just said you want to punish me? I know what that means to you."

"Yes, but you left your cozy little cottage and came out to the Golden State to try to retrieve that skull. That tells me what it means to you."

"What it means is what it will always mean. A way to catch the filth who was coward enough to kill a little girl and hide her body in the ground."

"Are you trying to make me angry?" His voice was amused. "There's nothing cowardly about killing in any form. Society totally rejects the idea of murder, they even seek to put to death those who have the courage to go their own way in spite of their stupid rules. To be clever and skilled enough to take a life and walk away a free man makes me far more remarkable than you and that detective, who are trying to find and punish me."

"You actually believe that?"

"Of course."

"And the act of killing is only a challenge no matter who the victim? A helpless child, an old man?"

"You sound so revolted. As you say, it's the challenge of the kill itself. I do appreciate the ending of a young life because it's regarded with such horror. But just the act itself immediately puts me in the crosshairs of do-gooders like you and Nalchek. If I make a mistake, you could bring me down. It's me against the system." He paused. "But I much prefer that it be me against you and Joe Quinn. So much more interesting. So why don't you come and see if you can take this reconstruction away from me?"

She looked at Joe, then said, "A trap, Walsh?"

"A challenge, Eve." He chuckled. "I'll e-mail you the location where you can find the skull, and you can take a look and see if you want to attempt trying to bring her home. Isn't that the phrase that you use? I read a magazine interview with you about your sculpting process. I was quite touched." His voice suddenly lost all hint of humor. "But now that you mention traps, if you try to load the dice against me and bring on police or FBI reinforcements, you will not only not see the skull to judge whether you wish to take your chances, but you'll see your fine reconstruction destroyed before your eyes. It's just between you, that fine lover of yours, and me. Do you understand?"

"I understand that you're trying to set us up."

"Then meet the challenge and try to win the prize." He hung up.

Eve drew a shaky breath as she turned to Joe. "What do you think?"

"I think he's a complete sociopath, and he wants you dead," he said harshly.

She nodded. "Jenny said that he meant to kill me, but he didn't have time after he stole the skull." She grimaced. "It's clear he didn't like my chasing after him."

"On the contrary, I think he did like it. Now he doesn't have to go back to the lake to finish you off. He thinks he can do it here."

Her e-mail pinged, and she looked down at the phone. "That's probably the location."

"The trap, you mean," Joe said. "Give me your phone and let me handle it."

"Joe."

"He wants to kill you."

"It's a chance to get the reconstruction." She looked at him. "It may be a chance to get Walsh. We have to get him, Joe. It's not only Jenny. I sat there all afternoon and read all those case files about those murdered children and their families."

"Too much risk."

"I can work around it."

"Good God, you're going to do it."

"I'm going to try. I'm not going to do anything suicidal. As soon as I can, I'll notify Nalchek and try to bring him up there to trap Walsh. But I'm going to see if I have any way I can retrieve that skull. If I can't, I'll see if I can learn anything, do anything to bring me closer to catching Walsh before he kills again."

He met her gaze for a long moment, then glanced at her phone. "Pull up the damn e-mail."

She pushed the e-mail access. "It has to be Walsh. It's a map." She scanned it and handed it to Joe. "Somewhere near

Tahoe. No X marked the spot. He's probably going to contact us later."

"When he's sure you're going to meet his challenge," Joe said bitterly.

"I can't do anything else, Joe," she said.

"Do you think I don't realize that?" he asked as he took her elbow and led her toward the car. "I was sitting right there beside you today. Do you believe I wasn't sick to my stomach? I wanted to kill the son of a bitch by the time I jerked you away from that computer." He opened the car door for her. "So I'll take you to Walsh. I'll try to keep you safe while you get that reconstruction. But if there's a choice between getting the skull or taking out Walsh, it will be Walsh. I won't care if you can't bring Jenny home." He slammed the door and strode around to the driver's seat. "She'll have to be satisfied with my sending her killer straight to hell."

CHAPTER

9

He was coming.

He would be here soon.

Margaret sat absolutely still beside the creek, waiting. She was excited, she realized. Was there an element of fear with that excitement? Maybe. Strange. She was seldom afraid.

But everything she'd been feeling since she'd arrived in these woods was somehow . . . different.

He had stopped just beyond the trees. He was looking at her. Excitement again.

Don't let him see it. "Are you going to stand there and gape at me? I promise I don't have any explosives strapped to me to-night, either, Nalchek."

"How do I know that?" He came toward her. "You're an unknown quantity. Eve may trust you, but I don't." He stopped a few yards from where she sat. "And I don't know how she can trust you, either, with what little she knows about you."

Margaret chuckled. "We have a sort of history, and I was

able to help her when she needed me. That must count for something in the balance." She tilted her head. "Haven't you ever run into a situation that warranted a little faith in the face of suspicious circumstances?"

"No."

"I think you have." She studied him. He was all lean hardness, and his eyes were cool and intent. But there was a barely contained explosiveness beneath that restraint. She knew how strong he was, and she could sense that at the moment, he was barely able to stop himself from lashing out. "Maybe not lately. Why are you here, Nalchek?"

"Because you're here." He dropped to his knees beside her. "I could ask you the same thing. You know you shouldn't be in these woods."

"And how did you know I was here?"

"I assigned a man to watch the hotel and report if you left it."

"Why?"

"Because I wanted to keep my eye on you." He added roughly, "And you hitchhiked here again, dammit. How stupid can you get? That's inviting an attack."

"I'm a pretty good judge of character." She smiled. "And I can take care of myself."

"I didn't notice that last night."

"You surprised me. Besides, I knew right away that you were probably no threat."

"Then you were wrong. I am a threat to you."

She went still. The fear was back. Her gaze flew to his face. Then she relaxed. "You're bluffing. You just want to be in control. You wouldn't hurt me unless you had to." She paused. "But I'm surprised you would want me to believe it. I don't think it's what you'd ordinarily—" She nodded suddenly. "You want something from me, and you're not sure I'll give it to you. What is it?"

His expression didn't change. "What do you think I want?" He reached out and touched her cheek. "Yes, I do want to be in control. Why do you think I became sheriff?"

Her cheek was tingling beneath his fingers. She could feel a tightness in her chest. "Because you're one of the good guys?"

"How do you know? Oh, that's right, you're such a great judge of character." His hand moved down to cup her throat. "Bullshit, Margaret."

She could feel her pulse beating hard against his hand. It felt strange and rhythmic and completely sexual. "I am a good judge of character." She moistened her lips. "And you would never use your office to either hurt me or for sexual gratification. You're just angry or frustrated about something, and I'm handy to vent." She took his hand from her throat and leaned back. "And the fact that you can't put me in a convenient pigeonhole is making it worse." She met his gaze. "But I'm no one's whipping boy, so tell me why you're being an ass. What do you want from me?"

He stared at her for a moment. "I'm beginning to think of all kinds of things."

"Don't start that again. I'm not your type. You thought I was a college kid. You probably like them tall, leggy, and sophisticated. I'm not any of those things."

He smiled faintly. "No, you're not. But you're undoubtedly interesting."

"You're damn right." She got to her knees, her hands clenching into fists. "Why did you come looking for me? I'm sure it wasn't to make sure I made it safely here to the woods."

The corners of his lips deepened. "You look like you're going to take a swing at me."

"I'm tempted. I don't like being used."

"I didn't use you. Well, maybe a little."

"I don't like being manipulated, either."

He shrugged. "I only tried, I didn't succeed. I guess I didn't appeal to you."

He knew that wasn't true. That moment had been brimming with sexual tension, and Margaret was aware she was usually transparent as glass. "Why?"

His smile faded. "I'm tired as hell of being the outsider. This is my town, my case, and Eve would never have been involved with that little girl if I hadn't sent her the skull. Then she brings Quinn and you into it and leaves me out in the cold. That's not going to happen."

"She doesn't regard it as a competition. She's grateful for your help."

"As long as she calls the shots."

"You weren't this angry earlier today." Her eyes narrowed on his face. "What happened?"

"She phoned me from Sacramento and wanted to know Jenny's blood type. When I asked her why, she said she'd call me back."

"And she didn't do it?"

"No, and when I tried later, the call went to voice mail." He smiled crookedly. "So I decided I'd go and search for answers from someone else who belongs to the club."

"Me?" She shook her head. "I don't know why she'd want to know that. I haven't heard from Eve since she left the hotel." She frowned. "She doesn't want to involve me any more than

she has to, Nalchek. At least, she doesn't feel guilty about contacting you."

He didn't answer.

"Oh, for Pete's sake, she called you, didn't she? Why are
you being so possessive about the little girl in that grave?"

"Don't be ridiculous. It's my job."

"It's more than that," she whispered.

His gaze flew to her face. "More?" he repeated softly.

Fear again. Yet she had just said that she knew he wouldn't
hurt her. It didn't matter. Unreasonable or not, the fear was
here.

She braced herself to try to break through it. "Did you
know Jenny before she was killed, Nalchek?"

He was suddenly rigid. "What?" She could see he hadn't
expected that question and could sense the shock. "What the
hell do you mean?"

"It's a clear question, isn't it? Did you?"

"There's nothing clear about it. Are you asking me if I had
something to do with her murder?"

"No, but I'm asking you if you had reason to be so obsessive
about Jenny's death. Eve just accepted it because she's obsessive about her, too."

"But you don't accept it. And you're confronting me about
it while we're alone, and you couldn't be more vulnerable."
He leaned closer to her. "Which makes my point about the fact
that you're about as able to take care of yourself as the little child
in that grave."

"Stop it." She drew a deep breath. "Answer me. I'm not
going to back down and let you intimidate me. I stand by my
guns."

"Except you don't have a gun or any other weapon."

"I know karate and several varieties of street fighting." She glanced down at his holster. "And, besides, I'm sure you wouldn't shoot me. Did you know Jenny?"

He didn't answer for a moment. "Why would you think that? And don't give me that obsession bullshit."

"You're answering a question with a question. You first, Nalchek."

He gave a half shrug. "No, I did not know that child before I pulled her out of her grave. Did it occur to you that I went to a hell of a lot of trouble to find out her identity if I already knew who she was?"

"Yes, but it would seem the innocent thing to do, wouldn't it? I had to ask."

His brows rose. "And you believe me?"

She nodded. "But I had to hear you say it."

"Because you're such a great judge of character?" he said sarcastically. "And I passed the test?"

"You passed the test."

"If you had any suspicions about my having something to do with Jenny's death, you should know that I was still in Special Forces at that time and based in Afghanistan."

"I know," she said. "But that doesn't mean you might not have been in a position to— I understand your missions weren't entirely confined to Afghanistan. You're very clever, and you could have finagled something."

"Finagled? That's a fancy word for a good ole country boy like me."

She snorted. "A country boy who majored in mathematics at MIT and turned down two prestigious European scholarships to enlist in the army."

"Now how did you know that?"

"I dug. The same way that you probably went about trying to find out everything about me."

"But I have a number of investigative sources at my disposal."

"And I only have one. My friend, Kendra Michaels. But she has all kinds of friends in police and FBI circles. Though she did say that prying any information out of the military about you was like pulling teeth. Some of the things you did are still considered classified."

"And why did you put her to that trouble?"

"I had to be sure."

"But you're still not entirely sure, are you? Why? Why not accept me as I am? Why dig?"

"Tit for tat?" She made a face. "You're not going to like it."

"I can't say I liked much of what's transpired tonight," he said dryly. "Well, maybe a few things."

His hands on her throat that should have been a threat and became . . .

She veered quickly away from that memory. "I couldn't be sure of anything, so I had to check. There were questions about you . . ."

"What kind of questions? Who was asking them?"

She hesitated, then went for it. "Sajan."

His jaw dropped. "Oh, my God."

"I told you that you wouldn't like it."

"A coyote has questions about me?"

"Not exactly. You were just jumbled in with Walsh when I was melding with him." She stared him in the eye. "But it confused me. Because Walsh wasn't the only one searching in this forest. Sajan saw you, Nalchek. Not once, but many times."

"When? Anyone can tell you I've been practically living in this forest since we found Jenny."

"I didn't get the impression that's what Sajan meant. I believe it was before that."

"But you're not certain."

She shook her head. "But I believe in my instincts. I believe that I'm good at what I do. Sometimes that's all that I've had to hold on to."

He stared at her. "I could almost believe you, too." He grimaced. "What am I saying? Sorry, I refuse to be placed under suspicion by the blurred meanderings of your guardian coyote."

She suddenly grinned. "There wouldn't be any suspicion at all if you'd tell me the truth. Of course, I don't expect you to do that. You must have had an important reason to be in the woods—important to you, at least. And you would have told Eve if it wasn't confidential. I only wanted to know that you weren't involved in Jenny's death. That's all I care about."

"Is it?" He reached out and touched her cheek. "You're fairly incredible."

"That probably means you think I'm weird."

"A little." His hand dropped away from her face. "But a lot of people think I'm weird, too. It's usually a question of choices. I've made some pretty bad ones." He got up in one lithe movement. "But you're not old enough to have made many mistakes." He reached down and pulled her to her feet. "And I'm not about to let you start on my watch. No hitchhiking. I'll drive you back to your hotel."

"What if I'm not ready to go?"

"You're ready."

"How do you know?"

"I don't believe you were here communing with your coyote. I think you came out here because you knew I'd follow, and you wanted to talk to me." He shook his head. "Do you always take chances like that?"

"I have to trust myself," she said simply. "I don't have anyone else."

"Oh, shit. Now what am I supposed to say to that?"

"Nothing." She started toward the trees. "Now I know that you may have your own agenda, but you won't hurt Eve." She glanced back over her shoulder. "And if I hear from Eve, I'll call you and tell you." She smiled. "I won't leave you out in the cold, Nalchek. I know how painful that can be."

"Not painful, just annoying."

She turned and moved ahead of him. "Whatever . . ."

TAHOE

"Three miles ahead," Joe said as he turned the curve. "If he's going to contact us, it should be soon."

"Yes." Eve glanced out the window at the glittering waters below. Beautiful, she thought. Incredibly beautiful and remote from the ugliness of Walsh. She had thought all during the drive up here to the mountains that this entire countryside was filled with glamour and breathless beauty. Yet she knew that Walsh saw only the trap he was setting for them. "Do you suppose he's watching us?"

"Probably. He'd have a good view from anywhere along those cliffs." He didn't look at her. "Opt out. Let me go it alone."

She didn't answer.

"Eve."

"I'm the one who should be saying that. I knew that was

what you had in mind when you insisted on stopping at that army surplus store on the way."

"Walsh is a professional, and he's bringing us to fairly wild country. I need to be prepared."

"See, it's all about you. Look, I'm the one Walsh wants. I'm willing to take a chance to get that reconstruction, but that chance doesn't include you, Joe."

"Then we won't take a chance." He smiled recklessly. "I'll make certain that it's a sure thing." He suddenly pulled around a curve and far over to the inside of the mountain. "And we'd better start now." He cut the engine. "Get out. This car is too much of a target."

Eve was already out of the car. "You're right." She moved over to the brush and pine trees bordering the road. "But I'm interested to know how you intend to—"

Her phone rang. "Walsh."

"Why did you stop?" Walsh asked mockingly when she picked up. "And I thought you were so eager to see me."

"You can't have it all your own way, Walsh," she said. "We're not going to blindly follow your orders as if you're some kind of Pied Piper."

He chuckled. "Funny that you made that comparison. You do know that the Pied Piper was paid to lead those creatures from the village to drown in the river. Don't you think that this magnificent lake is so much more impressive?"

"Joe and I have no intention of being your victims, Walsh."

"But you may have no choice, Eve. You've proved to be far too persistent, and you've attracted the attention of my employer. I was intending to dispose of you anyway, but now I have a direct order."

"From whom? If you're so certain that you'll be able to get rid of us, you shouldn't mind satisfying my curiosity."

"I'm not that arrogant. Nor that stupid. There's a possibility that you might slip away this time. Not a great possibility, but it does exist."

"Then tell me where I can find the reconstruction."

"You're almost there. Go another mile or two and look down the cliff. I've even been considerate enough to put a few Coleman lanterns to light your way."

"And make certain that we can be seen if we make the attempt."

"There is no if. You want it too much. You'll think that you can find a way. Tell me, is it really the idea of bringing that poor child home, or is it that you're more arrogant than even I've ever dreamed of being."

"Or is it that Jenny wants you dead and in hell and has picked me to send you there."

There was silence, and when he finally spoke, his voice was harsh. "The dead don't have power. I have the power just as I did when I killed the bitch. Now go find her skull before I blow it into a thousand pieces." He hung up.

"I believe you struck a nerve," Joe murmured.

"Or Jenny did." She slipped her phone back in her pocket. "What next?"

"We move." He went to the trunk and started pulling out the equipment he'd picked up on the way out of Sacramento. He put on the backpack. "On foot. And I lead."

"No argument." She fell in behind him. "Your qualifications as a SEAL far outweigh mine in this area. Just don't try to leave me behind."

He didn't answer as he moved up into the trees at the side
of the road.

One mile . . .

Bright moonlight on the lake below but only darkness here
in the trees.

Joe was moving fast, smoothly, every step springy and cat-
like. He was making no allowances for her, but then he never
did when he was on the hunt. He trusted her to keep up with
him and not hold him back.

"I see a light," he whispered as he stopped on the ridge ahead.
He fell to his knees and took out his infrared binoculars. "But
it could be only a decoy. Let's take a look . . ."

"Walsh said another couple miles." Eve knelt beside him.
"Why would he lie about—" She stopped. Why was she questioning why Walsh would do anything? You couldn't have any
expectations about that murderer. You couldn't believe anything he said. "Maybe he wanted to catch us off guard?"

Joe didn't answer as his gaze raked the surrounding terrain,
then he trained the binoculars on the steep, jutting cliff ahead.
"The light's being cast up from that cliff. But I don't have a
view of where it's coming from. I have to get closer." He was
rising to a half crouch. "Stay here."

"The hell I will." She drew her gun and crawled after him.
"Look, we see where he's setting up his trap, but if it appears
too dangerous we don't go for it. Okay?"

Joe didn't answer.

"Joe."

"You want that reconstruction."

"I want you alive. I'll find another way to get the skull."

"Not if he blows it up." He pulled himself onto a boulder.

"And, besides, the bastard annoyed me. He's too sure of himself."

She felt a chill as she recognized that tone. There was no one more competitive or deadly than Joe when he was zeroing in on the prey. "Maybe because he's holding the best hand right now."

"Possibly." He'd lifted the binoculars to his eyes again. "But there's almost always a way to get around that— There it is!"

Her gaze flew down the sheer face of the cliff to where he was staring.

A shallow ledge only twenty feet above the lake.

Two large Coleman lanterns illuminating an object sitting between them.

"What is it?" Her fingers dug into Joe's arm. "Was he lying?"

He handed her the binoculars. "See for yourself."

She raised the binoculars and focused.

At first she couldn't make out the shadowy object because of the brilliance of the light blurring everything around the lanterns. Then, as her eyes became accustomed to the light, she began to see details.

Familiar details. Winged brows, high cheekbones, pointed chin.

Jenny.

"It's her, isn't it?" Joe asked. "I only saw the completed reconstruction for a few minutes, but she has a face to remember."

She nodded. "It's Jenny. He didn't destroy the skull."

"Yet," Joe qualified. "But he has her set up as a target." He paused. "I think we'd better go get her."

"No!" She drew a deep breath. "How could we get down that cliff? There's only that single winding road, and once we reach the ledge, we'd be the targets Walsh planned. I told you that if it was too dangerous, I didn't want to make the attempt."

Joe was staring thoughtfully down at the road leading to the ledge. "He'd expect me to go down that road. I'd bet he's positioned himself to take the shot." His eyes lifted and slowly traveled over the terrain. "Probably in those boulders near the road. Or maybe in those pine trees about ten feet down the slope of the cliff." He tilted his head. "I'd bet on the pine trees and go down and take him out. But I can't do that because if I guess wrong, he might have time to destroy Jenny's reconstruction. Pity."

"Don't even think about it."

He smiled. "I won't. Because there's probably another way." He took out his phone and quickly punched in a topographical site. "He's expecting us to knock on the front door. But that would be boring, wouldn't it?" He smiled as he found what he was looking for. "That cliff juts out and then back in a few miles away from here. That side of the cliff doesn't appear to have another road and no ledges, but if I can make it around or under that ledge from the other side, I might be able to snatch and grab."

"It's not worth it." She moistened her lips. "Do you think that I could stand the thought of your dangling over that lake and risking getting shot just to get that skull for me? No way."

"Not just for the skull," he said quietly. "Not just for you, Eve. Maybe if I hadn't spent most of the day looking at the photos of Walsh's victims, you might have been able to convince me. But I don't think we can let Walsh win even one battle from now on."

She wasn't going to be able to persuade him, and it was scaring her to death. "Don't do this, Joe. Dammit, if you don't care about the risk to yourself, think about what you're doing to me. How do you think I'll feel knowing it will be my fault if anything happens to you?"

"I'll just have to make sure nothing does." He kissed her lightly on the forehead. "Stop trying to give me a guilt trip. Because you're right, everything that happens to me is because of you. I chose that path a long time ago, and I wouldn't have it any other way." He turned away. "But it's always my choice, Eve."

"We were only supposed to explore the possibilities," she said desperately.

"That's what we're doing. You stay here and keep an eye on that reconstruction and any move from Walsh." He handed her the binoculars. "If you can manage to kill the bastard, that would be fine, too. I'll go and explore the possibility of stealing Jenny away from him."

"It's only a skull, Joe. Jenny is dead."

He slanted her a smile over his shoulder. "Not to you, love."

He disappeared into the trees.

Shit. Shit. Shit.

Her nails bit into her palms as she stared blindly into the pines.

She wanted to run after him. She wanted to shout and pound her hands on the ground.

What good would that do? Only an exercise in frustration. Once Joe made up his mind, he wouldn't budge. All she could do was stay here in an agony of desperation and try to help however she could. Which meant do what Joe had said and watch and wait until she had an opportunity to move more actively.

If you can kill the bastard, that would be fine, too.

Yes, it would, and she had no doubt she would do it if given the opportunity, she thought fiercely. She hated violence, but Walsh was a monster, and that monster was a threat to Joe. Her hand instinctively closed on her gun. Then she forced herself to release it.

She wouldn't be able to do anything to help unless she located Walsh. Joe was vulnerable, and so was she as long as Walsh was hovering over them like a threatening cloud.

Find him.

Neutralize.

Or destroy.

Find.

Joe had said either that clump of boulders or the pine trees on the slope.

Find out which one.

She started to move slowly toward the boulders.

Joe moved through the foliage, bending and contorting his body almost as if by instinct. His SEAL combat training taught him to move stealthily. The brush around him barely moved as he made his way up the steep hill.

He glanced back. Eve hadn't been happy to be left behind, and knowing her, she was already taking a position to give him cover. He'd practically given her marching orders by pointing out the boulders and the row of young pines, but there were actually a half dozen other places where Walsh could be hiding.

Let me handle this, Eve. It's what I do.

And he couldn't deny the hunt was stirring all the adrenaline and excitement that it always did.

He half smiled as his pace increased. What was he thinking? Eve was going to do whatever the hell she wanted. Exasperating, yes, but also why he loved her so damn much.

Okay, Eve. That's how we'll play it. You've got my back, and I've got yours, just like always.

With certain limits . . .

He crouched and looked up at the reconstructed skull in the distance. He'd seen literally hundreds of Eve's reconstructions, but there was something so luminous, so lifelike, about this one that it gave him an eerie feeling to see the disembodied head apparently floating over the hillside.

We're coming to get you, Jenny. Eve wants to bring you home.

Joe glanced around as he slowly pushed ahead. Someone had been on this path. Recently. Leaves had been freshly torn from bushes, and several branches were bent away from the others. It had clearly been a one-way journey toward the plateau but not back. He'd have to be careful; that could be a sign of possible—

Sproing.

Joe froze. The sound was almost imperceptible but unmistakable.

He looked down and saw, beneath his left foot, a familiar, oval-shaped outline.

Shit.

He'd just stepped on the triggering pedal of a Dieter land mine.

Great. Just great.

He remembered "skill with explosives" had been on Walsh's résumé that he'd been sent by Interpol. Evidently the bastard had made careful preparations for his trap.

The triggering device had been buried on the trail. Now, if he lifted his foot, he'd be blown to bits.

There was movement up ahead, in the brush. Dammit. He was a sitting duck.

The movements drew closer. Joe crouched, keeping his foot planted squarely on the triggering pedal. He drew his Winkler field knife from its sheaf and angled himself toward the sound.

Come and get me, you sick son of a bitch. I'll be ready for whatever you're dishing out.

Not at the boulders.

Her heart was pounding as she drew back from the moss-covered rocks and moved back toward the road.

But that didn't mean that he might not have been there and moved on.

It didn't mean that he couldn't be anywhere in the darkness.

She jumped as her phone vibrated.

Walsh.

"Where are you, Eve?" he asked mockingly. "You've been too quiet. Did I discourage you? I have to admit that it's a challenge that would intimidate most people."

"It's a trap, not a challenge. We both know that." She paused. "And neither Joe nor I are foolish enough to walk into it. Did you really believe we would?"

"Oh, yes. I still believe it. Why do you think I arranged the bait with such care? I had to make sure you could see all the fine details you'd installed in that reconstruction. Such a pity to have it blown to bits and sunk into that icy water. What do you think the chances are that you'd ever be able to retrieve it?"

"Science is a wonderful thing. There's a possibility."

"You're bluffing. You haven't given up. You're probably frantically plotting with your lover about how you're going to manage to get the best of me." He added softly, "I'll give you another forty-five minutes to study your handiwork and decide whether you're going to make a try at it. After that, I'm done. I'll destroy it as I intended to do in the beginning."

"And why didn't you do that, Walsh?"

Silence. "I didn't get around to it."

"Really? Then maybe it was fate," she said mockingly. "Maybe you were never meant to have it. You don't seem to have handled it very professionally since the moment you killed that poor FedEx driver in Georgia."

"That's a lie," he said harshly. "There's no one more professional than I am. I tell you, I just didn't get around to it." He changed the subject. "Forty-five minutes, and you'll see all your work vanish as if it had never been." He hung up.

Forty-five minutes.

She almost wished that Walsh would destroy the skull now.

If Joe heard the shot, then he'd know there was no reason to go after that reconstruction. He would be safe.

But she couldn't rely on wishes. Don't think about what Joe was doing.

Think about what she could do to make him safer.

She quickly dialed Nalchek. "I need your help." She quickly gave him the location. "Walsh is here. I don't know how much time we have."

"Not my jurisdiction. I'll have to—"

"I don't care. Get someone up here." She hung up.

Now find Walsh.

•   •   •

Joe cocked his head, listening for the rustling brush. The sounds had stopped. Whatever or whoever it was was only fifteen feet away, maybe twenty. Had he been spotted?

Doubtful.

But he couldn't stay here, that was for sure. The bomb beneath his left foot clearly put him at a serious tactical disadvantage.

Understatement.

He looked down at the half-buried mine. He knew what he had to do, but it wasn't going to be easy. Shit.

He jabbed his knife into the ground beside him and grabbed the short blade from his ankle scabbard. He'd been taught a trick that might work, but, of course, his teacher had been missing his right arm and half his face, Joe remembered ruefully. From a mine a hell of a lot less powerful than this one.

Joe thrust his hand into the soft earth and moved his fingers underneath the mine. He stretched his thumb over the top triggering pedal and gripped its muddy surface next to his boot. It was slick and wet, and the spring pushed against his clenched fingers.

One slip, and he was a dead man.

Joe slowly, carefully raised his foot, eyeing the triggering pedal to make sure that it remained in place beneath his thumb.

His foot was free. Now for the tricky part.

He pulled the mine from the damp earth, wincing as his thumb slid over the slippery pedal. He looked at the mine for a moment, keeping it at arm's length from his face. As if that would help if it exploded. The temptation was strong to just throw the damned thing, but there would be only a second between release and the deadly blast.

And it was probably how his old instructor had lost half his face. No, he had to take care of this another way. Joe slowly turned over the mud-encrusted explosive device and looked at its underside. The top half fit cleanly over the bottom, almost like an oval-shaped shell. A thin ridge separated the two parts, a ridge just wide enough for . . .

Joe looked at the short blade in his left hand. It *seemed* about right. He'd know soon enough.

He slowly loosened his grip on the mine. The spring-tensioned top half rose slightly . . .

He stopped. Hopefully, the thicker part of his blade would catch and keep it from rising any more. He probably had only a few more millimeters to play with.

He loosened his grip even more.

It didn't move. The wedge was holding.

He held his breath.

So far, so good. Here goes nothing . . .

One . . . two . . . three!

He let go.

And the pedal held in place.

He let out his breath. He cradled the mine in both hands. He bent over and carefully, gently, placed it on a large rock.

He backed away and moved toward a denser area of brush. Climbing would be harder this way, but less likely to yield another nasty surprise.

He wiped his brow and realized that his face and hair were soaked with perspiration. As he slid through the brush, he looked up at the reconstructed skull, still glowing in the lights trained on it. What other traps did Walsh have waiting for him up there? It wouldn't take much, of course. A rifle scope and a decent perch would do the trick. But the psycho had also shown an affinity for explosive booby traps.

So . . . How to get that reconstruction without getting shot or blown up?

Joe stopped. There might be one way to pull it off.

He shrugged off his backpack, unzipped it, and pulled out a thin, plastic bag. He tore into the bag and unfolded a six-by-six piece of mosquito netting. Joe pulled it taut between his hands. Thin, light, and reasonably strong. He put it on the ground and surveyed the trees around him. He unsheathed his knife and sliced off two thin branches, each about eight feet long. After a quick pruning, he attached the netting between the branches with wire from his backpack.

He held the two branches in his hands and practiced twisting and turning them for a moment. Not the most ideal contraption, but it could work.

He unholstered his gun and turned toward the reconstructed skull on the hillside. He'd have to get as close to it as he could while still maintaining a line of sight to the rock with the rigged land mine. This would require a near-perfect aim and split-second timing.

And a little bit of luck.

CHAPTER

10

Eve crouched low as she moved through the bushes, muttering a curse as every step crunched and crackled. If only she could move through the woods as silently as Joe. With all the racket she was making, how could Walsh *not* know she was coming?

She stopped, looking up at the reconstruction. Where would Walsh go to keep watch over his prize? Her eyes darted around the area. If it were she, where would she go? She looked up.

Of course.

A tree.

But which one? There were hundreds. Thousands. But she could immediately discount many of the smaller trees, and the ones without low-hanging branches to provide an easy foot-hold for climbing.

That still left a sizeable—

Boom.

An explosion rocked the woods, just a hundred yards west of her.

Joe!

Her head jerked toward the blast, which momentarily lit up the night sky. Oh God, Joe had been heading in that direction. Had he run straight into Walsh's trap?

Maybe not, she prayed. There was a chance—

She had turned back toward the reconstructed skull.

The skull was gone!

It was like some kind of magic trick. It had been there just moments before, and now the two battery lanterns were aimed at . . .

Nothing.

Absolutely nothing.

She smiled.

Joe.

Walsh stared in disbelief at the spot where the skull had just been. The land-mine explosion had practically knocked him out of the tree, and by the time he recovered, Eve's reconstruction had vanished.

There were two paths up there, and he'd secured both with explosive booby traps. And if anyone tried another route to the skull, he was ready with his rifle.

Except in the few moments after the land mine exploded behind him. Dammit. Had Eve or Quinn used his own explosive as a distraction?

Very clever, but it wouldn't make any difference. Eve Duncan wasn't leaving this forest alive.

Walsh slung his rifle over his shoulder, and he jumped to the ground.

•   •   •

Success!

Under the cover of darkness and the thick underbrush, Joe yanked his mosquito netting free of the two branches and wrapped it around the reconstructed skull. He'd been taught to fashion his mosquito net to capture small game in survival situations, but he'd never thought he'd one day use it to snag a human skull.

Thanks, SEAL Training Sgt. Peter Fallon, USN.

He'd dislodged the short blade from the mine with a single bullet, which bought him just enough time for a long-reach grab for the skull.

Joe bundled it under his arm and ran through the woods, dodging the obvious paths that might hold even more booby traps. After a few minutes, his phone buzzed in his pocket. Without breaking stride he glanced at the display. Eve.

He answered. "I have the skull."

"Good." Walsh replied. "And I have Eve."

Joe stopped. "Walsh."

"Oh, yes. And you also know there's only one way I could have Eve's phone."

"Walsh," Joe said slowly and precisely. "If you've hurt her, I will kill you in the most painful way imaginable."

"Such violence. Joe Quinn the caveman, swinging his club to protect his mate . . . Does that kind of thing still work in this day and age?"

"Put her on the phone. Now."

"So demanding . . . Especially when I'm holding all the cards."

"Now."

Eve's voice cut in quickly. "Joe, take the skull and get the hell away from—"

She was abruptly cut off, and Joe heard what he was sure was the sound of a blow being struck. Walsh returned on the phone. "I never bluff, Quinn. I don't need to."

Joe looked toward the ridge where he'd last seen Eve. She had to be somewhere near there. He started moving as he spoke into the phone. "Then what do you want?"

"You're holding it. Bring that skull back to me."

"And you'll let Eve go?"

"We'll negotiate."

"Why in the hell should I believe you? You already had the skull before this night ever began."

"Conditions change. You brought about that change. Well done, by the way."

"We've both been trained in the same school. If you hurt her, I'll show you why I graduated cum laude."

"You're quite capable. I get that. Bring me the skull, and we'll talk."

Eve's voice cut in again, this time in the background. "Joe, don't! Get out of here."

He pulled the phone away from his ear, but he didn't hear Eve's voice in the open air. They had to be farther away than he thought. He quickened his pace.

Walsh's voice was muffled for a moment as he said something to Eve. Then he returned. "I suggest you do as I say, Quinn. Eve is starting to annoy me."

"Where do I bring it?"

"There's a small clearing just on the other side of the ridge."

"You'll be there?"

"Where I'd make myself a target? Be serious. But that's where I want you to be. We'll be close enough to see you. Do as I say, and you'll see Eve."

"I'd better see her unharmed. I'm warning you."

"What happens to Eve in the next fifteen minutes entirely depends on you. Do as I say, Quinn."

Walsh cut the connection.

"If you want to live through the night, you'll let me go," Eve said quietly. "You don't know who you're dealing with. Joe is in his element out here."

Walsh tugged on her nylon wrist restraints as he pulled her through the woods. "You have a high opinion of your Joe Quinn."

"It's well-founded."

"Your faith in him is touching. He was lucky. I'm better than he is. Look who's on top now."

"For the moment." Eve studied Walsh, looking for weakness, as he pulled her around a clump of bushes. He held his handgun high in his right hand, and he used his left hand to guide her. "But all you've proved so far is that you were able to overcome me, and that was only because you took me by surprise." He was very good. He'd appeared out of nowhere with a gun leveled at her head. A complete shock.

And, if they couldn't find a way out, in a few moments, he'd have Joe and the skull.

"You were easy. A woman who sculpts faces on skulls? Though you did do an amazing job with reconstruction," Walsh said. "You brought that little girl back."

"No. There's no coming back from what you did to her."

A range of emotions suddenly played across Walsh's face. Eve tried to decipher the expressions. Doubt. Fear. Anger. Was that a weakness? Probe a little and try to find out.

"Jenny had her entire life ahead of her," Eve said.

"How do you know that's her name?" Walsh snapped.

"That is her name, isn't it?"

He was silent.

Eve smiled. "She told me."

"Bullshit."

"Believe what you want. I know the truth."

And he knew it, too, Eve realized. Jenny had definitely reached out to him.

"We'll wait here." He stopped and pointed through the trees at a clearing. "That's where your Joe Quinn will be meeting us. Don't make a sound, Eve, and it may be over soon, with a minimum of pain for you."

In less than five minutes, Joe appeared in the clearing. He was holding the bundle under his arm. Run, take the skull, and get the hell out of here, she wanted to tell him. But she had said it all before, and he wouldn't do it now any more than he had then.

Joe looked around. "Walsh?" he called out.

Walsh responded, still in the cover of the surrounding trees. "Put the skull down, Quinn. And take the gun from your holster and throw it into the woods."

"Let me see Eve."

Walsh nudged her.

She called out. "I'm here, Joe."

Joe tossed his gun, then rested the mosquito-net-wrapped bundle on the ground. He stepped back. "Here's what you wanted. Now let her go."

Bam.

Walsh fired his gun, and Joe went down.

Joe!

Blood spurted from his right side. He rolled over and looked up at Eve.

Walsh stepped forward. "So sorry, Quinn. But Eve here has been selling you as quite the formidable opponent. I couldn't take the chance."

Eve tried to run to Joe, but Walsh held her back.

"He can still survive, but you need to be smart, Eve. I promise you, my next bullet will finish him."

She whirled back toward him, her eyes glistening. "He did everything you asked," she said fiercely.

"That remains to be seen. Open the package for me, Eve. Let's see your creation."

Eve turned toward Joe. He was doubled over on the ground, pale and in pain. She wanted to run to him.

Walsh shoved her toward the package. "You're wasting time."

Eve knelt on the ground, just feet away from where Joe lay. She pulled away the mosquito netting and froze. She looked up and locked eyes with Joe.

"Well?" Walsh said.

Eve turned and raised the reconstructed skull in Walsh's direction.

He lowered his gun and stepped toward her, his gaze fixed on the skull. He had that odd expression on his face again.

Fear. Awe. Anger.

Eve slowly reached down into the folds of netting and picked up the present Joe had hidden for her there.

His 9mm Beretta.

She gripped the handle and whirled around, firing at Walsh.

The first shot hit him in the shoulder. His gun flew from his hand.

The second shot grazed his temple.

Walsh screamed in pain and ran into the woods.

Eve kept firing until the cartridge was empty. She grabbed Walsh's gun and turned back toward Joe. "I need you to walk. Can you do that for me?"

He shook his head, and whispered, "Go. Run."

"No way. Not without you." She linked her arms underneath his and dragged him out of the clearing.

His eyes fluttered. She was losing him.

She tore off her overshirt and pressed it against his wound. "Hold this here. I've called Nalchek. He should have been here by now."

She punched the number. The buttons became sticky with blood. Joe's blood.

"Nalchek," he answered.

"Where the hell are you? Joe's been shot. We need help *now*."

"You'll get it. The police helicopters are on their way."

She cut the connection and turned back toward Joe.

She fell to her knees beside him.

Blood.

Staining his shirt. So much blood.

"They're coming, Joe. He said the helicopters are on their way."

"I think . . . I hear them."

So did Eve, but so far away.

"It's okay," he whispered. "Shh, it's okay, Eve."

"It's not okay," she said brokenly. "Dammit, he shot you."

She was frantically searching for the source of the blood. "You shouldn't have done it. Not any of it. And you stood out there and let him shoot you."

"Knew it wouldn't be . . . a kill shot if . . . he wasn't sure he had the skull."

"You didn't know, you took the chance. And you took a chance he'd have me unwrap the skull."

"It would have been . . . hard for him to unwrap it and keep an eye . . . on both of us. Reasonable . . ."

"There wasn't anything reasonable about it. You shouldn't have done it. We should have left when I asked you to do it. I told you that reconstruction wasn't important. Not in comparison to—" The wound was in the upper right chest.

How deep?

Don't think about it. Just stop it.

She applied pressure. "Keep breathing. Don't go to sleep. I'm going to keep you with me, Joe. There's no way I'll let you slip away."

"Yes, ma'am." His smile was faint, and so was his voice. "You bet you won't. Gone through too much together . . . Wouldn't let a scumbag like Walsh get between . . ."

"Just hold on. Those helicopters are closer, almost on top of us. They should— Joe!" His eyes were closing. "Don't do that!"

"I won't let you down. Promise. Just for a little while . . ."

He was unconscious.

But not dead, she thought frantically. She could feel the beat of his heart beneath her hand. He was alive, and he'd stay alive.

She wouldn't let him go.

• • •

Son of a bitch.

Walsh's foot slammed down on the accelerator, and the car jumped forward.

He could feel the blood trickling down his cheek and the searing sting from the bullet Eve Duncan had fired at him. An inch more, and the bitch would have blown his head off.

She had taunted him and gotten in his way, then had almost killed him.

The rage was tearing through him. It wasn't enough that he had, at last, probably taken down Joe Quinn. He had to have Eve Duncan. He had to show her how superior he was to her. He wanted to crush her, destroy everyone she cared about, then show her how much pain he could inflict.

Die.

She had to die.

In the most agonizing way possible.

CALIFORNIA PACIFIC MEDICAL CENTER
SAN FRANCISCO, CALIFORNIA

"You look . . . beautiful," Joe said.

Eve opened her eyes and leaned forward in her chair toward the hospital bed. "Awake at last? You must still be woozy from the anesthesia if you think that." She took his hand. "The surgeon said that the operation went very well, and you're definitely out of danger. How do you feel?"

"You are beautiful. More . . . beautiful than usual."

She chuckled. "I've already addressed that comment. No one but you would ever think I'm anything but interesting-looking, and it's so dim in here, I'm sure you can barely see me. Now let's talk about—"

"Interesting is beautiful." He smiled. "And I can see you well enough to see your strength and the way you hold your head and the set of your lips. I think I was dreaming about you before I came around, and you defied every expectation. You always defy expectations."

"Bullshit." But even recovering from surgery, Joe was behaving oddly. "What is this all about, Joe?"

He chuckled. "How suspicious. Every word is true."

"And?"

"Maybe I wanted to distract you a little from agonizing over this wound that's causing me a few problems. When I opened my eyes, I could see all the strain and the edginess."

"A few problems?" she said harshly. "You were out of control. You could have been killed."

"But I wasn't, thanks to your very nice shooting that put Walsh on the run." He tilted his head. "Of course, I was being exceptionally skillful myself, but I have to admit you saved the day."

"I don't care about saving the day." Her hand tightened on his, her voice uneven. "I only care about you. I could *hit* you. Don't you ever do that again. I told you that we weren't going to take any chances. Yet you strode off like some kind of Gary Cooper wannabe gunning for your own personal *High Noon*."

"Not entirely personal. You wanted the skull."

"It was personal," she said fiercely. "You've told me that everything between us is personal. I know that, but I can't stand the thought of your risking—" She broke off and drew an uneven breath. "And you can't tell me that you didn't want to try to take Walsh down. You didn't care about the risk."

"Wrong," he said quietly. "I wouldn't have risked leaving you alone with Walsh out there. I would have pulled back if I hadn't thought I could do it." He lifted her palm to his lips. "And I did do it, didn't I? Or rather, we did it. Was there any damage to the reconstruction?"

"A little. But it won't take me more than a few hours to repair it." She leaned closer. "But I don't want to talk about the skull. I want to talk about promises. I can't stand the thought of this happening again. I want your word that you won't—" She stopped. He was shaking his head. "Joe, dammit."

"You won't get it. Why are you even trying? This is who I am. Every bit of me belongs to you, but I can't change who that person is." His hand tightened on her own. "Hey, do you think that I don't want to run your life so that you'll be safe forever? Sometimes I try to do it. But I'm never going to ask you to be someone else because sometimes I get scared. I'll just work around it."

As he'd done when he'd tried to convince her not to go to Tahoe. He'd accepted, then applied every ounce of his intelligence and strength to make the decision work for him. She was silent, gazing at him. "Like you did tonight."

"Yep. But that's not so bad. We've done pretty well so far."

All the years, all the love. "So far . . . But tonight it almost crashed and burned." She stood up and leaned forward to kiss him. "I'll be back soon. I'll go and tell the head nurse that you're awake."

"Fine. When am I being released?"

He wasn't going to like this. "The doctor will be in later, but he's going to err on the side of caution. He said the earliest will be four or five days."

"Bullshit," he said flatly.

"Talk to him. The surgery wasn't all that easy. He said if you rip those stitches before they're healed, you could bleed to death." She heard him mutter a curse before she hurried from the room. "I'll see you later."

"How is he doing?"

Eve turned away from the nurses' station to see Nalchek walking down the hall toward her. "Not bad. Could be a lot better. But I'll take it. Unfortunately, Joe isn't likely to agree. They're going to have to fight to keep him here for more than a day or two. He's stubborn as hell."

"I got that impression." He glanced down the hall at Joe's room. "And damn tough. The Nevada PD said he pulled off an amazing stunt out there."

"He's always amazing." And strong, and smart, and more complex than anyone would dream. "And I've got to figure a way to keep him from bolting out of here."

"I could ask the PD to find a minor crime with which to charge him." He made a face. "But I don't want Quinn for an enemy. I don't believe he's one to forgive and forget."

"No way. My problem." She turned to look at him. "Any news about Walsh?"

"Nothing good. They found an abandoned rental car on the shore a few miles away, and forensics is going over it. He probably had a speedboat waiting."

"I'm grateful for your responding to my SOS and getting us out of those mountains. Thank you, Nalchek."

"I'd say you're welcome, but I'm still pissed off that you didn't involve me in the beginning," he said grimly. "It might have turned out differently if I'd been there for backup."

"We were playing it by ear."

"And leaving me out."

"Yes. We didn't know what to expect."

"That's not going to happen again," he said grimly. "You owe me. I want to know everything you know about Walsh."

He was right, they did owe him. "I didn't mean to exclude you. It just . . . happened." She quickly filled him in on everything they'd learned or suspected about Walsh. "I agree that we have to share information. It's only sensible."

His lips twisted. "But you and Quinn are so close that you practically finish each other's sentences. I can *see* it. I'll have to watch you like a hawk to keep you from doing it to me again." He met her gaze. "You need me. I should have been there for you. You'll notice you didn't seem to do too well if that—"

"Maybe not," she interrupted. "We lost Walsh. But we got the reconstruction."

"So you told me when you phoned. Where is it?"

"In a canvas bag at the administration office. I left it there when they checked Joe into ER."

"I want it. Let's go down and get it."

"Not yet. I have to make a few minor repairs. Then I'll hand it over." She rubbed her temple. "Then I have to call Margaret. She has a right to know what's happening."

"I already called her."

She glanced at him in surprise. "You did?"

"After we knew Quinn wasn't going to die. I thought you'd want her to know."

She nodded. "Thank you."

"She said she'd be at the hospital as soon as you let her know you need her." His lips twisted. "She's probably planning on hitchhiking. I'll see that she has a ride."

"You're being very cooperative."

"Haven't you heard? Margaret says I'm one of the good guys. Not with sterling qualifications, and I could fall from grace at any moment." He shrugged. "So I have to work on keeping on her good side. She might set her coyote on me."

"I doubt it."

"I don't doubt anything about what she might do. She's one of a kind, and I'm not certain what kind." He changed the subject. "How quick can you manage to repair that skull?"

"I should have her finished by this afternoon." She paused. "But I want to know what news sources you're going to go to with the reconstruction."

"You don't trust me?"

"I didn't say that. But I lost her once. I don't want that to happen again. I want to be able to control the distribution of her photo."

"I suppose I shouldn't be surprised if you're being proprietary, but might I remind you that I'm the one who sent Jenny to you." His gaze narrowed on her face. "You didn't by any chance get a call from Margaret since you've been here at the hospital?"

"What?" She gazed at him in bewilderment. "I don't know what you're talking about. You're the one who told Margaret about Joe."

He nodded curtly. "Just a thought. Margaret and I haven't been on the best of terms since we met. You were prepared to trust me before."

"Trust has nothing to do with it. I'd just feel better to be involved all the way through the process."

"I could confiscate the skull."

"Yes, you could. But then you'd have me on your back instead of by your side. You don't want that."

He didn't speak for a moment. "No, I don't." He turned

away. "Let me know where you'll be working, and I'll be there to pick it up this afternoon."

She had a thought. "Come here. I'll try to get permission to do the repairs here in Joe's room. I want to keep an eye on him, and it might make him a little more complacent if I'm with him, and he feels part of the process." She added ruefully, "Complacent? That term doesn't apply to Joe in any sense of the word. Oh, well, I'll have to do what I can."

"And that appears to be pretty impressive." He paused at the elevator. "I'll give the hospital administration a call and rattle off your credentials so that they won't give you trouble about bringing a skull onto the floor. Sometimes they can be a little touchy about things like that."

"I can do that myself."

"You're shutting me out again." He punched the button. "I'm law enforcement. Use me."

She shrugged. "I'm accustomed to doing everything for myself. No offense."

"None taken." He got on the elevator. "And I'll let you tag along with me when I take the skull to a few reporters with whom I've had good luck. You might be an asset."

"Thank you. I can't tell you how I appreciate your cooperation," she said with gentle sarcasm.

"Now you know how I've been feeling."

Before she could answer, the elevator doors closed.

She wrinkled her nose as she turned away. It was clear she hadn't handled Nalchek with any great degree of diplomacy and had managed to annoy him.

Too bad. She respected and admired him but she couldn't please everyone, and the main issue was to get Walsh before he could kill again. But he was right, it was time to use him.

But not right now. She wearily rubbed the back of her neck. She would call and arrange for her supplies to be sent to the hospital. Then she would beg a bed for the next few hours and sleep before she started to work.

But first she would go back to Joe and fill him in on the current plan and try to make it as palatable as possible for him. It would not be easy. As she had told Nalchek, Joe did not forgive and forget. He would have planned to go after Walsh even if he had not been shot. Now he would be totally relentless.

And that's what she must be until she managed to stop Walsh. She might have only a few days before Joe was on the hunt again, and he was hurt and vulnerable. Yes, she would use Nalchek and anyone else to find Walsh before Joe had to face him again.

He's dead, you bitch. And you'll be dead, too. You can't stop me.

The hell I can't. Watch me.

"Quite a setup." Nalchek was standing in the doorway of Joe's room, his gaze on Eve, who was standing at a makeshift stand across the room, working on Jenny's reconstruction. "Is she much worse for wear? She doesn't look it. That sketch you drew looks just like her."

"Not much damage." She shook her head at Joe. "He took better care of her than he did himself."

"I wasn't about to let it be destroyed," Joe said as he glanced at Nalchek. "I suppose I owe you thanks for the way you responded to Eve's call. You got those police helicopters out to us with amazing speed, considering that they were out of your jurisdiction. I know how difficult it can be bridging the red tape when it's not your own guys."

Nalchek shrugged. "I've made it a point since I became sheriff to establish friendly relationships with other police departments both statewide and in close neighboring states. You can never tell when you're going to need a favor."

"You must have done a good job. I was impressed."

"But they didn't snag Walsh."

"No, but we'll get him. That bastard isn't going to take anything from us ever again."

"Sounds good." Nalchek smiled at Eve. "Don't worry, I'll keep an eye on both her and the reconstruction."

Oh, shit. He couldn't have said anything that would have made Joe feel his helplessness more. Eve could see the immediate tension that tautened Joe's body. She said quickly, "Not your job." She picked up the towel on the worktable and wiped her hands. "But it is your job to take Jenny for her first viewing." She nodded at the box on the chair. "Pack her up, and we'll be on our way."

"Okay." He moved across the room and carefully took the reconstruction and placed it in the box. "If you still want to go with me."

"I told you I did. Which journalist did you place first on the list?"

"Terry Brandell. She writes a weekly column and has national syndication. But she's very popular in California and Oregon. She's helped me out before a couple times." He closed the box. "Though never with anything quite like this. She's more into tough, investigative police work than lost and found."

"This is definitely investigative police work."

"But that face is . . . wrenching. Children always evoke an emotional response. She prefers the cool, analytical approach."

"No, there's nothing cool and analytical about anything to do with Jenny." She moved toward the bed and gave Joe a quick kiss. "I'll call you." She headed for the door. "Let's get this over with, Nalchek. The sooner your reporter gets Jenny's face in her column the better."

"I suppose Nalchek told you that this kind of curiosity/ human-interest stuff isn't really my cup of tea?" Terry Brandell asked as she looked down at the box. "I'm surprised he brought this skull to me."

"He said you would give it the greatest amount of coverage," Eve said bluntly. "And this reconstruction is not a curiosity. It's a little girl who was murdered and needs the justice she never had. If you think that's a human-interest story, then we disagree. Personally, I believe it's a terrible tragedy that deserves being exposed and rectified. If you're willing to do that, then we've come to the right place. If not, say it now, and we'll find someone else. I have no intention of begging you to do the right thing."

The journalist blinked. "I can see that." She glanced at Nalchek. "And I like her honesty. When you called me, I did a little research, and when I checked her credentials, I was thinking of doing an interview. How about a trade?"

"No," Eve said. "I'm not the story. This little girl is the story, and I won't have her cheated or overshadowed."

"You heard the lady." Nalchek was smiling. "I'm open for a deal on future information for your articles, but this one is off the table, Terry."

"Interesting." She tilted her head. "Particularly since this isn't exactly what I'd think you'd be involved in, Nalchek."

"Yes or no," Eve said. "I don't know how much time we have."

"You can't convince me there's a hurry. She's been dead eight years."

Eve didn't answer.

"Or are there new breaks in the case?"

"How can there be?" Nalchek asked. "We don't know who she is. That's how you're going to help us."

"Maybe."

Eve shook her head. "Yes or no."

Terry shrugged. "Yes. Why not? I always like to have Nal‐chek owe me." She reached for the box. "Show me the kid."

Eve opened the box and carefully drew out the reconstruc‐tion. She put it on the desk in front of the journalist.

Terry Brandell studied the skull. "Very unusual. Are you sure that you didn't indulge your creativity a bit on this one, Ms. Duncan?"

"I'm sure," Eve said. "When you locate a photo of her, I'd bet that the similarity will be very close, Ms. Brandell."

"Terry. *If* we locate a photo." Terry's gaze was fixed on Jenny's delicate features. "But if someone has seen her, it's likely she would be remembered."

"That's what we thought," Eve said. "How soon can you publish the photo?"

"A few days."

Eve shook her head.

Terry Brandell grimaced. "Pushy. Very pushy." She turned to Nalchek. "Tomorrow. Give me an hour to get my photog‐rapher on it." She added brusquely, "And I want an exclusive if you come up with the kid's killer."

"Done," Nalchek said.

"And you can come back later today to pick up the recon‐struction."

"No, we'll wait," Eve said. "She's not going to be out of my sight until you've taken those photos. Things sometimes get . . . misplaced."

"I don't imagine skulls are high on that list," Terry said dryly.

"You'd be surprised." Eve sat down in a chair by the door. "I won't get in your way."

"Suit yourself." She asked curiously, "Are you always this intense?"

"It depends on the job. This one seems to require it."

Terry turned to Nalchek. "I'm beginning to become intrigued. Want to have dinner and discuss it?"

"No," Nalchek said. "I'll take a rain check. Thanks for helping, Terry."

"I won't give up, you know." Her gaze went back to the reconstruction. "Now that I study it, there's something familiar . . ."

"Someone compared her features to those of a young Audrey Hepburn," Eve said. "That's probably what you're seeing."

"Maybe." She stared for a moment, then shrugged. "Maybe not. I'll think about it."

"Why else would she be familiar?" Eve asked. "She's been buried for eight years, and she was only nine. You said that missing children weren't your cup of tea."

"They're not. And I'm probably imagining things." She reached for her telephone. "I'll get my photographer up here and get those shots. Fill me in on the backstory about where she was found, Nalchek."

CHAPTER

11

They didn't leave Terry Brandell's office for another three hours. By that time, the photographs had been taken and the story written.

"She's right," Nalchek said as he opened the passenger door of the car for Eve. "Pushy. Very pushy. We're lucky she didn't tell us to hit the road."

"We didn't have time to be diplomatic." She settled herself in the seat. "But I wasn't rude, merely insistent. And I saved you from having to be the one to pressure her. You might need to use her services later. I don't have to deal with her after she publishes that photo tomorrow."

"So you did it out of the kindness of your heart."

"I did it because I have to get this wrapped up before Joe gets out of the hospital." She fastened her seat belt. "And before Walsh decides to move on that little girl in Carmel. That child must have parents or guardians, and I'll bet that the photo will look like their child. All of the other victims bore a definite resemblance to Jenny. Maybe seeing the article will cause something to click. Or it could be that they'll make some kind of connection with Jenny." She wearily shook her head. "If they just see it, and it scares them about the possibility of something like that happening to their own child. If it makes them a little more careful, I'll take that, too."

"So would I," Nalchek said grimly. "And if we don't hear anything in a week after Terry's article, we'll go to another reporter."

"Old news," Eve said. "It will be harder the second time."

"I'll get it done."

Eve could imagine he would. There wasn't much that Nalchek wouldn't be able to accomplish if he put his mind to it. "Let's hope Terry's article will do what it's supposed to do." She paused. "She said that she looked familiar. She's a journalist, is it possible that—" She broke off. "Not likely. I'm reaching . . . I'm just hoping that something is going to go right for a change."

"Maybe someone else will think she looks familiar," he said quietly. "That's what this is all about." He started his car. "Where do you want to go? Back to the hospital?"

"Not yet. I've made reservations at the Fairmont Hotel. I want to check in and have a shower and change of clothes before I go back to the hospital."

"Sounds like a good idea. Anything else I can do?"

"Yes, you can bring Margaret to see me. Ask her to stop in my room at the inn and get my other suitcase."

"Today?"

"Yes, please."

He shrugged. "Okay, it will take an hour or so."

"Whatever. It will give me a little time to myself."

"Then you'd better call her and tell her to make herself

available." His lips twisted. "She's probably back in the forest communing with that coyote."

"I don't like her being there alone. That's not what I meant to happen when I asked for her help."

"I can't keep an armed guard on her constantly. I've told her not to go into the forest, but she's not listening."

"She's listening. But probably not to us." She shook her head. "And I'm the one who set her to trying to find out what was happening in that forest. But now it scares me."

"Me, too."

Eve looked at him. "You?"

"I don't give a damn about the fact that she thinks she talks to— Hell, maybe she does. Or maybe she's just nuts. I don't care. I don't want her running around that forest and getting herself killed. That's my county, my town." He said fiercely, "Keep her out."

"I'll try," she said. "I'll tell her I want her to leave the area. Okay?"

"If she listens to you."

"I don't know if she will," Eve said ruefully. "And, if I tell her to go, I don't know where that will be. She seems to drift from place to place. She makes friends, but Kendra Michaels, who found her and sent her here, and my adopted daughter, Jane, are the only ones who appear to be close to her. I don't know how much they even know about her."

"I'll find out before this is over."

"You haven't yet." She waved a dismissive hand as she saw him frown. "It's not important. I only want to keep her safe and make sure that she's not collateral damage from our going after Walsh."

"She wasn't the target in Tahoe. You were the one Walsh wanted to lure to your death. Joe Quinn was the one who took the bullet, but it could have been you. Didn't you tell me that he said he had orders to take you out?"

She nodded. "I was getting in his way. I was too close." She shivered. "God, I hope I'm close. I don't seem to know anything." They had pulled up to the front entrance of the hotel, and the doorman opened her car door. "That's got to change, Nalchek." She got out and nodded at the reconstruction she'd placed on the backseat. "Take good care of that skull. I hope we don't need to use it again. Tomorrow will tell the tale, won't it?"

"I hope so," Nalchek said soberly. "There's something I should tell you. I've persuaded the SFOPD to assign an officer to keep an eye on you while you're at the hotel or hospital. If you go anywhere else, call me, and I'll make sure you're safe. Don't be alarmed. We both know that Margaret isn't the only one who is at risk." He smiled faintly. "I'm sure Quinn would approve."

"Without a doubt." She added, "I won't argue. Anything to get Walsh." She turned and headed for the front entrance. "I'll call Margaret and have her ready for you."

"You can try," he said dryly. "So far, I've found that she's not only ready, she's a step ahead."

"Then I'll tell her to be kind to you." Eve wrinkled her nose at him. "Poor Nalchek, so put upon . . ."

SONDERVILLE FOREST

Margaret felt a chill as she closed her eyes and tried to delve through the confusion she was sensing in the coyote's mind. It was difficult. She had been struggling to understand what Sajan was trying to communicate since she had made contact over an hour ago.

"He's coming."

"Why are you afraid of him, Sajan?"

"Same as the other one. Rage. Violence. Just like the other one."

"What other one?" she asked patiently.

"The grave."

The chill was spreading. "The one who put the little girl in the grave?"

"Shouldn't have done it. Shouldn't have killed. His fault I have to be here."

"Whose fault?"

"Shouldn't have done it. Don't like any of this. Why should I be here?"

"I have no idea. Talk to me. Maybe we can figure it out. Whose fault? I need—"

"Coming now! Hide!"

He was gone.

And she was left alone in the darkness of the forest.

Coming.

Who was coming? Walsh?

Or the other one Sajan said was the same.

"Margaret?"

The other one.

Nalchek.

It could be a mistake. Sajan was confused, and she hadn't been able to clarify anything in the short time she'd had to work with him.

But the image she'd gotten from him was definitely Nal-chek. The power, the tiger ferocity, the sleekness.

"Margaret." More impatient now.

Trust her own instincts? Or Sajan's jumbled memory?

In the end, she always had to trust herself. If she was wrong, she was now prepared to deal with it.

"Here!" She stepped out of the trees. "It's about time you got here." She strolled toward him. "I've been waiting for you."

"Then you should have told me where to find you. I guess that didn't occur to you." He was frowning. "The officer I had watching you told me you were still in your room at the hotel. It took a little while to determine you'd given him the slip."

"And you came immediately here."

"I told Eve that this was where you'd probably be." He shrugged. "But there was a chance that I might be wrong since she'd asked you to bring her suitcase."

"No problem. Eve travels light." She nodded down at the small flight bag she was carrying. "And Joe Quinn evidently never unpacked his luggage when he got here. It's probably still in his rental car."

"Are you going to tell me why you slipped away from my officer? If you'd insisted, he would have brought you back here."

"Not necessary. I met a college professor in the coffee shop, and he offered to give me a lift."

"That's no answer."

"It's all you'll get from me." Then she shook her head. "That was rude. I'm a little on edge." More than a little, she thought. As usual, she was experiencing a multitude of emotions at being this close to him. Nalchek was all power and keen intelligence, and she was drawn to both. And now there was added the chilling uncertainty of what she'd learned tonight. Forget it. She'd made a choice. She'd chosen to trust herself . . . and Nalchek. Deal with the consequences. Which meant dealing with Nalchek. She met his eyes. "I don't like to be watched. I'm sure your officer is very courteous and only doing his job, but he made me uneasy. I won't permit anyone to be able to put his hand on me at any given time."

"Why?"

She smiled. "My nature? Or something more devious? I'm sure you're busily trying to find out."

"Yes, I am."

"Why? Because you're a police officer, and you don't trust me or what I am?" She nodded. "That would be reasonable . . . if one looked only on the surface."

"What's that supposed to mean?"

She hesitated. Back off, or respond as she usually did. Backing off would be more suspicious. Nalchek was very sharp. "Because you're not what you appear to be, either."

"You're wrong, I'm exactly what I appear to be. My public record is open for anyone to read. I couldn't have been elected to this office if I were hiding a shady past."

"Really? Everyone hides something. At least, everyone interesting. Animals are different. They're much simpler. Except felines."

His gaze narrowed on her face. "I don't believe we'll change species in this particular conversation. Just what do you think I'm hiding?"

Probe a little. "I don't know. Not your military career, you were a hero. Not during your college days. You were too intelligent to get involved with drugs or all that nonsense."

"Then do you think I'm a crooked cop?"

She slowly shook her head. "I don't think so. That would be an opportunity for corruption, but you grew up with a father who had strict values and believed in the law. That would have rubbed off. I'd bet you're well thought of by your officers as well as the people who elected you."

"Then it appears you're running out of scenarios for me to indulge in my wicked nature," he said mockingly. "Where did you find out all this about me?"

"The Internet. And I have a few friends who have buddies in high places. Not to mention those who wallow in low places." She stopped as she reached his car. "I don't have your advantage with access to all those databases and stuff."

"They haven't done me much good . . . yet."

"But you're still hopeful. I like that about you, Nalchek. Hope is a wonderful thing."

He opened the car door. "So we've both drawn a blank."

"Not me." She got into the car. "When I become confused about direction, all I do is go back to the beginning."

"And where is that?"

She looked out the window at the forest. "Back there. Whatever you're hiding is back there."

He got into the driver's seat but didn't turn on the ignition. Had she gone too far?

He looked straight ahead. "I'd like to know how you made a guess like that."

She could feel his tension. Very dangerous moment. She should be afraid. But she wasn't: excitement, anticipation, curiosity—no fear. Did that mean that he was no threat?

No. The threat was there, but it didn't mean that she couldn't handle it.

"How do you think?" she said lightly. "My friends aren't only the two-legged variety. But that shouldn't worry you since you have a healthy skepticism for any connection I have with them. And how could Sajan possibly tell me anything that might hurt you?"

"Skepticism doesn't preclude curiosity." He still hadn't started the car. "Why don't you want to tell me what you think I'm hiding?"

"Because you're very intense. If I struck too close to home, you might have to make a decision."

"And as long as I don't know, I can just coast along and not worry?" He shook his head, and said roughly, "Margaret, you're a fool. You can't be that naïve. You shouldn't have said anything at all if you thought I was a possible threat. Instead, you put yourself in a vulnerable position, then decide to tell me that I might have reason to remove you."

"I'm always vulnerable," she said simply. "Though I've been trying to correct that lately. But I have to work with what I have. I have intelligence and instincts and judgment. I never let myself get in a situation that my judgment says I can't get out of. Of course, there are triggers that can change everything."

"Like an unexpected decision that might cause an explosion."

"Or might not. I like to avoid having to worry about it." She looked him in the eye. "May we go now?"

"Nervous?"

He mustn't go down that path. Nervousness was too close to fear. And fear could be looked upon with suspicion. Red herring. Distraction. "A little, but it's more excitement, I think. It's just that Eve said that she had to get back to the hospital and wanted to see me."

He didn't move. "Excitement?"

"You know. Sex." She smiled. "I feel very sexual whenever

I'm around you. They call it chemistry, but I've always thought of sex as basic and primitive."

"I . . . see."

"Oh, did I make you feel awkward? It's not as if I'm making a move on you. I know I'm not your type."

"Oh, do you? Dark, leggy, and sophisticated. Isn't that what you said?"

She nodded. "That's right, and anyway, the sex urge isn't always reciprocal regardless of appeal. And the initial excitement can vanish as quickly as it comes."

"Stop talking about sex."

"Of course. I only wanted to explain that—"

"You only wanted to throw me a curve and take control," he said bluntly. "Because you thought that it was a safe ploy. It's *not* safe." His voice lowered, and the words came fast and hard. "And you don't have any idea what kind of women I like to screw. You *do* appeal to me. And if you weren't such a weird nutcase, I'd have had you in the backseat, tearing your clothes off, and coming into you three minutes ago."

"Really?" She cleared her throat. She hadn't expected that response, and she suddenly felt out of her depth. "Then I guess it's lucky that I am that weird. You'd be having all kinds of second thoughts that would—"

"Shut up." His hands were on her breasts, kneading, pulling, stroking.

Heat.

Tingling electricity.

Fullness.

She couldn't breathe.

She couldn't move.

His mouth was on her throat, his tongue moved down to

the hollow of her breasts. Her shirt was suddenly open, and his mouth was on her nipple.

She arched up to him with a low cry.

"*Yes.*" His teeth were pulling, his mouth . . .

She instinctively moved closer, offering more.

He froze.

"Nalchek . . ."

He took a deep breath, then he pushed her away. "Keep away from me."

"I don't want to keep—"

"I don't care what you want." He leaned over the steering wheel. "I care what I want. And it's not to screw some kid who wants a quick thrill and a little experimentation. For God's sake, the first time I saw you, I thought you were a teenager."

"I'm . . . twenty-one." She was trying to get her breath. "And I'm sure that you've done your share of experimentation. Though that wasn't what I meant—" She stopped. "And you were right, I only intended to take you off guard. I could see that you only thought of me as a kid, and I believed it was a safe way to distract you." She steadied her voice. "It kind of . . . blew up."

"You bet it did," he said grimly. "You had me so hot that I wasn't going to stop."

"But you did." Her fingers were shaking as she buttoned her shirt. "And now the best thing is clearly to forget it happened."

"Is it?" He was watching her fingers on the buttons. "Why? Didn't you say I excited you?" He made a violent dismissive gesture. "Forget I said that. But it's not that easy. I came close to raping you."

"No, you didn't." She looked away from him. "You wouldn't have done that. I know about rape."

He went still. "Do you?"

"See? You're getting all protective. You wouldn't have used force."

"When did it happen?"

"When I was twelve. It was when I was hiding in the woods from my father. Two hunters found me and decided to have a little fun."

Nalchek cursed.

She shook her head. "It's over. It took a long time to get over it, but I was lucky that I was in the best place in the world to learn that rape sometimes happens, but so does survival. It was all around me. It's all part of nature. You just have to turn your back on the pain and accept the joy." She tucked her shirt in her jeans. "Now I think you should take me to Eve."

He sat looking at her. "Yeah."

Then he turned on the ignition. "Did you know their names?"

"The men who raped me? Yes, it seemed important at the time."

"Who were they?"

She shook her head. "It's not important now."

"I want their names."

"What are you going to do? Arrest them?"

"Maybe."

She shook her head. "After all this time? More pain than gain."

"I don't agree." His foot pressed the accelerator as he reached the highway. "Let me put it in a way you'll understand. In nature, there's rape, there's survival, but you left out one other important element."

"What's that?"

"Revenge."

•   •   •

"Here she is," Nalchek said when Eve opened the door to her hotel room. He nudged Margaret into the room. "Though what you want with her, I don't know. She's big-time trouble."

"Problems?" Eve asked as her gaze shifted between the two of them. Nalchek was obviously tense and . . . something more explosive. Margaret was more subdued than usual. "You were longer than I thought you'd be."

"My fault." Margaret smiled. "I wanted to spend a little more time in the woods before he picked me up. I didn't tell his officer, and it led to . . . disturbance."

"Yes, it did." He met her gaze. "And it could have been worse . . . or better. Don't play games with me again, Margaret."

"I won't." She smiled as she lifted her chin. "I learn from my mistakes. Do you, Nalchek?"

"Yes, but that doesn't mean I don't repeat them. It depends if it's worth it. I asked you a question, then allowed you to sidle out of answering. Next time, you will answer, Margaret."

"What's going on, Nalchek?" Eve asked.

His gaze shifted back to her. "I'm not sure, but I'd bet that you'll know before I do." He turned to leave. "I'll call you after the story comes out tomorrow. If you need me, you have my number."

Eve nodded and watched the door close behind him.

She turned to Margaret. "Did I detect friction?"

"Among other things." She handed Eve her carry-on bag. "I know you wanted to change before you went to the hospital."

Eve nodded. "I only had one change of clothes, and I ruined those when Joe was wounded."

"How is Joe?"

"He'll be back in action within a few days." She headed for

the bathroom. "And that might be too soon. I'll be right out. There's one of those beverage servers on the dresser. Help yourself."

"I will. Maybe some tea. I could use a little caffeine."

"You don't look it. You look . . . charged."

"Appearances can be deceiving," Margaret said.

But she didn't think that was true in this case, Eve thought. Margaret's cheeks were flushed and her eyes sparkling. Whatever had gone on between her and Nalchek, it didn't require the aid of stimulants.

Eve quickly changed clothes and washed her face and hands before she went back into her room. Margaret was sitting curled up on the couch, cradling a cup of tea in two hands.

She looked up and smiled. "I love the scent of Earl Grey. I got used to drinking it while I was on the island."

"It does smell wonderful." She folded her arms across her chest. "But I don't have time to discuss tea, Margaret. I have to get back to the hospital. I've been gone most of the day."

"Go on. You're in a hurry. I'll curl up here and see you in the morning."

"No, I've arranged a room for you. Your key is on the coffee table." She took her handbag from the coffee table. "But I do have time to have you tell me if there's something I should know about why Nalchek is so pissed off at you. Does it concern Walsh?"

"Sort of . . . in a roundabout way."

"I've discovered that's not unusual with you."

"Yes." She took a sip of her tea. "But then what can you expect?" Her expression was suddenly sober. "Well, it's not really about Walsh. At least, only on the outer edges."

"Margaret."

"Nalchek is hiding something." She shook her head. "I

think it's bad. Though I can't be sure. Sajan was pretty confused. He kept comparing Nalchek to the other one."

"What other one?"

"The one at the little girl's grave," she said simply. "Sajan thought that he was like him. Angry. Violent."

"Walsh."

"Yes, it must have been him. But I don't know how true it was. As I said, Sajan was confused, and he's not a reliable witness." She grimaced. "And that damn coyote was pretty angry, too. He didn't know why he was supposed to be there, but he didn't like it."

"You said that before."

"He kept repeating it. Sajan is definitely not a stoic."

"Are coyotes supposed to be?"

"No, but I got tired of the whining."

Eve's gaze narrowed on Margaret's face. "You're talking a lot about this coyote and waltzing around Nalchek. Is it because you think that your furry friend may be all bullshit?"

"It could be." She was silent a moment. "I hope it is. But Nalchek can be angry. And I think he can be dangerous. He showed that side to me tonight."

Eve stiffened. "He hurt you?"

"No." She was suddenly grinning. "He called my bluff. But it was still a revelation." She waved a hand to shoo Eve out of the room. "Go see your Joe. Nothing happened to me tonight. I wish I could say I learned something more to tell you, but that wouldn't be true. I only found out more questions to ask."

"And I certainly can't confront Nalchek with an accusation that he might be in cahoots with Walsh on the testimony of a coyote," she said dryly. "Particularly since you don't have a good deal of faith in it."

"I did when Sajan was thinking about it," she said slowly. "He believed it, Eve. He made me believe it."

"But you don't now?"

"Like him, I'm confused." She finished her tea. "But I think you can't rule out anything."

"I'm not about to do that." She opened the door. "I won't be back tonight. Don't stay here. Go to your own room and lock the door. I'll call you tomorrow."

"You're afraid Walsh will come after you."

"Yes, I made him very angry, which means I'm an automatic target. Besides the fact that he's afraid I'm going to find out too much about Jenny. Yes, he'll come. But maybe not before he goes after that child in Carmel. She may be first on his agenda. He's been looking for her for a long time."

"And you're going to try to find her first?"

She smiled. "With a little help from my friends. I can't have Joe know where I'm going, but I might need help in canvassing the areas in Carmel. That's why I wanted Nalchek to bring you here. I hope that the news story tomorrow will give me a lead, but if it doesn't, we'll be heading there anyway."

"Without Nalchek?"

"I'm not going to invite him along. Though he did help at Tahoe, I'm just not going to put my faith in him." She smiled. "Someone told me not to rule out anything."

CALIFORNIA PACIFIC MEDICAL CENTER

The lights were out in Joe's room and he'd already been given his medication.

"Where have you been all my life?" Joe's voice was a little slurred. "In particular the last eight hours of it."

"Hi." She took her seat in the chair beside his bed. "I told you I was going to a hotel and get some of the stench of that hillside off me." She held out her arm. "Smell. I'm fabulous."

"You were fabulous before." He sniffed. "But a vast improvement. Lemon. I like your vanilla better."

"Never satisfied."

"And you like it that way." He pressed his lips on her forearm. "So do I . . ."

"Go to sleep. I'm sorry I didn't make it before you had your meds. We'll talk in the morning."

"Come to bed."

"I'm right here."

"Come to bed."

"Joe, they'll kick me out."

He kissed her forearm again. "I'm not insisting on conjugal privileges . . . maybe. I just want you next to me. I can't sleep without you."

"You're almost asleep now."

"Okay, I *won't* go to sleep without you. And you know I've been trained to do without sleep."

"Stubborn bastard." She hesitated. "They *will* kick me out, Joe."

"We'll face that when it happens." He painfully shifted to one side. "In the meantime . . ."

"Don't move again. I'll do it . . ."

A moment later, she was lying beside him, holding him. "Now go to sleep," she whispered.

"Soon." His cheek was rubbing her shoulder. "Tell me about your day."

"I told you when I called you. Very boring."

"No, there are always nuances. I want to know what I'm missing."

So that he could think and put all the pieces together. "Something is going on between Margaret and Nalchek. She's not sure she trusts him."

"Why?"

"The usual reasons with Margaret." Her hand was stroking his hair. "Nothing concrete."

"You're not concerned?"

"I'm concerned. But I have too much on my plate right now to let it become major."

"And I have nothing on my plate." He felt her stiffen, and his lips brushed her throat. "I'm not bitter. But I'm getting zilch from those databases. I'm frustrated and trying to work around it and be useful. I just have to have all the info available so that I can do it."

She felt relieved. She knew he was chomping at the bit, and it was only a matter of time before he exploded. But he also knew that he wasn't at full capacity and was willing to wait . . . for a time. "I'll have Margaret call you tomorrow. She's staying at the hotel with me, but she could come here if you like."

"No, I don't need help. I'll do it myself. I like the idea of your having someone with you."

"Nalchek said he was assigning someone to watch me."

"Oh, you mean our great sheriff who Margaret is so uneasy about?"

"We had no doubts about him before."

"But now I'm doubting everyone. Probably the result of this damn frustration."

"It may be over soon. Maybe someone will recognize Jenny's face tomorrow in the article."

"And maybe they won't." He drew her closer. "Either way we'll make it work for us." He yawned. "And now I think that I'll go to sleep. Don't you dare move unless one of those nurses shows up with a bazooka."

"Yeah, you stake me out for disciplinary action, then nod off to sleep."

"That's the plan. Someone's got to take the heat, and I'm wounded and unable to cope."

"Not true." She was aware of a subtle difference in his demeanor. He might be frustrated, but he was not on automatic. Joe's mind was clicking, formulating, and that might be good or bad for her plan of keeping him out of the action. "Wounded, yes."

"And that's causing you to agonize and try to—" He broke off. "Go ahead, agonize, it will put you right under my thumb. I've been trying to get you in that position for years. And all it took was a bullet."

"All?" She gave him a quick kiss. "Shut up. And I'll keep you safe if I want to do it. You have nothing to say about it."

"Yes, ma'am." His eyes were closing. "I'm in your hands . . ."

For the moment, he was in her hands. Tomorrow or the next day, it might be different.

But she would take tonight and hold it close.

CHAPTER

12

"Time to get up." Elena Delaney opened the door and stuck her head into Cara's room. "Past time. You're late. You overslept. If you don't hurry, you'll miss the bus."

Cara raised her head. "I'll make it." She yawned. "And if I don't, I can walk with Heather. She says she does it all the time."

"No," Elena said crisply. "We've discussed that. Get up and get going. You're going to be on that bus."

"Okay." Cara swung her legs to the floor. "I'll skip breakfast and be down there in front of the apartment on time. I promise, Elena."

"You won't skip breakfast." She turned and started to leave. "I'll make a grilled cheese sandwich, and you can eat on the run." She stopped, and looked back over her shoulder, her gaze going to the dark circles beneath Cara's eyes. "The nightmares again?"

Cara nodded. "But they're getting better. I haven't had one for two weeks. Maybe they're starting to go away."

"And maybe they're not. When you have one, you don't sleep for the rest of the night."

"Honest. They're getting better." She started for the bathroom and then stopped. "Should I know an Eve, Elena? Do you know someone named Eve?"

"What?" Elena frowned. "No, why?"

"No reason. She was just part of my dream." She disappeared into the bathroom.

Elena shook her head and hurried toward the kitchen. She had to get Cara on that bus and be at the restaurant where she worked as a waitress forty-five minutes later. It would be fine. She was good at multitasking. She put butter into the frying pan to melt as she turned on the TV to get the local weather. Then she opened the front door and picked up the newspaper and carried it back to the kitchen. She put the two pieces of bread in the frying pan and poured herself a cup of coffee.

"Cara," she called. "How are you coming?"

"Almost there."

"Five minutes, and you have to be out the door." She flipped through the newspaper. Usual depressing stuff. North Korean threats, terrorists beheading people, politicians feathering their own nests. She didn't know why she even paid to have a paper delivered.

Because it might be more dangerous to ignore the news than to have to put up with it.

Ignorance could be deadly.

And Elena had her own nightmares that she never told Cara about.

But maybe Cara was right, and everything was getting better . . . for both of them. Maybe it would be—

Dear God.

She was staring down at the face in the newspaper.

Cara's face.

No, not Cara's. Jenny's face. But close enough. Those distinctive features . . . The two girls had always looked alike even though there was six years difference in age.

Now Jenny's green eyes were staring out of this paper at her, and Elena was starting to shake as she remembered that last night.

Not my fault. I would have saved you if I could. You shouldn't have run away. Then I had to choose.

Stop shaking and read the story. See how bad it was going to be for them.

She quickly scanned the article, then pushed the newspaper away.

"Something's burning."

Cara was standing in the doorway of the kitchen.

Elena glanced at the toast in the pan that was now smoking and blackened. She tried to gather her composure as she quickly took the pan off the burner. "Sorry, something distracted me. Grab a health bar and get out of here." She pushed the newspaper aside. "I'll see you this afternoon."

"Right." Cara grabbed her red book bag and a honey oat bar from the cabinet. "See you . . ."

"Wait."

Cara stopped at the door and looked back at her.

Elena couldn't let her go like this. She hadn't been thinking straight. It might be okay, but having this skull out there for everyone to see could be a disaster. She couldn't chance the connection to Cara. "We're going to have to leave, Cara."

Cara stiffened. "Again?"

"It's best." She moistened her lips. "I'll pack up our suitcases and meet you at school. Do you have your phone in your back-pack?"

"I always have it." She stood there, stunned. "I like it here, Aunt Elena. My school . . . I've even started to make a few friends. Do we have to leave?"

Elena nodded. "Maybe we can come back someday. We just have to leave right now."

"We won't come back," Cara said. "We never come back."

No, they never went back. They'd had to go on the run several times in the past years, and they'd never returned. Elena was always afraid that they might have left some trace, some clue behind.

And there might be someone waiting for them.

"New places are good, too. You always do well."

"You said the money had run out. How are we going to get settled again?"

"I'll find a way."

"I like it here."

"Cara, go get on the bus. Don't argue with me."

Cara nodded and turned toward the door. "No, I won't argue. It doesn't do any good, does it?"

"Cara . . . I don't want to do this."

"I know. I'll be waiting." She left the apartment.

No arguments. No questions. The first few times Cara had asked questions, but even then she had not protested. She had just accepted.

Which made Elena wonder if that doctor she'd taken Cara to had been right, that she had no real memory of that night. She hoped that was true. Cara had been a child of three, and what she'd experienced had been enough to traumatize an adult. Yet there must be subconscious memories because the nightmares remained. She would wake crying and shaking in the night, but nothing could get her to tell Elena about them.

But if even scanty memory remained somewhere in that child's mind, it might be reason for her not to argue about fleeing at even the hint of danger.

She looked back down at the photo of Jenny. So alive, so incredibly lifelike for a child killed all those years ago. She felt a wrenching regret.

I'm sorry, Jenny. I can't help you now, just as I couldn't help you then. All I can do is try to keep Cara alive.

Get moving. Get packed. Hope that someone hadn't seen this story and decided to call the cell number listed. Someone who had noticed the curious resemblance to Cara . . .

CALIFORNIA PACIFIC MEDICAL CENTER

"Any word?" Eve asked Terry Brandell when she answered her cell. "It's almost noon. Have you heard anything?"

"We've had a few calls but nothing definitive," the journalist answered. "A lot of curiosity seekers and one pastor who thinks that you should have left the remains to return to dust."

"No one who recognizes her face? I can't believe it. She's very memorable. You even thought you recognized her."

"But I haven't been able to tell you from where," she said. "Could be imagination. I've got to go. I'll let you know if I get a solid lead." She hung up.

Eve turned to Joe. "No luck yet."

"So I heard. It's early."

She braced herself. "I can't just sit here and do nothing."

"I've been waiting for that." Joe's lips tightened. "I was

hoping for that same miraculous call you did, but it isn't happening. You know that these photos sometimes pay off and sometimes don't. No one knows that better than you."

"If it doesn't happen the first day the photo is published, the chances get slimmer and slimmer."

"And so do the chances of that little girl Walsh is targeting." She leaned forward and took his hand. "I have to go to Carmel and see if I can find out anything more."

"The school photographers? One of the first things we checked when we were going through those photos at Sacramento PD were the ones from that city. We didn't come up with any photos that bore any resemblance to Jenny."

"But maybe she didn't pay to have her school photo taken. If her parents knew she was targeted, they might have refused to let her do it. But I was thinking, club photos, organizations, yearbooks. She might be in one of those."

Joe was silent.

She suddenly realized why. "You thought of that, too," Eve said. "You didn't bring it up."

"At the time, we had enough victims to worry about. You were practically overwhelmed."

"No, that's not it." She was studying his expression. "You were going to go back on your own later and check it out. You thought that it might be a danger zone, and you didn't want me there."

"Guilty," he said warily. "No reason to be upset. It was only a possibility."

"Yes, but you were going to do it again. The same thing that happened at Tahoe. Close me out and take over." She was shaking with anger. "Dammit, you *can't* do that, Joe."

"It was just a question of training and experience. You told me yourself that you realized where my expertise lay."

"Of course I do. You were a SEAL. But that doesn't mean that I'm going to let you get yourself killed trying to protect me. I brought you into this. Jenny is *my* reconstruction. Everything that's happened since that day I accepted her is tied to that decision. I'm the one who is responsible. You know I feel that way." She jumped to her feet. "I've been tiptoeing around trying to keep you from doing too much, trying to keep you from exploding and finding a way to get out of here before you were ready for release." Her hands clenched at her sides. "Well, I'm through with that. You want to help? You stay in that bed and help."

"I can't promise that, Eve."

"No, probably not. But I'll pull out a couple wild cards that will slow you down. As long as you stay here, I'll call you and tell you what's going on. You have my word on it. But I'll also call Nalchek and ask him to have a guard outside your door to follow you if you leave. If you lose him, he'll call me." She paused. "And that will be the end of my checking in with you. I'll disappear, so that I don't have to go through another Tahoe."

"That wouldn't be smart." His eyes were glittering in his taut face. "We need to work together."

"And we will, but not if you keep closing me out." She turned toward the door. "Here's your first report, I'm going to check on those photographers and look through current year-books. If I hear from that journalist, I'll follow up. I'll take Margaret with me, and we might be able to split up the work-load." She looked back over her shoulder. "I'll always answer your calls, always be ready to share . . . as long as I know the call comes from this hospital."

He looked at her, his expression enigmatic. "Tough. Very tough, Eve."

"No, I'm being easy on you. Think how I felt when I was holding you, trying to stop that damn blood."

She left the room. She was still shaking as she walked down the hall toward the elevator. She was torn by anger and regret and loneliness. She hated this. She had known for years that Joe would always be protective of her, it was his nature and the nature of the years and events that had formed their relationship. It was based on love, and how could you condemn him for loving her too much?

So she had accepted and protested but never fought it.

She had to fight it now. She couldn't bear the thought of what could have happened at Tahoe. She had exploded when she had guessed that Joe had been going to investigate that lead without her, but it had all gone back to the basic problem. They had to come to terms.

She was punching the elevator button as she dialed Margaret. "Hi. I'm leaving the hospital now and coming to pick you up. I should be there in fifteen minutes. Meet me in the lobby."

CARMEL, CALIFORNIA

She was being followed.

Elena felt the muscles of her stomach clench as she looked in her rearview mirror after leaving the restaurant where she worked.

She was sure it was the same tan Toyota she had noticed when she had left the apartment this morning.

But how could they have found her so soon? The photo had just come out this morning.

There were thousands of tan Toyotas. She could be wrong. There were several turns on the way from her work to Cara's school. If she was right, she mustn't let the driver of the Toyota know that she was aware she was being followed. That would automatically put him on the defensive. Drive a few blocks, take two turns, and see what happened.

She took the first turn and slowed.

Tan Toyota.

Her heart was beating hard.

She took the second turn.

Tan Toyota.

Oh, God, it was happening. All those years of waiting and terror, and it was happening.

Calm down. Think. How could she protect Cara?

Go by the plan. Don't try to change anything.

She reached for her phone and dialed Cara.

"I can't talk, Elena," Cara whispered when she answered. "I'm in English, and they'll—"

"Listen. Act as if you're sick to your stomach and run out of the classroom. Do it now."

"But I can't—"

"Do it now." She hung up and waited for a few minutes and called back. "Where are you?"

"In the bathroom down the hall. I thought that would be—"

"That's fine. Look, you can't wait until I come to get you. Something has— You can't wait."

"I don't understand."

"You don't have to understand. You just have to get out of there and go to the cave. We have to put the plan I taught you into effect. You still have the money I told you to keep in your backpack?"

"Yes."

"Remember that trip we took after we moved into the apartment? The bus station, where to get off, how far to hike down to the beach?"

"I remember. You had me do it by myself, so that I wouldn't forget."

But she was frightened, she was sensing Elena's own fear and reflecting it. "It will be fine. You're very smart. I'll be there as soon as I can. But you have to go now."

Was the Toyota closer?

Maybe.

"If I don't get there right away, don't leave the cave. Try to hide if someone comes. Don't trust anyone. Don't get in any cars that aren't familiar to you."

"I can tell you're scared. I'm scared for you. What's going on?"

"Sometimes bad things happen." She paused. "But we can beat this, Cara."

Cara was silent. "It's going to happen again?" she whispered.

"Not if we can help it," she said. "But you have to do as I say. Get out of there. You know what you have to do. We've talked about it. Just follow the plan. Be strong. Call me when you get to the cave." She was about to press the disconnect, but she couldn't leave her like this. "I love you, Cara. I've . . . always loved you." She hung up.

She drew a deep breath. It would take another fifteen minutes to get to Cara's school, and, hopefully, Cara would be long gone by the time she pulled up in front of the building. But she still had to give her any extra time she could. She would wait there at least another thirty minutes before she left the school.

Then she would try to lose that Toyota before she made her way down Pacific Highway.

But she doubted if the driver would allow her to do it. If it was Walsh, then he was expert at all kinds of deadly games. He would have probably only been tailing her until she picked up Cara. Then he would have had both of them in his sights.

Don't think about what might happen next. She had a gun in her glove compartment. The two of them had survived this long. They would get through this, too.

All she had to do was stall and give Cara time to get away.

CALIFORNIA PACIFIC MEDICAL CENTER

Screw those databases, Joe thought, as he watched Eve walk down the hall. There wasn't time to go through the effort again. He had stored enough information in his head; now he needed to analyze and put it all in perspective. Then he had to lay out the pieces of the puzzle and put them all together.

Fast.

Sounded simple, he thought grimly. It wasn't going to be simple. There were all kinds of variables and possibilities.

But it had to be done. Eve was getting close, and that meant Walsh would be targeting her. He had to be ready for him. He couldn't do that without knowing his strengths and weaknesses.

And his objectives.

He sat up in bed and reached for his yellow pad. Start at the beginning. List everything he knew about the main principals and locations. He drew three columns. WALSH. JENNY. Then he hesitated and added one more column. NALCHEK.

"All I want to do is see the yearbooks," Eve said patiently. "I'll be glad to give you references with the Atlanta PD and several other law-enforcement organizations in California. I've no desire to pose a threat to any of these students."

Josie Coultan was still not convinced. "I don't know that." She took the card that Eve handed her and gazed at it suspiciously. "And anyone could have cards made up."

"Absolutely right," Eve said. "And I applaud you for being careful." It was the truth. This woman was completely different from that first photographer they'd run across in Sacramento, but they evidently had similar values. But she wished she wouldn't be quite this careful. Josie Coultan's photography studio was the third one she and Margaret had visited this afternoon, and she felt as if time was running out. "Just call Sheriff Nalchek, and we'll wait until you're satisfied." She got to her feet and moved to look at the photos on the wall. "These wedding photos are amazing, Ms. Coultan."

"Josie. My specialty. I just do the school photos to add to my income." She frowned as she started to dial the number. "But you have to be careful with kids. I don't know if it's worth the trouble. You have parents thinking that I didn't do justice to their darlings, you have divorced couples who battle who is going to pay me."

"That's not what we're looking for. We're trying to find a child who didn't want to have her picture taken."

"Oh, there aren't many of those. When? How old?"

"We're thinking ten, eleven," Margaret said as she knelt

to stroke the white Persian cat sitting on a turquoise pillow on the low table. "This boy is amazing. What do you call him?"

"Royal. I've had him for four years."

"You need to change his diet. He doesn't like that new cat food you're giving him. He's been losing weight."

"What?"

"Weigh him. Your husband feeds him, doesn't he? He's not been paying attention, and Royal is getting very pissed."

"What are you—"

Eve stepped in quickly. "Margaret volunteers with a local vet office." Lord, all they needed was to have Margaret start a family feud. "She has a good eye, doesn't she?"

"Perhaps." Josie spoke into the phone. "Sheriff Nalchek, I have two women here who gave you as a reference. Will you confirm that it's . . ."

"And he hates the name Royal," Margaret said in a low voice to Eve. "He thinks it's pretentious. He doesn't need that nonsense."

"Do me a favor and let Royal handle his own dietary needs."

"Don't worry, he intends to do that. I just thought I'd hurry things along. He was going to start a hunger strike to scare them tomorrow."

"Sheriff Nalchek informs me that you're no threat," Josie said behind them as she hung up the phone. "I'll get those yearbooks. I did the work at four area schools during the past five years. I always request a complimentary copy of the actual book. I'll go get them for you." She got to her feet and headed for a door that led to the back of the shop.

"Like pulling teeth," Margaret murmured.

"At least she's cooperating now," Eve said. "We'll split up

the books to get through them faster." She turned with a smile as the photographer returned burdened by the yearbooks. "I can't tell you how much I appreciate your help." She took two of the books and handed two to Margaret. "But I wonder if we might hurry things along if I showed you a photo that was in the paper this morning. It could trigger your memory." She handed her the folded newspaper. "It's a reconstruction I worked on several days ago."

Josie glanced at the photo. "I saw this photo this morning. I was thinking how appalling the photography was. I could have done much better."

"But you didn't recognize the child."

"I didn't pay much attention. You see one kid, you see them all."

"Really?"

She made a face. "I suppose I shouldn't say that? But I'm so sick of having to do those photos. Every one is the same. No grace, no glamour, like a wedding photo."

"And no fat price to sweeten that glamour," Margaret said.

"They're not all the same," Eve said quickly. "Look at her face. We believe that the girl we're looking for might be a relative of this dead child."

Josie studied the photo. "Nice bone structure. Very photogenic. I'd probably remember if I took her photo."

"But you don't remember her?"

She shook her head. "It's like an assembly line. There's no way I can make any of them stand out. No grace. No drama. I'd probably try with this one, but if she didn't pay to have her photo taken, I wouldn't bother. But what a bride she would have made someday. Pity that she—" She stopped. "Maybe I do remember . . ." She snatched last year's yearbook from Eve. "A bride . . ."

"Not old enough," Margaret said. "Except maybe in India or—"

"No, of course not," she said impatiently. "But it was the gown . . ." She was rifling through the pages. "I arranged the folds, and it turned out—" She found the page she was looking for and turned it around. "The girl at the end of the second row. You see how beautifully I draped that collar around her neck?"

It was a photo of a girls' choir. All the girls looked to be between the ages of ten and fifteen, and all were dressed in flowing white robes.

The girl at the end of the second row . . .

Small, dark hair, high cheekbones, winged brows, delicate features.

"Bingo," Margaret said softly.

Not Jenny, naturally. But so close . . .

Eve couldn't take her eyes from that picture. "What school?"

"Ronald Reagan Middle School," Josie said. Her finger was going down the name list. "Second row . . . Cara Delaney."

She was flipping through pages again. "That appears to be the only organization to which she belongs . . . No, here she is again in the band photo. Violin."

Choir. Violin.

I got to keep the music.

And Cara had also been permitted to keep her music.

Eve closed the yearbook. "May I borrow this? I promise to return it."

Josie nodded. "See that you do." She was smiling. "I really

made that robe look good, didn't I? You should see what I can do with an entire wedding party. Magnificent."

"I'm sure that's true. Thank you." She headed for the door. "Is that school near here?"

"About twenty minutes north." She was frowning down at her Persian gazing balefully up at her. "Do you know, I think he *has* lost weight."

"You set the GPS while I call Joe," Eve said when they reached the car. She wasn't sure that what she had promised him would be enough, but she'd keep her word. "I think we've found her," she said as soon as Joe answered. "Cara Delaney. She looks so much like Jenny that they have to be related. We're going to the school now and try to find out more about her."

"We always thought that it might be a family resemblance we were looking at," Joe said.

"No might about it now," Eve said. "She has hazel eyes, not green, but everything else is right on."

"Jenny's sister?"

"I don't know. It would be my guess. But she would have had to be only about three when Jenny was killed. What were two children doing out there in those woods? And why was Jenny murdered, and Cara—" She stopped. "Too many questions and not enough answers. But Cara Delaney has to have parents or guardians. At least I'll have someone to ask. I'll call you again after I get to the school and find out more." She paused. "How are you?"

"Healing as fast as I can. And I haven't jumped that guard Nalchek put outside my door. Though don't count on my holding out past tomorrow."

"I had to do it, Joe."

"No, you didn't. But you thought you did. What you really want to know is am I angry with you. Yes, I'm no saint, and I hate being thwarted." He added, "Keep safe, and you may get your way . . . for a little while." He was silent for a moment. "But those two girls pose interesting questions. Why? Where? What? I'm keeping myself occupied trying to work up some scenarios. I believe I'm getting there. Good-bye, Eve." He hung up.

He *was* angry, Eve thought. He had been absentminded, almost cool, and that was something Joe had seldom been with her.

Too bad.

She had done what she had thought necessary and would have done it again.

"Trouble?" Margaret asked.

"Some." Eve started the car. "Nothing we can't work out. At any rate, I can't think of it now. Do me a favor and call Nalchek and have him pave the way with the school administration before we get there." She looked down at the GPS. "We should get there before school is out. I'll go to the administration office and see what information I can gather before I speak to Cara."

"That sounds like a plan," Margaret said. "Not a bad start for a day. I'm excited." She smiled. "We thought that we were going to find out so much from the reconstruction article but it turned out differently. You can never tell, can you?"

"No, you can't," Eve said. "But I'll take it."

She could still see that little girl in the photo. Jenny, but alive and well and not threatened by monsters. No, not Jenny.

She kept thinking of that little girl who had exploded into her mind and life, but this was another child.

Cara, who was almost certainly Jenny's kin.

Cara, who loved music as much as Jenny.

Cara, who was also threatened by monsters.

CHAPTER
13

"Cara Delaney." Mrs. Karpel looked down at the transcript on her desk. "Eleven years old. Her parents were killed in an automobile accident, and she's in the custody of her aunt, Elena Delaney."

"How long has she attended this school?" Eve asked.

"Two years. She transferred from Fresno Elementary."

"Any problems with attendance or grades?"

"No, she's a good student and always obeys the rules. In the entire two years she's been with us, she's had only one absence, and she brought a doctor's excuse."

"We saw a photo of her in the choir. Did she belong to any other groups?"

"Just the band. She's an amazing violinist. Mr. Donavan, the band director, wanted to give her a solo in the spring festival, but her aunt refused to sign the permission slip."

"Have you had any contact with her aunt?"

She shook her head. "But that's not unusual. The school is overcrowded, and unless the student causes a disturbance, there isn't a lot of reaching out from the teachers. There just isn't time. Sad, but true." She tilted her head. "What's all this about? Is Cara in trouble?"

"I hope not," Eve said. "But I'd like to have her aunt's address and phone number. And I'd like to talk to Cara before she leaves school today."

"Certainly. Elena Delaney works as a waitress at a local Waffle House, and I'll give you her work number, too." The administrator was already writing out the information. "I'll have Cara paged to come to the office." She tore off a Post-it with Cara's name, got up, and moved toward the front desk.

"No photos. No problems that would draw attention," Margaret said.

Eve nodded. "Cara faded into the background. And her aunt Elena appears to also be very elusive. I definitely have to speak to that aunt."

"I'm sorry." The administrator was back. "Cara became ill in her English class this morning and ran out of the room." She was frowning. "I spoke too soon about her obeying the rules. She should have reported to the nurse's office, but evidently she called her aunt to pick her up instead."

Eve tensed. "Evidently?"

"Her aunt didn't answer her phone when Cara's advisor tried to call her. But Cara's friend, Heather Smallwood, saw her aunt waiting outside the school. She must have picked her up without checking her out." Her lips tightened. "I'll have to have a talk with Elena Delaney."

"And so will I." Eve got to her feet. "Thank you for your help. If you hear from Cara or her aunt, I'd appreciate your contacting me."

"Of course. I'll get in touch the first minute I know anything. This is very disturbing."

More disturbing than she knew, Eve thought grimly as they left the building.

"We're going to her apartment?" Margaret asked.

"Right. I don't like the fact that on the morning that photo was published, Cara got suddenly sick, and her aunt decided to whisk her out of school. I think that Elena Delaney knew that the little girl was targeted, and they were hiding out. That photo of the reconstruction was a red flag that made her panic."

"And you're afraid she'll take Cara on the run?"

"It's possible. I knew that there might be a response from publishing that photo. I hoped it would be positive." She got into the driver's seat. "But, yes, we're definitely going to her apartment and see what we can find out."

They were only a few blocks from the apartment when Eve's phone rang. Terry Brandell. She put the call on speaker. "Hello, Terry. Do you have something for me?"

"Yes, I got a phone call regarding the reconstruction," Terry Brandell said when she picked up. "Nothing very promising. It was from a young girl who said she went to school with a girl who resembled that sculpture. She was all excited at the thought of being part of the case. She kept asking about a reward or her picture in the paper if she could get the family to acknowledge that the dead girl was a relation."

"And this schoolgirl's name?"

"Heather Smallwood. She lives in the same apartment building. I told you it wasn't very promising. The only reason I told you was because you asked me to pay attention to any calls from Carmel."

"You're wrong, it's promising," Eve said. "Thanks for calling, I'll get back to you." She hung up. "It seems that Heather Smallwood had reason to be on the lookout for Cara's Aunt Elena. She was looking for a payoff." She pulled to the curb in front of the apartment building. "And all signs are pointing to Cara Delaney. Let's go find her."

Elena's hands tightened on the steering wheel as she gave another nervous glance at her rearview mirror.

The tan Toyota was still following her.

And he was no longer trying to hide the fact. When she had pulled away from the school without picking up Cara, any hint of subtlety had ended.

There had been a change, a boldness, a determination in the way he had resumed tailing her. He was not about to let her get out of his sight.

But she *had* to get out of his sight, she thought desperately. She had to get to Cara. She had promised she would take care of her. She couldn't leave her alone and at the mercy of the people who had killed her sister.

She might even have to go to the police.

No! She knew better; she had been warned all her life that she mustn't ever go to the police. Cara wasn't the only one in danger. She loved her, but Elena's own family could be slaughtered if she disobeyed the rules.

So find a way to lose him.

And if she couldn't do that, lead him as far away from Cara as she could . . .

"Elena Delaney quit her job, picked up her paycheck and her niece, Cara, and hit the road," Eve said in frustration when she called Joe two hours later. "And it can't be a coincidence. Cara has to be Walsh's target. We're at their apartment now, and we've been looking around for anything that might give us a clue as to where she might be going. I talked to Cara's friend, Heather, when she came home from school, and she said that Cara hadn't mentioned going anywhere today. They might be friends, but not close enough for Cara to confide in her. She did say that Cara was very quiet when she got on the school bus this morning. But Cara didn't ever talk much. It wasn't until Heather was in her current-events class this morning that she saw the reconstruction on TV and got all excited." She shook her head. "That's why she was on the lookout for Cara. She wanted to talk to her about it. She's very disappointed."

"And she saw Cara get into her aunt's car?"

"No, she had to go to her next class. But she recognized her car, a dark blue Camaro." She paused. "Can we find it?"

"If she doesn't get rid of the car and buy a new one. Give the license number to Nalchek."

"You can't do it?"

"I'm a little busy right now. Give it to Nalchek."

She was silent. "Okay. I don't believe she would have gotten rid of the car. Nalchek arranged for me to look through the apartment. Obviously, very limited means, and you don't usually have ready cash if you're a waitress at Waffle House."

"Nalchek is local, and he might get a faster response." He paused. "If you don't think he's dirty. Evidently, you must have some faith in him. You seem to be using him quite a bit today."

"I don't know either way. I can't put credence in Margaret's take on him when even she's not certain. It just seemed involving him was the easiest way to get things done."

"Since I'm obviously out of the action." His voice was without expression.

"Even if you weren't. You said you were going to use him, too."

"And so I will." He added mockingly, "But that doesn't mean that I don't intend to construct a few scenarios that would fit into Margaret's view of our bold sheriff. After all, I have to keep myself busy."

As long as it was at the hospital. "By all means, construct away. I'll call you if I hear anything else." She hung up.

"Do I detect trouble in paradise?" Margaret murmured.

"No. Paradise? Joe and I have never had an idyllic relationship. It's much too real."

"It seemed pretty close to it to me," Margaret said. "I was with him when he was trying to find you after you were kidnapped. I would have settled for someone's loving me like that." She shrugged. "But what do I know? I've never really had a relationship, period. Sometimes it seems very confusing when applied to me. Like Nalchek said, I'm a little too weird for a normal relationship."

"Did he say that?"

"Or words to that effect. He was a little upset with me at the time." She changed the subject. "But I'm sorry that Joe is upset with you."

"He'll have to get over it. He can't have everything his own way." She looked around the apartment. "Did you find anything else that might give us a lead?"

"A few things. Not much. It looks as if they left in a hurry, and Elena just threw things in suitcases and took off." She held up two yellow tickets. "Two expired bus passes. One adult, one child." She handed Eve a small, tan book. "And this. It was in the drawer of the bureau. I think you'll find it interesting."

Eve slowly took the book and opened it. Two photos, faded with time. Two little girls, both evidently sisters with those very familiar features. Dressed in shorts and T-shirts, their dark hair wind-tousled. They were smiling at each other: love, closeness, warmth. . . . "Jenny and Cara," she said softly.

Margaret nodded. "It looks as if the photo was taken on board a ship. Blue sky. Blue sea . . ."

"But where?" She looked on the back. "Not a professional shot. Maybe if Joe sends it to the FBI, we might be able to find out. They know all kinds of technical tricks."

"We can try." She studied the bus pass. "It's a local pass. West route. Why would she have a bus pass there when her job is here in the southeast?"

"We'll have to find out," Margaret said. "Are you ready to get out of here? I don't like this place."

Eve could see what she was talking about. The apartment was neat and clean, and there were even rose and yellow colors in the pillows on the couch. But it was too neat, like a hotel room instead of a home, and there was a coolness about it. It looked . . . temporary.

"Yes, I'm ready." She turned toward the door. "I need to get hold of a city map, compare it to those expired bus passes, and see if I can see anything." She grimaced. "But heaven knows, it would help if I knew what I was looking for."

The bitch was scared out of her mind, Walsh thought with malicious satisfaction. Elena Delaney had tried three times to lose him in the past hour, and now she was going faster, trying to escape through sheer speed. She'd be lucky not to be pulled over by the highway patrol.

Would she be tempted to tell them she was being followed?

No, she knew what would happen to her family if she did. She would be polite, accept the ticket, then get back on the road. But that would give him his chance to catch up to her.

No matter what she did, he would eventually have her.

And after a short but very painful time for her, he would also have Cara.

Eve didn't call Joe again for another two hours. "I'm on my way back to San Francisco. Margaret and I went to the bus company and asked a boatload of questions but came up with zilch. The passes were paid for in cash and no one remembers Elena Delaney. It would have been too much to hope that she had a cozy conversation with the clerk about where she was going and why she needed a pass."

"Sometimes it happens like that. Not often. Where does that bus go?"

"On the Pacific Highway, then into some of the subdivisions in the suburbs. I asked to talk to the bus driver who drives the route, but they had to check their records." She added wearily, "And probably my credentials before they give me his telephone number. It's been a question of hurry up and wait all day. I'm not getting anything done. I thought I'd start again tomorrow morning."

"You're being too hard on yourself. It's a suspicious world. You know that no one wants to give out information unless forced by authority." He paused. "Sounds like you need a cop."

"Joe."

"Just a thought."

"Not a good one. You have two more days."

"Maybe." He said, "In the meantime, I've been looking into Nalchek."

Eve glanced at Margaret next to him. "Building scenarios?"

"It's hard to build any case against him. He was in Afghanistan when Jenny was killed. He came back over a year later and worked with his grandfather at his vineyard until his death. His father resigned as sheriff eighteen months later, and Nalchek ran for office himself and was elected by a sound majority." He added, "No hint of corruption, and he won the Silver Star when he was in the service."

"So he's clean?"

"I didn't say that. I've seen pastors who seemed above reproach turn out to be serial killers. I said that on the surface it appears it's going to be difficult to dig up anything derogative."

"I don't want derogative. I want the truth."

"And that's what you'll get. But not in a few hours," he said. "I've got a call coming in from Sonderville. I'll talk to you when I know something." He hung up.

Eve glanced at Margaret. "You heard him. Nalchek evidently appears eminently respectable."

Margaret looked away. "I heard him."

"But you don't believe him."

"If Nalchek was a holier-than-thou type like that pastor Joe was talking about, I'd have more trouble. But he's very human, and people make mistakes. I believe Nalchek's capable of everything and anything. Just as we all are if the circumstances fall into line."

Eve's brows rose. "You appear to have made a study of him."

Margaret shook her head. "Sometimes, I don't think I know him at all. But I do know he's very human."

CALIFORNIA PACIFIC MEDICAL CENTER

Joe opened his eyes when Eve pulled back the sheet and slipped into the hospital bed. "Hi, I wasn't sure that you'd be coming back here tonight. I thought you'd go to your hotel."

"You thought wrong. I dropped Margaret at the hotel and came to you." She kicked off her shoes and pulled the sheet over both of them. "And if the nurse tries to kick me out, I'll tell her I'm in dire need of therapy, and you're the only one who has the qualifications."

"What type of therapy?"

"Not the one you're thinking about. I'm not an exhibitionist. Though I would never be ashamed of anything we do together. It's all good. Would you?"

He pulled her close and cradled her head against his shoulder. "Hell, no," he said gruffly. "I feel sorry for anyone who's missing out on what we have." He brushed his lips against her temple. "What therapy?"

"It's hard being away from you. It's harder not to be able to say yes, to not give you anything you want."

"You didn't show it."

"But you knew it. If you didn't after all this time together, then we'd have a serious problem."

"And the therapy you require?"

"Just this. Just to know that no matter how much we disagree, in the end, this is the only thing that's important."

He was silent. "You're not going to get your way if I see a danger, Eve."

"And I'll do exactly what I told you I'd do." Her voice was low. "And tomorrow night, I'll come back to you like this and you'll hold me and everything but what's between us will fade away. Isn't that true?"

He was silent again. Then he chuckled. "Who am I to deny you therapy? I seem to need it myself."

"Say it, Joe."

"Words?" His voice was silken soft. "Yes, it's true. In the end, everything else just fades away . . ." He kissed her, then abruptly sat up in bed. "Turn on the lights."

"What?" she said, startled.

"Do it. In the end everything else fades away. But this isn't the end, and I have to fill you in."

She was gazing at him in bewilderment as she got up and turned on the lights. "What are you up to?"

"Doing the only thing you allowed me to do. Pull up that chair." He took his yellow pad from the bedside table. "I think I've got most of it figured out." He showed her a pad full of notes and crossed-out sentences and questions. "Though there are a few things that didn't make sense."

"I can't make sense of any of it."

"Okay, take it from the beginning as I did. Walsh. What do we know about him? Yes, he's a child killer, but what else?"

"You know the answer. Burglar, murderer, human trafficker, drug dealer, and who knows what—"

"Stop right there. Human trafficking. That's the only crime most likely to connect to Jenny or any other child if you rule out serial killer. We've both noticed that Walsh is different; he's in control, and though he enjoys the kill, he doesn't let it rule him. He's an enforcer, and he lived a good life obeying the Castino family. He wouldn't let a careless, self-indulgent kill interfere with that life."

"Human trafficking . . . You're saying he kidnapped Jenny and was going to sell her?"

"That was my first thought." He shook his head. "But everything connected to her death is too complicated. Why kill her instead of sell her?"

"Impulse? Emotions?"

He shook his head. "Then why spend years hunting down her sister? There had to be a reason that would impact his wallet or reputation."

"And that would be?"

"I think this is the way it went down. Walsh was working for the Castino cartel in Mexico City right before Jenny was killed, according to Interpol. It's logical that the chain started there. Castino was dipping his hands in human trafficking as well as his other criminal pursuits, and it would be natural for Walsh to be involved as his enforcer. So I called Mexico City Police and asked some in-depth questions. You know I spent a few weeks down there this year at that cartel seminar."

"I remember. You made quite a few contacts."

"And one of them was Detective Máñez, who has been investigating the cartels for the past twelve years. I believe we managed to work it out together."

Eve leaned forward. "Tell me."

"Castino's is only one of several cartels in Mexico. Probably the most powerful, but there are others who are constantly at war with them. Needless to say, the fighting gets very vicious. No holds barred. A man can make a fortune playing both sides."

"Walsh."

"Juan Castino had a beautiful Russian wife, Natalie, and they had two children. Unfortunately for her, both were girls. Our macho Castino wanted boys. But he would never admit something he owned wasn't perfect. He made a big play about being besotted with the girls. Which made them automatic targets. Kill the girls, hurt Castino. The police think Walsh was hired by Alfredo Salazar, who runs a rival cartel, to double-cross his boss and do it. But it was too dangerous to do it on Castino's home turf, so he waited until he was due to escort a group of slave laborers to Southern California to work the fields down there. He arranged to kidnap the girls and send them in the trucks bound for the fields. It was a quick and easy way to transport extremely hot merchandise. When he got there, he was supposed to kill them and safely dispose of them. No one was supposed to know that Salazar had funded the kill. It would have started a messy gang war. Salazar wanted the satisfaction of destroying the children Castino cared about and wanted to be able to gloat without consequences. It was important that no bodies be found. So Salazar chose an expert, Walsh."

"A monster . . ."

"But something evidently went wrong. He wasn't as efficient as Salazar had hoped. One disposal clumsily handled, one child escaped and went on the run. That probably had something to do with Elena Pasquez, who might have helped the children to escape."

"Who?"

"Elena Pasquez, a young nursemaid, who disappeared at the same time as the children, probably also kidnapped by Walsh."

"Elena Pasquez. She changed her name to Elena Delaney?"

"That would be my guess. She probably changed her name many times while she was on the run."

"But if she helped Cara to escape, why not just go to the police?"

"Her entire family was involved with the cartels. No one ever went to the police, and those who did usually ended with their entire family being targeted."

"So Elena was alone and trying desperately to hide from Walsh. He must have been relentless."

"We both know how egotistical Walsh is. I believe he's been trying to rectify that mistake for the past eight years. Not only did he have to keep Castino from knowing he'd sold him out to Salazar, he had to make the correction to preserve his spotless reputation."

"And Jenny had to remain lost and unknown. Cara had to be found and killed, no matter what the cost."

Joe nodded. "That about covers it."

"How did it all go wrong? What happened in that forest?"

"I haven't gotten that far yet. I have a few ideas. I think I'm getting close. It's all beginning to fit together. I have to make a few more calls." He tapped the Nalchek column. "And I haven't developed any valid scenario for him, except for a feeling that he *could* be involved in something dirty." He smiled faintly. "Give me another hour or so."

Eve stared at the yellow pad. "You've accomplished an amazing amount as it is."

"I had to know him. *You* had to know him. Any questions?"

"Yes, are we sure that these Castino daughters are Jenny and Cara?"

"I'm sure. Máñez e-mailed me the newspaper stories about their disappearance. Natalie was the typical heartbroken mother who only wanted her children back. Bragging about her Jennifer, who was a brilliant pianist and always entertained her guests. Wishing vengeance on the monsters who had done this foul deed. According to Máñez, she didn't mention that the girls were always in the care of servants and seldom saw either of their parents."

Jenny. Brilliant pianist . . .

They didn't take away the music.

And other than her little sister, the music was all Jenny had.

Eve could feel the tears sting her eyes.

"Hey." Joe reached for his phone. "Stop feeling sorry for her. She was awesome. I had them send me a few pictures." He handed her his phone.

Jenny at the piano in her white dress. Her expression intent, totally absorbed, lost in her music, almost ecstatic.

Jenny at a tall window looking out at the sunset, dreamy, wondering.

Jenny on the ship with Cara, laughing and full of love.

"I saw this last photo at the apartment. She loved her sister, didn't she?" She shook her head. "No, she *loves* her. Present tense. What else is this all about?"

Joe nodded. "That's what it's about."

She looked down at the photos again. "She *was* awesome. Thank you for showing them to me, Joe."

"I thought you had to see them. All you've seen of her has been death and sorrow. You needed to see what she was, what she could be, what she should be. The complete package."

"If Walsh hadn't killed her."

"No, you believe Bonnie hasn't changed except to become more of herself now that she's crossed over. You have to believe the same of Jenny. Walsh has to be punished, but he did nothing to damage what Jenny was or is."

She cleared her throat. "I know that."

"Then don't forget it again."

"I won't." She got to her feet and turned out the light. "But right now, I want to hold you. Is that all right?"

He pulled her into the bed with him. "I believe I could put up with it."

She was silent for a moment in the darkness, listening to his heartbeat beneath her ear. "You're an amazing man, Joe Quinn."

"I keep telling you that."

"And I'm a lucky woman."

His lips brushed her temple. "Damn straight. And don't forget that, either."

She nestled closer. "I won't. I promise . . ."

Something was wrong!

Eve's eyes flew open.

Panic.

Darkness.

Wrong. All wrong.

Eve sat up in bed, her heart racing.

All wrong.

Her first thought was Joe.

No, he was still asleep, his breathing normal.

All wrong.

She swung her legs to the floor.

"Where are you going?" Joe asked drowsily as Eve slipped out of the bed and reached for her shoes. "What am I? A one-night stand?"

"I don't believe that's an accurate term since we didn't have sex." She stood up, leaned over, and kissed him. "I'm going to the hotel to shower and change. I want to get an early start on locating that bus driver." He opened his lips, and she put two fingers on them to silence him. "I love you. I'll keep you informed." She hurried out of the room before he could protest.

All wrong.

She leaned against the wall of the elevator, trying to overcome the sickness as the car zoomed downward.

Crazy.

Everything was okay. She just needed some air. She'd keep the car windows open as she drove to the hotel. The tension of the day must have been more enervating than she had dreamed.

She was feeling less sick but still shaky as she pulled out of the hospital parking lot. Stop it. She was fine. Everything was fine.

"No, it's not. It's all wrong, Eve."

She stiffened, her gaze flying to the passenger seat.

Jenny.

Pain.

Eve could feel her pain and despair.

"It's been a long time, Jenny. I thought we were working on this together."

"I told you that I'd never be sure when I could come to you," she said. *"It's so hard. He's so hard. He fights me. He won't believe me, and sometimes he makes me think that he's right. That I'm . . . nothing."*

"No, he's not right. Don't think that."

"It's only sometimes. Most of the time, I know I'm getting stronger, and I'll soon be able to stop him."

"Stop him?"

"The way he stopped me," she said. *"The way he stopped her."*

"Her?"

"Elena. He shouldn't have done that. It was all wrong."

"Jenny, what are you saying?"

"*He followed her. I couldn't do anything. I couldn't make him listen. He wouldn't hear me.*"

"Jenny, what did he do?"

"*I don't know. The car . . . I don't know. He wanted to hurt her. I think he did it.*"

"He hurt Elena?"

"*Yes. He shouldn't have done it. So kind to me. So good to Cara.*"

"Cara. You know about Cara? You know that she's the little girl Walsh was targeting?"

"*Of course I do. Who else? It had to be Cara.*"

"You didn't know before."

"*I told you, I'm getting stronger. Things are coming back to me. Soon I'll know everything.*"

"And you know that Cara is your sister?"

"*Of course she is. She was Marnie. Now she's Cara. Elena had to change it.*"

"And Elena isn't really her aunt?"

"*No, she was our nurse. She took care of both of us before Walsh took us from our home. He thought having her with us would make it easier for him on the trip, and he made her come along.*"

"But it didn't make it easier, did it? She helped you to escape from him?"

"*Yes, but it didn't work. He was too smart. He came after us. He was too close. He was going to catch Cara. I couldn't let him do it. All I had to do was run away and make a lot of noise, so he'd follow me. But I had to leave her alone. I told her that I'd keep her safe if she'd just do what I said.*" She moistened her lips. "*And I did it. I can't let it all be for nothing. I can't let her die now. I saved her the last time. I have to do it again.*"

"Is it Cara who Walsh is hurting now?"

"*No, not yet. I told you . . . the car. Cara wasn't in the car.*"

"She wasn't in Elena's car? But she picked her up at school."

"No, she fooled him. She had to fool him. She couldn't let him get Cara."

"Then where is Cara?"

"I don't know. I can feel her. She's scared, so scared. Like she was that night. There were tall trees around her then, but now there's only rock. And she's all alone."

"Does Walsh know where she is?"

"I don't think so. Maybe. He hurt Elena."

"Do you know where Elena is?"

"The car." Her green eyes were glittering with tears. *"It's the car. We have to help them, Eve. I've been searching. I have to find them before Walsh does."*

"We will. We found two bus passes that led up and around Carmel. Could that be near where she is?"

"I told you, I don't know. I have to—" She stopped and drew a deep breath and straightened her shoulders. *"I'm sorry. I shouldn't have put this on you. I always knew that I was the one who had to stop Walsh. Maybe the reason I was sent to you was that I had to learn to be strong enough to do it. Remember, you told me that I had to reach down and get the strength to fight him? Maybe I didn't try hard enough. Well, I have to do it now."* Her lips were trembling, but her voice was steady. *"I hope you can help me, but if you can't, then I have to do it myself. It's all wrong. It shouldn't happen again. I can't let it happen."*

"No, and it won't. We'll work it out together. It will be—"

But Jenny was gone.

Eve could feel her own eyes sting. "I wish you wouldn't do that, Jenny. It's hard enough without you wafting off to never-never land after you upset me."

She pulled into the parking lot of the hotel and turned off the car. She buried her face in her hands and tried to get control of herself.

Think.

Try to put it together.

If she was to believe Jenny, Cara was somewhere alone and on the run.

Elena Delaney? Eve was afraid to make a guess. She leaned back in the seat and took a deep breath.

Wherever Elena was, she must be in danger . . . or worse. She had to be found. How?

"Car . . . it's the car."

She took out her phone and dialed Nalchek. "I need your help."

"In the middle of the night?" A pause followed immediately by, "Have you found Walsh?"

"Not yet. I'm worried about Elena Delaney. I'm afraid that Walsh may have located her."

"Not the kid?"

"No, I think Cara and her aunt may have split up."

"Why do you think that?"

Awkwardness again. "I had a tip."

"Another anonymous source?"

"Yes."

"That you're not going to divulge."

"Sorry."

"So am I," he said dryly. "And how am I supposed to help?"

"You were going to try to locate Elena's car. Have you done it?"

"Yes. I've been on the phone twice with the local police."

"Could you call them now and go up the chain of command to try to get someone to find her car right away?"

"I could ask them, but I have no proof to show real grounds for the pressure."

"Kidnapping. Tell them that you suspect that she kidnapped Cara, and you're trying to verify."

"She's supposed to be the kid's aunt."

"Which you can say was based on forged documents."

"And they'll have my ass when they find out I'm lying."

"It could be true. We don't know why she was with Cara. We don't know anything."

"Your mysterious source didn't tell you?" he asked sarcastically.

She didn't answer. "Will you do it?"

"You haven't given me a good reason."

"Walsh is after Elena. She's going to die if we don't find her before Walsh does."

He was silent. "So Walsh is directly involved and on the move? That has a certain substance. I'll give Carmel PD a call and phone you. Are you still at the hotel in San Francisco?"

"I won't be by the time you get back to me. I'll be on my way to Carmel."

"Then I'll see you there. I'm staying at the Radisson."

"In Carmel?" she asked, startled.

"I started driving down there after the last time you called me. Things were happening, and I figured that was the place to be. You were getting close."

"Not close enough. Cara Delaney slipped away."

"Closer than I've been before. This time I'll get him," he said grimly. "Is Margaret still with you?"

"Yes."

"Leave her in San Francisco. She'll get in the way."

"No. Call me when you find out anything." She hung up.

The news that Nalchek was in Carmel had come as a surprise. She supposed it shouldn't have been a shock. She couldn't expect the sheriff to stay in the background while she was asking for help. She had known from the beginning that he was a dominant personality. But she was uneasy knowing he had not bothered to tell her he was coming to Carmel. He had just quietly and efficiently complied with her every request and compiled all the information she had gathered for his own investigation. Then he had positioned himself where he might be able to use it for his own advantage.

Nothing wrong with that. She and Joe had not been over-generous about sharing their information, either. It had not been easy to explain Jenny.

Easy?

Impossible.

And Margaret's distrust of Nalchek had influenced her whether she wanted to admit it or not. He must sense that reaction, as well.

But that distrust hadn't stopped her from calling him for help again. Just be careful, strike a fine balance, and let him help her.

And hope that help included finding Elena Delaney.

CHAPTER
14

"Are you going to tell me what this is all about?" Margaret asked quietly. "You tumble me out of my bed in the middle of the night and whisk me back here with the briefest explanation possible."

"I was wondering if I should even bring you," Eve said. "I think I did it because Nalchek told me not to. And because I found myself making excuses for him. I want to believe him, Margaret. You, on the other hand, have doubts. I needed the balance."

"That's clear," Margaret said. "Maybe. But how did you find out that Elena didn't pick up Cara?"

She didn't answer.

"Ah, the anonymous source again? That must have driven Nalchek crazy."

"He wasn't happy."

"I can see that he wouldn't be." She didn't speak for a few minutes. "Sources he can't identify will upset him. I'm the prime example." She grimaced. "Sometimes I wish I could pull up a mysterious but entirely understandable and plausible 'source' myself every now and then. But it never works for me."

"What are you trying to say?"

"Nothing. Can't you tell? I'm being diplomatic. I've got pretty good instincts, and I know all kinds of strange things happen in this world. I think I knew when you had no trouble accepting what I am. I just want you to know you don't have to make any explanations to me. I'm not going to ask you any questions, and I'll accept what you say without delving."

Eve didn't know what to say. "Thank you."

"You're welcome. So does your 'source' think that Elena is—"

Eve's phone rang. "Nalchek." She hit the speaker. "We're almost there, Nalchek. Are you at your hotel?"

"No. I'm at highway marker fourteen Pacific Highway. Meet me there."

"Why?"

"Because I didn't have to ask the local police to look for that car. They'd already found it." He hung up.

"My God." Eve pulled over to the side of the road and jumped out of her car. She ran to the edge of the cliff and looked down the steep slope.

The dark blue Camaro was a twisted hunk of metal on the rocks below. It must have been on fire because it was still black and smoking. She could see the forensic teams trying to make their way carefully around the rough terrain to do their investigation.

"She couldn't have survived that," Margaret whispered beside her.

That's what Eve had been thinking. "We have to find out."

She was gazing around the area, looking for Nalchek. She spotted him a few seconds later, talking to a tech holding a clipboard several yards down the slope. "Nalchek!" She half ran half slid toward him down the steep slope.

He caught her as she would have slid past him. He muttered a curse. "Be careful. All we need is another victim in the mix. I would have come to you."

She was gazing down at the blackened, smoking car. "Another victim? Elena Delaney was in that car?"

"They can't get close enough to determine that," he said. "But they should know soon. It's almost a foregone conclusion. They've searched the slope and rocks, and she wasn't thrown from the car."

"They're sure it was her car?" Margaret said as she came to stand beside them.

"They found the license plate. It was blown over on those rocks when the gas tank exploded. Half-melted but readable." He looked back at Eve. "It looks as if Walsh found her."

Eve nodded as she looked down at that charred wreckage. She felt a wrenching pity. She knew little about Elena Delaney, but she had risked her life to save that little girl. She didn't deserve to have that monster do this to her. "Terrible."

He nodded. "But the question is, did this happen before or after he found her?"

"What?"

"Did he fake this accident after he found out what he wanted to know from her? Or did she go off the road while she was in a panic, trying to get away from him?"

She shook her head. "I'm afraid I'm not thinking too clearly. My first thought was that Walsh did it."

"And probably the right one. I'm so frustrated, I'm grasping at straws. I don't want him to get what he wanted." He said through clenched teeth, "I wanted *him*."

So had Eve.

This can't happen again, Jenny had said. It's all wrong.

But it was happening, and Eve hadn't been able to stop it.

She looked back down at the wreckage. "We should know soon enough if he managed to chalk up another victim."

"She won't be down there in that car," Margaret said quietly.

Eve's gaze flew to her face. "What?"

"I think that Nalchek is probably right, and he faked the accident to stall us."

"Why do you think that?"

She lifted her gaze to the sky and pointed. "Because they're flying over that hill on the other side of the road."

Eve's gaze followed Margaret's.

Vultures. Black vultures wheeling in wide circles in the sky.

"Shit!" Nalchek whirled to face Margaret. "Could they be sensing death or injury in that car?"

"Not likely. They have extraordinary smell, but that car was burning, and smoke would have masked the death scent." She looked back at the vultures across the road. "They think that their meal is up there somewhere."

"Shit!" Nalchek started running up the slope at top speed.

Eve and Margaret were right behind him.

"She's dead?" Eve asked. "Is that why—"

"She may not be dead yet," Margaret said. "But it must be close. Actually, they think she's alive. Movement. That's why they're still just hovering. They won't go in until they believe there's no fight left in the victim. That's the way they prefer it."

"Then we have a chance of saving her." They had reached

the road, but Nalchek was already on the other side and entering the woods. Eve ran after him. "There's a chance."

"Eve . . ." Margaret was running after her. "Don't get your hopes up. Those vultures *smell* it."

Smell death.

Eve ignored her and tried to catch up to Nalchek. He was glancing on either side of the trail as he climbed the hill.

No sign.

He reached the top of the hill.

He stopped, gazing at something below him.

Eve had a cold, sinking feeling.

It didn't have to be bad.

But Nalchek was just standing there.

She caught up to him. "Do you see—"

A small, slender woman was lying crumpled near the bottom of the hill. She looked like the description they had of Elena Delaney. Midthirties, brown hair with a pink streak . . .

Or was that blood?

Her white T-shirt was soaked in blood.

She looked . . . broken.

White bones were sticking out of those thin arms. And her neck was at an odd angle.

"Why are we just standing here," Eve said unevenly. "Margaret said she could be alive."

"That fall alone should have finished her," Nalchek said.

"But maybe it didn't. We have to try." She started slipping and sliding down the hill. "We've got to help her."

She heard them behind her but didn't wait for them. She reached Elena and knelt beside her. She checked the pulse in her throat. Faint beat. Very faint.

"She's alive. Call 911 and get an ambulance up here."

"Right." Nalchek pulled out his phone and started dialing. "Those are knife wounds all over her torso. I doubt if—" He broke off and started speaking into his phone.

Try to stop the blood, Eve thought.

Where could she start? Which one of those knife wounds had done the most damage?

"Eve . . ." Margaret was behind her, her hand grasping Eve's shoulder.

"I've got to help her," Eve said unsteadily as she gently pushed up Elena's shirt.

Elena's eyes opened. "Who . . . are . . . you?"

"Eve. A friend." She took Elena's hand. She didn't know if she could give her anything but comfort. "A friend to you and Cara and Jenny. We're here to help you, Elena."

"Eve . . . Cara said . . . Eve . . . Too late for . . . me. It's Cara. Got to save Cara." Her eyes were frantic. "So that God will forgive me. I told him. He kept stabbing me, and I told him. How could . . . I do it?"

"Walsh? You told Walsh?"

"God will never . . . forgive me. I told . . . Walsh, and he laughed. Then he stabbed me one more time. He picked me . . . up and threw me . . . down here. He . . . thought . . . I . . . was dead. I should be . . . dead. Don't deserve . . . to . . . live. Told . . . him."

"What did you tell him, Elena?"

"Where . . . Cara. The strip . . . seventeen-mile . . . I told him . . . about the cave."

"What cave?"

"Spider's nest . . . spider's nest." Her voice was fading. "She won't have a chance . . ." Her hand tightened on Eve's.

"Please. Save . . . her." A trickle of blood ran from the corner of her mouth. "So that God will forgive—"

"We'll save her. I promise you." Her throat was tight. "And God will forgive you. There's no need. You've been a very good woman, and there's nothing to—"

But Elena's eyes were closed.

She was dead.

"Damn." Eve sat back on her heels and drew a deep, shaky breath. "Damn him."

"Yes." Nalchek hung up the phone. "We can't stay here. It would have taken Walsh a bit of time to stage the car accident to stall us, but he has at least an hour's head start."

Eve nodded jerkily as she got to her feet. "And we have no idea where we're going yet. But we'll find out. You go ahead in your car, Nalchek, and head back toward town and check the map and try to locate any reference to any caves near the seventeen-mile strip. I don't remember ever hearing about any. Margaret and I will stop at the crash scene and question the local police and see if they know anything before we join you in Carmel. Local cops usually know their towns better than anyone." She looked down at Elena. "And get someone to come and take care of her before those birds . . ." She started up the hill. "I'll be in touch as soon as we get on the road. We've got to hurry. I made her a promise."

Promises.

She had made a promise to Elena and to Jenny.

And the strongest, deepest promise was to herself.

She had to keep that little girl alive.

"We're heading toward town right now," Eve told Joe after she had filled him in on what had happened to Elena Delaney.

"Margaret is checking Google, but I don't think she's finding anything. I talked to the police at the crash scene, and they'd never heard of a cave in that area. It must not be well-known. I thought I'd let you have a go at checking on it. We need all the help we can get."

"And I'm so conveniently on the sidelines." He followed immediately. "That's not fair. I'll get to work on it immediately. You're right, we're heading for the homestretch, and there's no way Walsh will get there before us."

"Thanks, Joe."

"Is that all you need?"

"Yes." She paused. "No. It was bad seeing Elena—I felt helpless. I'm missing you right now. I wanted to hear your voice. I wanted to be with you."

"You're always with me."

"Yeah, I know. Keep in touch." She hung up.

Joe slowly pressed the disconnect. Eve felt safe saying she wanted to be with him when she was almost two hours away, and she had arranged roadblocks to keep him here.

Sorry, Eve. Homestretch.

He sat up in bed and threw his sheet aside.

First, get to Carmel in the quickest way possible.

He was dialing his phone as he started dressing.

"Nalchek. I need you to do something for me."

"Forget it," he said curtly. "I don't have the time. I'm driving toward Carmel and trying to—"

"I know what you're trying to do. I need one phone call from you, then I'll leave you alone."

"You'll not get it. I'm busy and—"

"I want you to set up a helicopter to bring me down there right away."

"What? You think I can just blink my eyes and arrange for a helicopter?"

"Probably. You have connections. You did very well when you got those police helicopters so quickly to us in Tahoe."

"That was different."

"Then consider it a challenge."

"No."

"Yes. Or we'll discuss Bryland Medical, and I don't think you want to waste time on that at the moment."

Silence. "You've been digging hard and deep."

"And I'd just finished putting together the pieces before Eve called me. But I'm willing to put it aside until we take out Walsh." Joe's tone hardened. "Get me the helicopter. And while you're at it, get rid of that guard in the hall, or I'll do it myself."

Nalchek didn't answer for another moment. "I'll get it for you. Why should I worry about you killing yourself? That's Eve's job, and she'll probably kill you herself when she finds out what you're doing."

"I'll be out of here and downstairs on the street in ten minutes. Call me and tell me where to pick up the helicopter." He hung up.

Eve wouldn't kill him, but she would probably find a way to punish him, Joe thought ruefully. But as long as he didn't pull those stitches and bleed to death, she would eventually forgive him. It would be worth the risk.

Homestretch.

Eve, Margaret, and Nalchek pulled off the road and climbed out of the car. They were on the southern end of the scenic seventeen-mile drive, which offered some of the most stunning views of the Pacific Ocean Eve had ever seen. But now it looked anything but beautiful to her. The crashing waves were ominous, threatening. Jagged rocks jutted from the water like fingers clawing desperately upward. Dark clouds billowed off-shore, pulsing with electrical energy.

Margaret pulled her sweater closer around her. "The birds have all gone. Look around."

Birds. Eve's mind went instantly to the vultures wheeling over Elena's poor broken body.

Margaret knew what Eve was thinking and shook her head.

Nalchek turned toward Margaret. "And what does that have to do with anything?"

"There's a storm coming, and they know it." Margaret nodded to the clouds offshore. "It's going to be a big one."

Eve unfolded a map and spread it on the car hood. "One more reason to find Cara as fast as we can." She ran her finger up and down the coastline. "The way I figure it, she could be anywhere along here. Most of the scenic road is close to sea level, and there aren't many places to hide. It's only here at this section, with all these cliffs and rocks, that offers a real possibility."

Nalchek shook his head. "It's still a lot of ground to cover. I'll coordinate with the Coast Guard and local police to get some manpower out here."

"Do that. But we're running out of time." Eve looked up and down the shoreline. "Walsh has a head start on us. I'm going down to the beach."

"By yourself? That's not a good idea."

"No choice. Cara needs us."

Nalchek shook his head. "And what if I ordered you to stay here?"

Eve folded the map. "I'd remind you that I don't work for you." She turned to Margaret. "What do you think?"

Margaret pointed up the scenic road. "I'll head up this way on foot. I'll call you if I see anything."

"Sounds good." She turned to Nalchek. "It's a lot of ground for two people to cover. I hope you were serious about getting the cavalry on board."

"Why, Eve, don't you trust me?" he asked mockingly.

"Sometimes."

"Margaret has obviously been exerting her influence on you." He pulled out his phone. "The first wave should be arriving in just a few minutes. I'll coordinate from here."

Eve was already sprinting down the stone stairs toward the beach.

This had to be it, Walsh thought.

He stopped in the knee-deep water and gazed up at the jagged rocks before him. The opening wasn't visible from the road, and he wouldn't have even guessed it was there if that bitch hadn't told him.

Stupid woman. She should have known better than to try to outsmart him. All that running and hiding, and it had come down to facing his knife on that hillside. It had been pure pleasure to force the information from her. She was surely dead now, and soon he'd have Cara.

He sloshed through the water toward the cave.

He stopped.

There was a sound echoing in the cavern.

Whimpering. Crying.

He smiled. Of course she was crying. She was only a kid and afraid of what was coming. Not like her sister, whom he'd not been able to break until that final blow. Cara was different, probably softer, and she should be afraid. Because once he had her, he'd make her pay for those years when he'd had to hunt her—

Wait.

He listened. It didn't sound like crying. It sounded more like . . .

Laughter.

And it wasn't coming from the cavern at all. It seemed to be all around him.

He swallowed hard. A trick of the wind, he told himself. The gusts were stronger now, whistling around the rocks. That had to be what he was hearing.

The laughter stopped.

He let out the long breath he hadn't realized he was holding.

Time to end this. Time to end *her*.

He moved into the tall cave, then stopped just inside the entrance. It was much larger than he would have imagined, with its small opening quickly expanding to a gaping yawn of a cavern perhaps forty feet high. Sharp rock formations stabbed upward and downward, like teeth in the mouth of a giant monster. As he sloshed through the shin-deep water, the noise from the outside receded, replaced by the sounds of breathing and movements bouncing off the rock walls.

He smiled as he glanced around the dark cavern. Absolutely perfect. No witnesses, no one to keep him from what needed to be done.

"Cara?" he shouted.

No answer.

"I'm here to help you. Everything is going to be all right now."

Silence.

"Elena sent me. She wants me to take you back to her. She's waiting for us."

Movement above him.

He looked up. The motion had appeared to be on one of several ledges that extended to the dark upper reaches of the cave. Could she really be up there?

His eyes adjusted to the darkness. He saw there were footholds in the craggy rocks, more than large enough for a child to climb.

"Cara?"

More movement up above.

She *was* up there.

Walsh grabbed hold of the rocks jutting out and lifted himself up.

The spider's nest.

Eve gazed desperately around her as she hit the beach. What in the hell had the poor woman been trying to tell them? It might have meant absolutely nothing, of course. Elena had been out of her head, practically incoherent in her last moments on Earth.

But there was something about the way she had said those words with such conviction, such purpose.

The spider's nest.

Thunder rumbled in the distance. Eve looked at the dark clouds bearing down on her. She wasn't sure she'd ever heard thunder on the West Coast. How strange . . .

Margaret was right. There was a big storm coming. Waves crashed violently against the shore, dragging large clumps of seaweed behind them. Eve stopped, surveying the rocks around her. If Cara was here somewhere, the child couldn't stay for long. The tide was coming in.

"Cara!" Eve shouted. "Cara!"

It was no use. Her voice was lost in the roaring surf.

Her heart stopped. Just twenty feet ahead of her, she spotted a splash of red in the sand. Was it blood?

She ran forward. No. Not blood, she realized. Thank God.

It was a child's crimson book bag.

Eve picked it up. It had been dropped here, probably in just the past few hours. It still looked new, unsullied by the elements.

Cara's book bag? It was empty except for a few pens and Post-it notes, and she could only guess. Perhaps Cara had been in a hurry and hadn't wanted the weight of the bag.

Perhaps.

Eve looked down. Whatever footprints there had been were gone, erased by the rising tide.

But she was on the right track, she knew it.

She started running again.

"Cara!"

"Thanks for the lift, guys. I appreciate it."

Joe settled back in the rear jump seat of a San Francisco PD Bell 429 helicopter. Two police aviation officers were seated in front of him as they soared over the Bay and headed south down the coast.

The unit's mechanic turned around to look at him. "The local police evidently wanted you pretty bad down there. But I gotta tell you, the way you climbed in here, I'm not sure you should be going anywhere."

Joe grimaced. The mechanic was right. His wound hurt like hell. He glanced around. "Where's your tool kit?"

"That bronze handle next to you. What do you need?"

"I can get it." Joe pulled up on the handle and rummaged around until he found what he was looking for: a roll of silver duct tape. He slid out of his jacket and pulled the tape taut over his T-shirt. He wrapped it tight around his torso, pulling the roll around and around, creating a makeshift cast.

He turned in his seat, first to the right, then to the left. Better. Still not great, but definitely better.

He looked ahead. "How much farther?"

The pilot answered, "Just a few minutes, Detective Quinn. You should probably buckle up. It looks like we have some rough weather ahead."

Margaret ran along the Scenic Drive, her gaze searching the beach fifty feet below her.

She shook her head. She'd always been known as being optimistic. But not right now. Now she was afraid there was little hope for that little girl.

She looked out at the rolling ocean. The animals' desertion had unsettled her; it was almost as if someone had taken away her senses. Birds were especially sensitive to changing atmospheric conditions. She had long ago learned to follow their lead where the weather was concerned.

The sky had been growing darker by the minute, but the clouds above her parted momentarily, revealing a patch of blue sky and brilliant sunlight. Margaret turned toward the beach.

The sunlight speared past over half a dozen rock formations and cast long shadows on the shoreline below.

She gasped. She halted, transfixed.

The spider's nest.

The formations' shadowy tentacles did indeed look like the legs of a spider, extending over the tall rock features on the beach.

The spider's nest.

That's where she was.

Margaret pulled her phone from her pocket and punched Eve's number.

"I know where it is!" Margaret said when Eve immediately answered. "I'm looking at it. The spider's nest is right in front of me."

"Margaret, slow down. What are you saying?"

"The spider's nest. The shadow of those rock formations is the spider. Wait, I see you on the beach. It's just in front of you, Eve. Look at the shadows. They're the spider. And those rocks are the nest."

Even from over two hundred yards away, Margaret could see that she had stopped Eve in her tracks.

"Oh, my God," Eve said. "You *found* it."

Margaret's gaze was searching desperately as the sun once again disappeared behind the dark clouds. "There's no way for me to get down there from here."

"It's okay. Margaret, run back to Nalchek. Tell him exactly where to send the police when they get here. I'm going to go over there."

"Eve, no. You have to wait until—"

Eve cut the connection.

Eve ran faster as the giant shadow faded into the gloom.

The spider's nest. Right in front of her eyes.

Only now could she see that the rocks surrounded a large cave that faced the open sea. Cara had to be in there.

She wanted to shout the girl's name as she drew closer, but she stopped herself. There was every possibility that he was in there, too.

Walsh.

Thunder boomed, and lightning lit up the dark sky. Rain suddenly poured from the heavens, as if turned on by a giant spigot.

Eve stopped outside the cave opening. She knew what Joe would say right now.

Eve, dammit. Wait. Wait for the cavalry you know is on the way.

Bullshit.

That's what he would say, but she knew damned well Joe himself wouldn't wait. Not when the life of that little girl was at stake.

The thunder boomed again. Louder this time.

Eve's clothes were drenched. Her hair was soaked and matted against the nape of her neck. She took one last look around before she slowly ventured into the cave.

Walsh pulled himself onto the dark ledge. It was quiet now, and he was beginning to think he was wrong about Cara's being up here.

Then he heard rustling and the sound of feet moving across the rock floor.

Then he saw her. Cara had a red coat pulled tight around her, and she was now huddled against the far wall.

"Why, hello, Cara."

She didn't answer. She was frantically looking around, trying to find an escape route. There was none.

He stepped toward her. "Do you know who I am?"

She finally spoke. "Yes, Elena told me. El Diablo."

He laughed. "Is that what she said? El Diablo? The devil?"

She nodded.

"Perhaps she was right. But the devil is nothing less than an angel. A fallen angel, perhaps, but an angel nonetheless. And I'm your angel, little girl. You'll see. I'm here to end your suffering, all your pain, all your fear. You'll never know what it is to be hungry or afraid ever again. Your angel will do that for you."

"Do you think I'm stupid? You're not an angel. You're a horrible, horrible man." Her voice was suddenly defiant. "I was afraid of you, but I'm not any longer. She won't let you hurt me."

He stiffened. "She?"

"All the nightmares, all the running. And you call yourself an angel? I know what you are. You're a coward and a—"

He lunged for her and snapped his arm around her neck. "Don't fight. I've waited too long. One minute, and it will be over."

She was struggling fiercely but couldn't even summon the breath to scream.

He squeezed tighter. She was making him angry. He'd thought she'd be easier. "I said stop fighting me. Or I'll hurt you, just like I hurt your sister. Do you hear me?"

He froze. He was hearing that sound again.

Laughter.

What in the hell . . . ?

At first he thought it was behind him, but the sound traveled around to the space in front of him.

It was a child's laughter.

It was coming from the little girl he was holding.

No! How could Cara—?

He looked down.

It wasn't Cara anymore.

It was Jenny.

Blood ran from her green eyes and nose, just as it had all those years ago after he'd struck that final blow.

But she was looking up at him and laughing.

His hands fell away from her, and he took a hurried step back.

What was happening? This couldn't be real.

He continued to back away, squinting at her in the cave's dim light.

Then, she was suddenly Cara again. She was clutching her throat, coughing and gagging.

"No," he said harshly. "You're trying to play your tricks, but you can't stop me. Nobody can."

Cara looked at him, puzzled, as she scrambled back to get away from him. But even she seemed to realize he wasn't talking to *her.* "Horrible and crazy. Just like Elena said."

He moved back toward Cara. "You can't stop me. I'm finishing this, and there's nothing you can do to keep me from sending her straight to—"

"Stay away from her!"

Walsh spun around. Eve Duncan was now climbing on the ledge with them, holding a gun.

He grabbed Cara and lifted her in front of him as a shield. "After I've gone to all this trouble? Put that gun down, or I'll break her neck." He smiled. "I'm actually glad to see you. It's going to save me a good deal of time and trouble."

Eve took aim with her gun. "Let her go. Right now."

He shifted in place, moving Cara back and forth in front of him. "Go ahead. Maybe you'll kill us both."

"And maybe I won't have to do it," Eve tilted her head. "Listen."

Walsh was listening. It was raining harder outside the cave, but there were new sounds accompanying the thunder and crashing waves. Son of a bitch. There was a powerboat in the distance. And a helicopter.

Fury tore through him. "What have you done, you bitch?"

Eve kept the gun leveled at him. "You're not getting out of here. Where's that knife you used before, Walsh? Throw it out."

"I got bored using that knife today." He smiled savagely. "I wanted my hands on this one."

"If you even look like you're going to hurt her, I will shoot you."

Laughter, again.

He went still. "No."

Eve turned around.

"You hear it, too!" he shouted. "You can hear it?"

"Of course I can hear it. She has a lovely laugh, doesn't she? I haven't heard her laugh very much."

Jenny stepped from the shadows behind Eve. Still laughing, still bleeding from the eyes, nose, and mouth. Her clothes were dirty and rotting, as if buried for years.

Still holding Cara, Walsh hurriedly stepped back. "You can see that . . . creature?"

Eve turned back. "I see a beautiful young girl. Hello, Jenny."

"She's hideous. Rotting . . . Bleeding from her eyes."

"I don't see any of that. Jenny?"

Jenny moved past Eve and continued her slow walk toward Walsh. *"He sees what he made me. Or what he thinks he made me. We know better, don't we, Eve?"*

"Yes, Jenny," Eve said gently. "We do."

His grip tightened on Cara as he backed toward the edge of the ledge. "Stay away from me. Whatever you are."

"Why? Are you going to hurt me?" Jenny asked. *"You fool, you can't hurt me now."*

"No, but I can hurt her."

"No." Jenny's face suddenly twisted in anger, her green eyes blazing. *"Never again."*

Jenny sprang forward and flew toward his face with teeth bared!

CHAPTER

15

No!" Eve lowered her gun and leaped toward the edge, where Walsh had stumbled back away from Jenny, with Cara still in his arms.

She was too late. She barely stopped herself from going over, sliding on the damp ledge. She struck her head on the rock wall.

Stars. And blood.

Stay awake. Don't pass out.

Eve finally crawled to the edge, afraid of what she would see below on the cave floor. She froze.

Walsh was splayed on the rocks below, impaled by two of the stalagmites. He was looking up at her, struggling to free himself. Blood was bubbling from his wounds. "You." Rage and anger and terrible pain were all reflected in his face. "You did this to me."

"I wish it had been me." She shook her head. "But I only helped. It was Jenny."

"No!" He writhed in pain for a long moment. Then he fell back, dead. Blood trickled from the corners of his mouth.

But Cara, where was Cara . . .

Eve was praying that the child hadn't taken that same terrible fall as Walsh.

"Help . . . me."

She looked down, and her heart plunged. Cara was seven or eight feet below her, holding on for dear life. She had one foot wedged in the rock wall, but Eve could see that it was slipping even as she watched.

And Cara was dangling over the same sharp rocks that had impaled Walsh.

"Cara, hang on!"

"I'm trying," Cara yelled. "But I'm slipping. I'm going to fall!"

"No you're not." Eve threw her legs over the ledge, still trying to fight that dizziness. "I'm coming down to you. Hang on just another few seconds."

"No!" It was Joe's voice.

Eve looked at the cave's opening. Joe waded quickly through the water, which was now thigh deep.

Joe. What was he doing here? She was torn between joy and sheer terror.

Joe ran underneath Cara and called up to her. "I'm going to catch you."

"I'm afraid."

"It'll be okay. I need you to let go."

Okay? Eve's hands dug into the rocks of the ledge. If Joe caught Cara from that height, he could tear those stitches and bleed to death. If he didn't, Cara might fall on those rocks and die. Either way, there was a terrible risk.

Cara was looking down at the dead man just feet from Joe.

"Don't look at him," Joe said. "Just look at me. I'm going to catch you. Okay? You can trust me."

She nodded, gazing into Joe's eyes as he smiled up at her. "Okay."

Who wouldn't trust Joe, Eve thought painfully. Who wouldn't trust a man who might be giving his life for you? But Cara didn't know that, she only saw the strength and the warmth and the safety.

"I won't let anything bad happen to you, Cara. That's all over. I'm going to count to three, then I'll need you to let go. Understand?"

Again she nodded.

"Ready? One . . . two . . . three!"

She let go, and Joe leaped to meet her. He twisted his body, cradling her in his arms as they both plummeted into the water. Seconds later, they broke the surface.

Joe whispered something to Cara, and the little girl nodded. Joe looked up at Eve with a weary smile.

"Are you both all right?" Eve shouted. "Joe, tell me!"

He gave her a thumbs-up.

And the next moment, Eve collapsed, as the darkness overcame her.

Swirling darkness.

Pain.

Jenny.

Jenny standing there in the darkness, her eyes shining and filled with triumph.

"*Cara* . . . " Eve said or perhaps only thought. "*Safe?*"

"Yes." Jenny smiled. "*We did it, Eve. You and me and your Joe. Walsh can't hurt her any longer. He can't hurt anyone ever again.*"

"*Good* . . . " Profound relief soared through her. "*It was so close . . . I was terrified when Walsh took Cara with him off that ledge.*"

"*Not that close. I knew I could keep Cara from falling for a little while. And I knew Joe was almost here.*"

"*You seem to have taken huge strides since I saw you last. Walsh certainly . . . seemed to think so.*"

"*I had to do it. I had to keep Walsh from hurting Cara until some-one could help her.*" She smiled. "*You said I had to reach down into myself for strength. Instead, I reached out to you.*"

"*I think we reached out to each other.*"

"*I guess that's true.*" She took a step closer to Eve. "*I was right, I was sent to you for a reason, and it wasn't only to save Cara. But that was the big thing, and we did it. I had to stay to say thank you.*"

"*That sounds like good-bye.*"

"*Sort of. Not really. It's kind of confusing.*"

"*My entire relationship with you has been kind of confusing.*" She felt a wrenching sadness. "*I thought you'd be able to cross over once this was done. Is that what's happening?*"

"*Maybe not yet. I'm not sure, but I think that something special is happening. I'm going to be with Elena for a while, but later . . .*" She shrugged. "*Whatever it is, it's not over.*"

"*I don't doubt that something special is going to happen to you. You're a very special person. Wherever you're going, I'll miss you, Jenny.*"

"*You're sad. Don't be sad. I'll miss you, too. But I'm not sad. I'll always be close to you.*" Her voice was soft, intense, and her expression glowing. "*Remember, I feel what you feel. It's not going to end.*"

She shook her head. "*Jenny . . . don't hold on to me. I want you to be happy. Take that next step.*"

"*I am happy. Can't you see?*"

Eve could see. Jenny's expression was serene and certain as Eve had never seen it. "*Jenny, I don't know—*"

"*Neither do I. But I know everything is changing, and it's all*" *good.*" She was beginning to fade into the darkness. "*I have to go. Your Joe is fighting to get closer to you. I think he's going to bring you back to consciousness by sheer will alone. I'll leave you now. Thank you again, my dear, Eve . . .*"

"Eve!" Joe's voice was rough and demanding. "Open your eyes. I'm not going to let you go."

By sheer will alone, Eve thought hazily. Jenny had been right.

"Eve!"

"Okay." Her lids slowly opened. "I heard you."

Joe's face close to her own, pale in the moonlight. Joe's hand tightly holding hers. "Then pay attention. I think you probably have a concussion. The ambulance is on its way. You're not going to black out like that again. Do you hear me?"

"I . . . hear you. You're one . . . to talk. All . . . this is . . . very familiar. You're sure you're okay?"

"Thanks to the miracle of duct tape."

"Duct tape? Never mind, I don't want to know."

"Then be quiet. This isn't about me. Nothing is supposed to happen to you. Not ever." He kissed her, hard, fast. "Or don't be quiet if it keeps you awake."

She suddenly realized she was lying on the sand, outside the cave. "Margaret . . ."

"She's with the kid. She and Nalchek are trying to comfort her. The first thing she asked after she knew she was safe was about Elena."

"She was . . . the only . . . family Cara knew. Elena loved her. She felt terribly guilty that she'd told Walsh where to find her."

"Maybe she somehow knows that Cara is safe now."

"*I have to go and be with Elena for a while.*"

"Oh, yes, she knows."

"You seem certain."

"I am." She looked up at him. "I think it's over. Thank God."

"Maybe not quite. There's still Nalchek to consider."

"Nalchek?"

He shook his head. "Not now. You probably couldn't comprehend anything clearly at the moment. That was quite a hit you took."

She wasn't going to push it. He was right, she was still bleary. It was a struggle just to keep awake and not go back to the darkness.

But she wouldn't have to struggle long. She could hear a siren and see the flashing lights of the ambulance somewhere near the strip. "I'll be fine. A couple aspirins, and they'll let me go home."

"Screw it. You were out almost thirty minutes. I'm going to have them go over you from head to toe with a fine-tooth comb. Then, if they don't find anything wrong, I'll let you leave the hospital."

"You're not doing that because I wouldn't let them release you? Payback?"

"It's a thought. No, I'm doing it because you scared me shitless."

"Then I guess I'll let you get away with it."

"*Let* me? No choice. You know we both signed over medical powers of attorney years ago because we weren't married and were always running into red tape." His hand tightened on hers. "The minute you enter that emergency room, you're *mine*."

"Bully." Mine. Wonderful word that could mean so many

things when spoken between them. "I'll see about that." She was having to force her lids to stay open. "And it might not have been that I was really blacked out. Might have been Jenny . . ."

COMMUNITY HOSPITAL OF THE MONTEREY
PENINSULA, CARMEL, CALIFORNIA

"Eve?"

Margaret's voice, Eve realized drowsily as she fought to rouse herself from sleep. She slowly opened her eyes to see Margaret standing beside her bed. The hospital room was dark except for the light streaming in from the hallway. "Hi, what are you doing here?"

"Sneaking in where I'm not supposed to be." She smiled down at her. "Joe helped me, but he's not pleased. I wouldn't have done it except that the doctors said that you're not nearly as fragile as you looked right after you got that knock on the head."

"It must be important if you're barging in here in the middle of the night." Eve yawned. "Is everything okay?"

"No. But I think it might be something you can fix." She turned her head. "Cara."

Cara Delaney moved out of the shadows in the far corner of the room. "Is it all right that I'm here? I won't be any trouble."

"Cara." Eve held out her hand to her. "It's all right as long as we don't get caught. They seldom have middle-of-the-night visiting hours at hospitals." She glanced at Margaret. "But she'd be better off in bed."

"No, she wouldn't," Margaret said. "Nalchek pulled strings

to keep her out of a child-care facility, so she could stay in my hotel room tonight. But she kept waking up with nightmares. The last time she woke up, she said she had to come here to you. She was getting upset, so I stopped arguing and decided to try to negotiate our way in here."

"You evidently succeeded," Eve said dryly.

"I won't be any trouble," Cara repeated. "Just let me stay."

"She's very good," Margaret said quietly. "I wouldn't have brought her if I'd believed she'd be a hassle for you."

"I'll just sit here and be with you," Cara said. "Like Jenny would want me to do."

Eve went still. "What?"

"She didn't tell me that," Margaret said.

"No?" She was gazing at Cara. She looked so much like Jenny, yet there were differences. Her features were not as delicate, and her eyes were hazel, not green. She had Jenny's exotic cheekbones but they looked stronger, more defined. There were other differences; the years of living and being on the run had given Cara a reserve and quiet strength unusual in a girl her age.

And she was gazing steadily at Eve as if she were trying to tell her something.

Perhaps she was, and whatever it was, Eve wanted to hear it. "You can leave her with me, Margaret. We'll be fine together."

Margaret nodded and fetched a chair from against the wall and set it beside the bed. She turned on the lamp on the bedside table that cast a low glow in the room. "I believe you will." She headed for the door. "But you can expect Joe to peek in shortly just to make sure." She glanced over her shoulder at Cara. "Don't wear her out."

"I won't." The little girl settled in the chair, and added gravely, "I know I have to take care of her."

Margaret's brows rose. "Really?" She shrugged. "Whatever." She left the room.

"Do you want me to turn out that light? I don't want to keep you awake," Cara said. "I just wanted to be here."

"No, it won't bother me." She smiled. "And I'd like to see you. You've been the mystery in this puzzle. Joe and I have been searching for you and looking at hundreds of pictures to try to locate you. We couldn't find one until we saw you in that choir photo."

"Elena didn't want me to be in that photo. But she found out too late to stop it." Her lips were suddenly tight with pain, her eyes glittering with tears. "She always told me that we still had to be careful. Sometimes, I didn't believe her. I should have believed her."

"The young always believe the best," Eve said gently. "Elena considered it her duty to protect you from the possibility that the best wouldn't happen. She loved you very much."

Cara nodded. "I loved her, too." Two tears rolled down her cheeks. "Now she's gone, Eve."

She wanted to reach out and hold her. Instead, she took her hand. "Not really gone."

"I know," she whispered. "She's with Jenny. Jenny said that she'd make sure that she was safe and happy before she left her."

Eve stiffened. "She did?"

Cara nodded. "But it's still hard. I miss her."

"Of course you do." She paused. "When did Jenny tell you that?"

"In the dream tonight. I was having a nightmare, and suddenly Jenny was there, and all the bad stuff went away."

"I . . . see. And do you often dream about Jenny?"

"No, only lately. The first time was when we were still at the apartment, and I didn't know anything was wrong." She was smiling eagerly again. "It was so good to see her. I thought she was gone, but there she was, just like before." Her smile faded. "You think I'm crazy? I know she's dead. I knew it before she told me in that first dream. But she was *there*."

"No, I don't think you're crazy. I think something very special happened to you because of the bond between you and Jenny."

"She told me that you'd understand that first time she came to me. She said, Go to Eve. You'll begin to feel what she's feeling, just like I do. I didn't know what she meant. I didn't know who she was talking about."

A ripple of shock went through Eve. "She was probably preparing you to accept me if I tried to help you get away from Walsh."

"I don't know." She frowned. "But I don't think so. Because she said something like that again tonight. She said, Go to Eve and take care of her. She'll need you. And you'll need her."

"But you said yourself that it was a dream, Cara," Eve said gently.

"You don't want me? That's okay." She was speaking quickly. "But just let me stay and take care of you for a while. I promised her. I won't get in your way."

"Cara . . ."

"It's okay." She released Eve's hand and leaned back in the chair. "Now go to sleep, and I'll be quiet and not bother you."

"You're not bothering me."

"I'll just turn out the lamp." The room was plunged into darkness.

So that Eve wouldn't see the hurt she had inflicted by that gentle reminder.

But she knew it was there, and she wanted to heal it. How to do it when the situation was bewildering, and promises couldn't be given? It reminded her of that similar moment with Jenny in the early days when she had first come to her. But Cara was no spirit, she had her entire life to live, and mistakes could be made so easily.

"Cara, we'll work this out. I only want you to be happy and safe."

"I know. Don't worry. I'll be fine."

"Yes, you will," Eve said firmly. "I'll make sure of it. Just hold on and give me a little time."

"I'll hold on as long as you let me, Eve . . ."

Joe Quinn was standing in the hall when Margaret came out of the room. "Eve's going to let her stay?"

Margaret nodded. "She won't be a bother to her, Joe. She's a good kid."

"Even good kids can cause disturbance. Eve doesn't need it."

"I told Eve you'd be checking in on her. Judge for yourself."

"I will." His gaze was fastened on her face. "You look tired. It's the first time I've seen you without your usual vim and vigor."

"I'm not tired. I'm feeling a little at a loss. Everything is winding down, and there doesn't seem to be anything that I can do."

"No interesting coyote discussions to instigate?" Nalchek had just gotten off the elevator and was coming toward them. "What a pity."

"What are you doing here in the middle of the night?" she asked. "I called and told you that Eve was going to be okay."

"I could ask you the same thing." He smiled crookedly. "But I know the answer. You're one of those people who have to be there twenty-four/seven for those they care about."

"You still haven't answered me."

"I believe that Nalchek is here to see me," Joe said. "And the middle of the night is an excellent time for our discussion." He turned and headed for the waiting room. "I've been expecting you."

Margaret gazed in bewilderment at Nalchek.

He shrugged. "Come along. By all means, let me satisfy your curiosity. I don't give a damn any longer, now that Walsh is dead."

"I don't want to— Yes, I do." She followed them down the hall to the waiting room. "I have to *know*."

"Those were my feelings exactly." Nalchek turned to face Joe as he entered the waiting room. "I had to know."

Joe nodded. "Because you're like Margaret. You had to be there twenty-four/seven for those you care about." He paused. "Even if there was a chance that it might destroy you."

"What are you talking about?" Margaret asked.

"Bryland Medical Center," Joe said. "When Margaret raised a red flag where you were concerned, I started investigating you, Nalchek, and that included everything about you."

"I would have done the same thing."

Joe nodded. "I couldn't find anything in your past or public career. You were everything your voters thought you were. So

I dug a little deeper. Family. You had a very close and affectionate family relationship."

"Yes, I do."

"And that includes your grandfather, Marcus Nalchek, who owned the vineyard and several valuable farms to the south. You grew up on his lands, and he was like a second father to you. Your own father was the sheriff and very busy. You bonded with Marcus, and he considered you his son and heir."

"My father didn't cheat me of affection. He was great," Nalchek said. "Stop trying to make me into a martyr. We were all family."

"But you were close enough to Marcus to go to work for him when you got out of the service."

"I wanted a break. I loved those vineyards."

"But you found out that things weren't the same as when you went to Afghanistan."

Nalchek didn't answer.

"I checked with your grandfather's financial consultants and creditors and found out that around the time of Jenny's death, he was having a good deal of money trouble because of the drought that was devastating the state. He was close to going bankrupt."

"So were half the other farmers in the state."

"But Marcus Nalchek felt it as a personal failure. The vineyards had been in the family for generations. He was the head of your family, and he couldn't stand the thought of you all knowing that he'd failed you."

"He didn't fail us. It was the drought. Even if we'd lost everything, we'd still have been able to make a living. We still had each other."

"But he didn't look at it like that, did he? However, he

didn't have to face your father or you with how bad the situation actually was." He paused. "Because suddenly everything was all right, he'd managed to save all those properties in jeopardy. Even his financial advisors didn't know how he did it. But you found out, didn't you, Nalchek?"

Silence.

"I'm on the track," Joe said quietly. "I won't stop. I've talked to the personnel at Bryland, and they gave me a few hints about your grandfather's meanderings after his stroke. And the financial stuff will just take time."

"I could make you do the work."

"You could, but I don't think you will."

Another silence. Then Nalchek finally answered, "I didn't suspect anything. Not right away. It wasn't until after my grandfather's accident that I put it all together. Before that, I only thought that my grandfather had aged enormously since I had last been with him." He grimaced. "But after Afghanistan, I thought the whole world had aged and was going to hell."

"Your grandfather had this accident a year after you went to work for him," Joe said. "Would you like to continue?"

"No." Nalchek's lips twisted. "But I'm sure that you have an idea where this is going and are planning a follow-up."

Joe nodded.

Nalchek shrugged. "We found my grandfather in the wine cellars one morning with his head split open. I had reason to believe that it was no accident. He kept holding my hand and telling me that it was a warning. He kept saying the word over and over. Warning. On the way to the hospital, he had a massive stroke that affected both his body and mental capacity. My entire family was devastated. He was taken to Bryland for rehab, but we knew he'd probably never come out of it. So did he. We were right, he died six months later. It was a bad six months. Whenever I visited him, he tried to talk to me. He appeared wracked with guilt. I could make out a few words and those words were . . . chilling."

"He told you that he was the one who had arranged with the Castino cartel to bring in those forced laborers to work his properties," Joe said.

"What?" Margaret said.

Both of them ignored her. Nalchek nodded. "I found out that he'd had to salvage the harvest any way he could. He kept the vineyards out of the deal. It was his home territory, and any change would have been noticed. But he made a deal for forced labor for his farms to the south. He didn't realize the horror of the human trafficking . . . until he experienced it. He said . . . slavery."

"Did he mention anything about Walsh?"

He shook his head. "Do you think I wouldn't have gone after him, if he had? I think my grandfather tried to get out of the deal once he realized what he'd gotten into. Too late. I knew that someone had tried to keep him from confessing what he'd done when he was struck in that wine cellar. It must have been Walsh. But I had no names then. Not Walsh, not Castino. I even put out some feelers with the Mexican government, but nothing came of them. My grandfather was a powerful and influential man, and Walsh didn't dare kill him outright. The second-best deterrent was a warning. I'm sure it would have been followed by a deathblow if the warning hadn't worked." He added bitterly, "It turned out not to be necessary after that stroke."

"What else did he tell you at the medical center?"

"Not much. The three words I remember most clearly. Forest. Child. Grave."

Margaret felt a chill run through her.

"Anything else?" Joe asked.

"He mentioned a name. Elena Pasquez . . . Help her."

"He wanted you to help her?"

"Or he wanted to tell me that he had helped her. After he died, I went to his office at the vineyard and went through his books. He always kept meticulous records. Yet he'd destroyed all paperwork connected to his deal with the cartel. Not one name or contact. But I found an entry for Elena Pasquez for $75,000 deposited in a bank in San Francisco. No reason given for the disbursement. I checked, and all the money had been removed the day after he'd deposited it. Enough funds to keep Elena and Cara hidden and safe for quite a while."

"Elena must have come to him to ask for help when she was taking Cara on the run," Margaret said. "And told him about Jenny."

"Then she had to have been desperate," Joe said. "Marcus Nalchek could have been in league with Walsh."

Nalchek shook his head. "People trusted my grandfather. Any of the workers would have told Elena that she'd be safe with him. He wasn't like that scum. He made a terrible mistake. He tried to correct it."

"The grave," Margaret said. "Your grandfather must have been looking for Jenny's grave when he was in the forest." She met his gaze. "And so were you after he told you about it. You were Sajan's 'other one.' Both you and your grandfather, full of violence and rage."

"What?" He shook his head impatiently. "Will you keep

that coyote out of this, Margaret? I don't want to deal with him at the moment. Yes, I was definitely filled with both of those emotions. But I didn't even know what I was looking for. There was no sign of the grave. Walsh did his job well," Nalchek said. "Every now and then, I would go and look again. But I never found it." His lips twisted. "Until that freak series of heavy rains that washed away the dirt."

"And you found Jenny," Margaret said softly. "No wonder you were so determined to find her identity. You thought it would lead you to the man who was responsible for your grand-father's death."

"Partly. I didn't lie to Eve. Seeing that little girl made me sick, and I felt the same guilt my grandfather had felt."

"It wasn't your crime," Margaret said.

"I suppressed information. Even though I didn't know for sure that there was a body buried in that forest, and I still kept searching. I set up my grandfather's estate so that there would never be a possibility of any other human trafficking. And I tried to relocate the remaining laborers who hadn't already been moved to other areas by the cartel." He grimaced. "But for years, I protected my grandfather's memory so that it wouldn't hurt my family. That was all that was important to me." He looked at Joe. "You know as well as I do that's not acceptable."

Joe nodded. "Absolutely. Not that I wouldn't feel the same way under similar circumstances. It's a basic primitive drive to protect the tribe." He smiled faintly. "And I'm very primitive."

Nalchek went still. "And that means?"

"You discovered a crime that had happened in the past and assured that it would not happen again. The man who perpe-trated it is now dead and cannot be prosecuted. You bent every

effort toward finding the killer of one child and protecting another child." He turned toward the door. "It's not my case. This
isn't my jurisdiction. And I need to go and make sure Eve is
having a good night. You'll have to take care of it yourself."

Nalchek and Margaret watched as he walked down the
hall.

"Does that mean you're off the hook?" Margaret asked.

"No, it means that he handed the hook to me," Nalchek
said. "Not safe, considering my past record."

"So what are you going to do?"

"Well, I'm not going to hurt my family after all I've done
to protect them." He left the waiting room and started down
the hall. "I'll turn in my resignation as sheriff and say that I
intend to go back to the university and work toward an ad-
vanced degree. Everyone will understand, considering the fact
that they've all been thinking I've been behaving a little weird
about this case anyway."

"You're really going back to school?"

He shook his head. "Not right now. I just need to keep
away from my family for a while. They know me too well,
they see too deep. I don't know where I'm going. Someplace far
away from everywhere to clear my head and see where the
wind takes me."

"I know a place like that."

He turned to look at her. "You do?"

"Summer Island. It's an island in the Caribbean where I
spent a little time. It's perfectly beautiful, and they do wonderful experimental work on animals. They have a good security
force, but I know that a man like you would be a welcome ad-
dition."

"Interesting idea."

"I thought you might think so." She went past him toward Eve's room. "I used it as a haven when I needed it. I've been tempted to do it again."

His eyes narrowed on her face. "How tempted?"

"That would be telling." Her eyes were twinkling as she looked over her shoulder. "But you should be relieved to know that there's not one coyote on Summer Island."

"Cara Delaney is out in the waiting room," Joe said when he entered Eve's hospital room the next morning. "I got her a breakfast at McDonald's and sat her down with her iPad. She wanted to come back to you, but I told her that there will be doctors and nurses bustling in and out all morning." He sat down in the chair beside her bed. "We have to talk about her, and we don't have much time. I figure they'll release you by early afternoon, and something's got to be settled before they do."

"I'll second that." She took his hand. "What's going to happen if we don't step in?"

"It depends on whether ICE finds out that Cara Delaney is Marnie Castino. So far, no one of us has made a statement to that effect. If they do find out, she'll be deported straight to the loving arms of that cartel scumbag of a father."

"If she lives that long. She could be torn between those damn warring cartels. Walsh's employer was a member of the Salazar family. If he hears Walsh is dead, what's to stop him from hiring someone else to kill Cara before her family is even notified."

Joe nodded. "All that is true. So what do you want to do?"

"Keep Cara safe. Keep her as far away from Mexico and Castino and Salazar as possible."

He smiled. "That was my first guess. Ways and means?"

She hesitated. "Play it by ear?"

"Send her to a private school?"

"No," she said sharply.

He threw back his head and laughed. "I didn't think so. I was just testing you. You want to take her home with us."

"It may only be for a little while. Just until we can get her happily settled."

"And it may be for a long, long time." He leaned forward and kissed her. "Another Jane, Eve? Our Jane was only a little younger than Cara when we took her in."

"There will never be another Jane. Just as there will never be another Cara. We know where Jane is in our lives, and it's all love. Cara is a clean slate, and we don't know what will be eventually written in the relationship." She frowned. "But how do you feel about it, Joe? She's had a troubled life, it could be . . . difficult. Even if it's for only a short time."

"I've only spent the morning with her. She's quiet and withdrawn and polite. She appeared very grateful I didn't drop her when she threw herself into my arms. The rest I'll have to learn with experience. But I didn't know much more when we adopted Jane." He smiled. "But she'll be a challenge. Just keeping her alive will be a task in itself."

She shuddered. "I wish you hadn't said that."

"Face it. You haven't chosen an easy way. But we can make it work and keep her safe."

She nodded. "She said that Jenny told her I'd need her. And that she'd need me."

"It might be true. You've been feeling a little lonely since Jane left home. And Cara certainly is going to need you."

"Us," she corrected.

He nodded. "Us." He got to his feet. "And now I'll go and

talk to Nalchek and Margaret and make sure that they don't disclose anything to local law enforcement. Then I'll arrange to whisk Cara away from here as if she'd never been. Preferably before Salazar finds out that Walsh is dead."

"I guess I'd better talk to Cara. Would you send her to me?" She made a face. "Though I should really get up and go to her. It's ridiculous that I'm still lolling in this bed. I shouldn't have given in and let you talk me into a full exam. You know those idiotic tests aren't going to find anything, Joe."

"Can't be too careful. I figured it couldn't hurt. You're always too busy to go in to see the doctor." He headed for the door. "We'll get the results in another hour or so."

"Joe."

He looked over his shoulder. "Yes."

"Come back here."

He tilted his head as he saw her expression. "Delighted." He whirled, and the next moment, he was beside her, lifting her, kissing her. "Hey, did I forget something?"

"No, I did." She kissed him again. "I forgot to tell you that most of the time you meet my every wish and that I'm damn grateful." She pushed him away. "And that I love you, Joe Quinn."

"Most of the time?"

"You were supposed to stay in San Francisco at that hospital. Instead, you came flying up here smack in the middle of the fray. That was definitely not according to what I wanted, and you know it."

"Yep, but you knew there was a strong possibility. I'll just have to make it up to you in other ways to lull you into forgetting it." He straightened and turned toward the door. "And I'll start doing that right away, after I send Cara in to see you."

•   •   •

"So what do you say, Cara?" Eve asked quietly. "Is it something you might want to do?"

She didn't speak for a moment. "I'd live with you?"

"At least for a while. You wouldn't have to be committed to us for the long haul. We could try it out and see how you liked it."

"And how you'd like it."

Eve nodded. "We're pretty much strangers. I don't see why we wouldn't get along, but it's better that we make it a trial run."

"You wouldn't send me back to Mexico?"

"No, that wouldn't be best for you. Why? Do you wish to go back?"

"No, Elena told me that I mustn't ever go back there." She shook her head. "I don't remember anything about it except being with Jenny and Elena. But she said it would be bad for me, that I would be hurt."

"Joe and I think that's true. But it might be difficult for us to keep you from being sent back. That's why we thought that you should change your name. Okay?"

"Again?" Cara nodded. "If that's what you want. I don't care."

"Does that mean that you're willing to come to live with us?"

"Of course it does. I told you that I wouldn't leave you, that I'd hold on as long as you let me." Her voice was suddenly fierce. "And I don't care about all that trial business. I'll be so good that you'll want to keep me. Jenny told me that you'll need me, and I have to be there for you."

"Cara, come here." She held out her hand. "It goes two ways." She drew the girl into her arms and held her. Cara didn't fight her, but her body was stiff and unyielding. It might be a long time before she would be able to physically respond to anyone after the death of her Elena. She had told Joe it might be difficult to bring her into their home. Don't force her. Everything must be slow and easy. She released her and smiled into her eyes. "I know you love Jenny, but this is between you and Joe and me. Can you start thinking of it like that?"

Cara nodded jerkily. "If that's what you want."

"That's what I want." She kissed her on the cheek and released her. "Now let's make a list of everything that you'll need from your apartment. Don't worry about clothes. We'll take care of that when we get home to Atlanta. Any personal items?"

She shook her head. "I don't need anything. Only my violin. Elena would have taken it, but you said everything in her car was burned."

"Yes, it was. We'll get you another violin."

A brilliant smile lit her face. "Thank you."

They couldn't take away the music, Jenny had said.

And no one must take away Cara's music, either.

"You're welcome. I look forward to hearing you play."

She nodded eagerly. "Yes, that's something I can give you. It's part of me and—"

"Hi, everything settled?" Joe came into the room. "Yes, I can see that it is." He smiled at Cara. "We'll get everything finalized before Eve leaves here today. But there are a few things I have to go over with Eve first. Would you run out to the hall, where Margaret is waiting?"

Cara didn't move. "What's wrong?"

"Nothing."

But there *was* something wrong, Eve realized. Cara's instincts were right. She recognized the tension in the way Joe was carrying himself. "Whatever it is, it has nothing to do with you, Cara."

Cara slowly got to her feet. "If it's me, I'll make it right, Eve."

"It's not you," Joe said shortly. "I promise."

Cara gave him another troubled look as she left the hospital room.

"She has good instincts. You're not easy to read," Eve said. "I'm glad that it wasn't about her. It would have been difficult explaining a sudden change of heart. Do you know, I'm starting to look forward to having Cara staying with us." She shook her head. "Bonnie was talking about a change in my life. This may be what she meant."

"Not necessarily."

Eve went still. She couldn't miss that jerky roughness in his tone. "What are you talking about? What *is* wrong?"

"Not wrong. Strange. Bizarre." He shook his head. "I don't know what else."

"Stop playing around with words. Talk to me."

"I don't know how to say it."

"Just tell me."

"The hospital has the results from all the tests. The doctor stopped me in the hall to go over them."

"The results? Joe, I know you've been ramrodding everything connected to my treatment since you brought me to this hospital, but that's going a little too far. Why go over them with you and not with me?" She tried to smile. "Some terrible disease popped up that he thought you should break to me?"

"God, I'm not doing this right. No terrible disease. You're

very healthy and ready to go home. He just didn't want you to leave the hospital without knowing."

"Joe, what are you trying to tell me?"

"In my completely clumsy and inadequate fashion"—He reached out and took her hand.—"I'm trying to tell you that you're going to have a child, Eve."

READ ON FOR A BONUS SCENE FROM JOE QUINN'S POINT OF VIEW!

"You have a FedEx package," Joe Quinn said as Eve came into the cottage. "It's on your worktable. It came from somewhere in California."

She nodded. "Yeah, Sonderville. Sheriff Nalchek called me last night and asked me to bump his reconstruction to the top of my list." She made a face. "I almost told him to forget it. I'm swamped right now, and I don't need any more pressure."

Something was wrong, Joe realized instantly. Eve never complained about pressure, even to him. She just did her job and kept on moving to the next poor kid whose skull ended up on her worktable. But if something was wrong, she wouldn't want him probing. Keep it light, and let her tell him when she was ready.

"You're always swamped." Joe smiled teasingly. "You thrive on it. And it's natural that you're in demand. Everyone wants the world-famous forensic sculptor, Eve Duncan, to solve their problems."

"Bullshit." She went to the kitchen counter and reached for the coffee carafe. "There's usually no urgency about putting a face on a skull that's been buried for years anyway. It has to be done, but there's no reason that I can't do it an orderly fashion. Every one of those children is important."

He had heard that many times before, but it was clear she needed to express it again. "So why did you give in to Sheriff Nalchek?"

"I don't know." She poured her coffee and came back to Joe. "He wore me down. He sounded young and eager and full of the horror that only comes the first time that you realize that there are vicious people out there who can do monstrous things to innocent children. I got the impression that he was an idealist who wanted to change the world." She sat down beside Joe and nestled close, her head against his shoulder. Her cheek felt right, absolutely perfect against him. He wanted to hold her closer, but he could wait. He could sense the slight tension of her body, the disturbance that made her want to touch him. She probably didn't even realize that she was in need and wanted his touch to be comforting. But he knew it and would give her what she needed.

"He kept telling me that this little girl was different," she said. "That he was sure that he'd be able to find out who she was and who had killed her if I'd just give him a face to work with. Who knows? Maybe he's right. In cold cases like this, the chances are always better if the officer in charge is enthusiastic and dedicated."

"Like you." Joe's lips brushed her forehead. "Maybe he thinks he's found a soul mate."

"Oh, I'm dedicated. Enthusiastic?" She wearily shook her head. "Not now. I'm too tired. There have been too many children in my life who have been killed and thrown away. I'm not as enthusiastic as that young officer is. I'm only determined . . . and sad."

"Sad?" Joe straightened and looked down at her. "Yes, I'm definitely feeling the sad part. But it's not only about that skull in the box over there, is it?" His hand gently cupped her cheek. "Jane?" He had thought the root of Eve's depression might be Jane MacGuire, their adopted daughter who Eve had just dropped off at the airport to catch her flight to London. "I could have taken her to the airport. I thought you wanted to do it."

"I did want to do it. It may be the last time we see her for a while. She's off to new adventures and finding a life of her own." She tried to steady her voice. "Just what we wanted for her. Look what happened when she came back from London to try to help me. She got shot and almost died. Now she's well and going on with her life."

But Eve was having problems coming to terms with the fact that Jane's life as an artist often took her far away from her, he thought. He had seen this coming. In Eve's line of work as a forensic sculptor and his job as a police detective, sometimes the evil came close to home. Most recently Jane had been one of the targets. Those weeks with her daughter, while she had been recuperating, had been strained and yet poignantly sweet for Eve. Jane had come to them when she was ten years old and she had been more best friend than daughter to Eve. But that hadn't changed the love that had bound them all these years. For Joe, the relationship had been different, the love was there, but it had built gradually, and he'd always known that Jane belonged to Eve. That was okay with him because he belonged to Eve, too. She was his center and Jane had always understood. But now that Jane was out on her own and becoming a successful artist, it was terribly hard for them to adjust to the fact that most of the time she was thousands of miles away.

"It's exactly what she should be doing," Eve said. "What's here for her? Hell, I'm a workaholic and always involved with a reconstruction. You're a police detective who they tap to work cases that don't give you normal hours either. It was just . . . difficult . . . to see her get on that plane."

"And you didn't let her see one bit of that pain," Joe said quietly. "You smiled and sent her on her way."

"That's what every parent does. It always comes down to letting them go."

"And more difficult for you than for others. First, you had to let go of Bonnie when she was killed. Now Jane is moving out of our lives."

"Not out, just away." She made a face. "And evidently I couldn't let go of Bonnie because I insisted on keeping her with me, alive or dead. I was so stubborn that whoever is in charge of the hereafter let me have my little girl's spirit to visit me now and then."

And that had been the most difficult challenge of all for Joe to accept. He was a detective, and logic dictated that ghosts were off his radar. But logic had nothing to do with his feelings for Eve. Not from the day that Quantico had sent him down to Atlanta to investigate the disappearance and probable murder of seven-year-old Bonnie Duncan. He had been a Special Agent with the FBI at the time and had not even wanted to visit Eve Duncan's house or go over old material the ATLPD had already covered very efficiently. But he had gone anyway, and life had never been the same for him. He had only been in that house for a few hours with Eve Duncan before he realized that something extraordinary was happening to him.

"I'm not a fool. I grew up on the streets, and know all about the scum who are out there." Eve looked wonderingly up at him. "But I have to hope. She's my baby. I have to bring her home. How can I live if I don't hope?"

He felt as if he were breaking apart inside. He could feel her pain, and it was becoming his pain. "Then hope." His voice was hoarse. "And I'll hope with you. We'll explore every way we can to find her safe and alive. There's nothing I won't do. Just stick with me and give me a little help."

She hesitated, gazing up at him.

Believe me, he urged her silently. Put your hand in mine, trust me, let me guide you. Something strange is happening here, but it's not anything bad. I won't let it hurt you.

She stood staring at him. She could feel it, sense what he couldn't say, he realized. In her pain, she couldn't define the nature of what she was sensing, but perhaps it would become clear to her later.

As, God help him, it was becoming clear to him.

But it was years before Eve had healed enough to realize that they could become lovers instead of friends. During that time he had almost lost her. The depression had been too severe, the heartbreak of her loss a nightmare from which she couldn't wake. But then something happened, she had begun to dream of Bonnie. Or at least that was what she had told him. She had thought she was hallucinating, thought that grief had made her mind fly to any solace possible. Before that, she had given up on life and wanted only to be with her Bonnie. She had only been stopped by the realization that the visits from Bonnie were not hallucinations.

It had taken Joe a lot longer than Eve to accept the possibility, but he had finally done it. Bonnie had kept Eve alive when he was losing her. Screw reality. Accept whatever miracle had kept her here with him.

Eve drew a deep breath and gave him a quick kiss. "Which makes me luckier than a lot of people. I refuse to feel sorry for myself. I have you. I sometimes have Bonnie. I'll have Jane as she moves in and out of our lives." She nodded at the FedEx box across the room. "And I have a chance to help the parents of that little girl find resolution." She got to her feet and took a sip before she put the cup down on the coffee table. "So slap me if you see me go broody on you." She headed for the kitchen. "How about lasagna for supper? There's something about the smell of baking garlic bread that lifts the spirits and makes everything seem all right."

"Besides outrageously tempting the taste buds. Sounds good. Need help?"

"Nah, you know my culinary expertise is nonexistent. I'll do frozen."

"Eve."

She glanced over her shoulder.

He had to make sure that was the only problem. He was frowning, and his gaze was narrowed. "It's just Jane leaving? You've been pretty quiet the last couple weeks. Nothing else is wrong?"

He could see she was tempted to deny it and put him off but she couldn't do it. They had been together for years, and their relationship was based not only on love but honesty. "Nothing that can't be fixed." She shrugged. "I guess I'm just going through some kind of emotional adjustment. I wanted everything to stay the same. I wanted to keep Jane close to me. Mine. Though I always knew she didn't really belong to me. She was too independent and was ten going on thirty when we adopted her. And Bonnie was mine but then she was taken." She smiled. "And that spirit Bonnie, who comes to visit me now and then, is very much her own self now. Beloved, but only flashes of being mine." Her smile faded. "But I'll take it. I just want to keep her with me, too. I don't want anything to change."

"Why should that change?"

"It shouldn't change. That's what I told Bonnie. Nothing has to change."

His brows rose. He had hoped the problem wouldn't have anything to do with Bonnie. How the hell could he fix anything having to do with a spirit? "Ah, your Bonnie. She said something to disturb you? When?"

"A couple weeks ago. She scared me. She said she didn't know how long she'd be able to keep coming to me. She said everything was going to change."

"How? Why?"

"She didn't know. She just wanted to warn me."

"Very frustrating." He chuckled. Keep it light and off-hand. "If your daughter has to pay you visits, I'd just as soon she not upset you like this."

"That's what I told her."

He got to his feet and took her in his arms. "And so you should. Send her to me and I'll reinforce it." He kissed her. "Though I doubt if that's going to happen. She only appeared to me a couple times just to make sure I knew that you weren't hallucinating." He looked directly into her eyes. "I know you need Bonnie. She's the anchor that keeps you here with me. You were spiraling downward and almost died before you had your ghost visits from Bonnie. She brought you back, and I thank God for her." He paused. "But if for some reason she stopped coming, I want you to know that we'll make it all right." He had to make her believe it. Their love was strong and yet he could still remember how fragile she had been during those first years together. There were times when he hadn't been able to help her then, but he could now. There was nothing he wouldn't do, no battle he wouldn't fight. His voice was soft, urgent. "I have so much love for you, Eve. I'm full of it, you're my center. You always have been and always will be. If your Bonnie drifts away from you, I'll just pour more of that love toward you. I'll find a way to stop you from hurting. I promise you."

He meant every word. Was he overreacting? There was a good chance. He usually tried to keep the way he felt about her low key and not let her see the true depths. It was a throwback from the time when he'd had to pretend that love didn't exist. These days he tried to strike a balance and keep the intensity down to make sure it didn't overwhelm her. She was strong, but her career was difficult, and so was the knowledge that she knew what he felt for her bordered on obsession. Sometimes he couldn't pull it off. Casual and easy weren't in his DNA.

It was okay. She was gazing up into his face and he could see no pressure or stress, nothing but warmth and love in her expression. "Hey, I'm just having a few twinges, nothing major. It just seemed when Jane got on that plane that the changes were starting. A sort of harbinger of things to come." She pushed him away and turned back to the freezer. "But change can be good, too, can't it? After all, Bonnie wasn't definite about anything. Forget it." She took out the lasagna. "Jane told me she'd call me as soon as she got off the plane in London. I think I'll start working on the new reconstruction after dinner so that I'll be awake when she calls . . ."